SOPHIA

Cover art and interior design by Lance Buckley

Editing services by Julie Frederick

Books by M.D. House

The Barabbas Trilogy (Christian historical fiction)
I Was Called Barabbas
Pillars of Barabbas
The Barabbas Legacy
Sophia: Daughter of Barabbas (spin-off)

The Patriot Star Series (science fiction)
Patriot Star
Kindred Star

The Servant of Helaman (Christian historical fiction)

Amulek: Revenant (Christian historical fiction)

SOPHIA

DAUGHTER
of
BARABBAS

M.D.
HOUSE

This book has surprised me in a lot of ways, even more so than the books of the Barabbas Trilogy which preceded it and form its basis. What a fascinating and fulfilling experience.

Why did I choose the youngest daughter for the first spin-off from the trilogy? I'm not sure I know the answer, and it wasn't the original intent. After involving her character in more depth at the end of The Barabbas Legacy, however, it seemed natural—and, of course, the ending to that book was the tip-off.

You will love Sophia. She is a spitfire, but also an earnest disciple of Christ, and it was so much fun to get to know her, along with the apostle John and the former slave Onesimus (once owned by Philemon, and who labored with Paul). The timeframe is 72–82 AD, and once again, the geography is large, extending beyond the Roman Empire.

As with The Barabbas Legacy, I utilized the expert editing services of Julie Frederick, along with the design brilliance of Lance Buckley. It's not always easy to find good help, so when you do, rejoice in it.

Thank you for your interest in Sophia, her family, and the early Christian saints. Enjoy!

M.D. House
July 2023

CONTENTS

PLACES IN SOPHIA
Britannia
Sarmatia
Cremni
Verona
Odessa
Rome
Heraclea
Ephesus
Caesarea
Jerusalem
Leptis Magna
Alexandria

PROLOGUE

---

*This then is the message which we have heard of him, and declare
unto you, that God is light, and in him is no darkness at all.*

1 John 1:5

Sophia let the beautiful words of Onesimus's prayer lap gently against her mind. He really was a wonderful, kind-hearted soul, and his understanding of the gospel surprised her more every day.

"And now we humbly petition you, our Holy Father, that you strengthen our faith and prosper our path, as we unite with your apostle, the beloved John, in furthering your work and blessing your children. Yours is the kingdom, and the power, and the glory forever, by the name of your Only Begotten, even Jesus the Christ, Amen."

"Amen." The word passed her lips as barely a whisper, wrapped in reverence, as she raised her head and beheld the tears filling the corners of his eyes. Her own eyes were moist as well. "Thank you, Onesimus. I felt that. And I know the Lord did, too."

He regarded her with slightly drawn eyebrows. He never wanted to take credit for the good he did, but she had been trying to persuade him to accept a compliment, graciously.

"Thank you, Sophia. I have learned much since Brother Paul guided me toward the light. I still have a very long way to go, though."

Good enough. She smiled. "Ha. Not as long as I have. I think I'm finally starting to realize how little I know. My parents have warned me many times about becoming proud and thereby losing the Spirit."

Onesimus gave a contemplative nod. "I have seen it in others, quite often. I remember what happened to Demas. So strong in the faith. And then his head swelled, his motives shifted, and he fell. He even tried to discredit Paul!" He shook his head sadly. Sophia recalled what she had heard about that story from her adopted aunt Esther in Trento. She had a hard time wrapping her mind around it, even now. How could someone so good change so horribly?

She had no more time to contemplate that, as one of the sailors shouted, "Smoke! I see smoke in the direction of Ephesus!"

Sophia stood up from her stool on the deck of the ship and squinted in the direction the man pointed. They were still several miles from the city, which was their destination, but there was indeed smoke, and a great deal of it. She looked to Onesimus with a confused frown.

He shook his head and shrugged. "Perhaps a warehouse caught fire, and it spread. Rome has no enemies that would dare attack her here, or that even could."

She nodded. That made sense. But her unease grew instead of abating. Something wasn't right. Or maybe she was still anxious about being away from her family for the first time, especially her mother Chanah. She shouldn't be too worried. Unexpected things happened all the time. And none of it was unexpected to the Lord.

"Um … would you mind asking the captain what he thinks?" she asked, feeling like she was ten years old instead of twenty-two.

"Of course not," he replied, giving her an encouraging smile as he turned to walk aft. She went the opposite direction, eyes focused on the growing black smudges on the horizon. It seemed like the entire city was on fire, and Ephesus was no minor town. When she reached the bow, a sailor took position there, too, calling out what he could see. She remembered someone saying he had the best eyes among the crew, that he could see like an osprey.

"No heavy flames near the water!" he shouted. She supposed that meant they wouldn't encounter burning ships. "Moderate wind driving the smoke southeast!" Well, anyone could see that. "Not much coming from the center of the city!" That was good. She had experienced the Great Fire in Rome. Other places had seen such conflagrations, too. Fire was greedy, merciless, and incredibly fast.

Onesimus arrived, bending down to speak into her ear. "The captain isn't concerned. He thinks they've had a warehouse fire, and he says the officials in Ephesus are well prepared for such things. They will have it under control shortly."

"But what about …" She frowned as she turned toward him. "Oh, never mind. Thank you, Onesimus. I guess we'll find out shortly."

He straightened, placing his hands behind his back as he stared toward the thriving metropolis, home to many members of the Lord's Church. That included her adopted brother Elhanan and his family, along with Timothy, one of the Seventy. Elhanan was still bishop there, as far as she knew. The orphan boy who had become such an incredible man.

She purposely lost herself in remembrances of her family—in Jerusalem, on Melita, and then in Rome, such a fascinating place. They had traveled a lot, too. She had been to Ephesus before, and Antioch, and Trento in the far north of Italy, even all the way to Armenia, where Mary Magdalene still lived. She had seen Pella, where a large body of saints now resided, those who had heeded the chief apostle Philip's warnings to flee Jerusalem, which was subsequently decimated. Those thoughts rang a somber requiem. Close to a million Jews dead. Judea was no more. Many Romans had already started calling it Palestina. But though she was Jewish by blood, the Jews were not 'her people.' The Christians were. She was the Lord's, which was why she had agreed to Philip's request that she join the apostle John for a time in his ministry.

"The captain was partially right," said Onesimus, and she started, realizing she had been daydreaming … on her feet! She brought the oncoming coastal city back into focus. They were much closer now than she expected. How long had her mind been wandering?

"What do you mean?" she asked as she tried to make out what was happening.

He raised a finger and pointed. "There are indeed some warehouses that have taken flame, but see, there … and there." His finger moved, her eyes following. "Some fires are scorching the center of the city, and there's even a pair on the hills. They cannot be naturally connected."

"Okay, so … what do you think is happening?"

His hand dropped, and she watched him ponder that question for several moments. A few muffled shouts began to reach them over the water, sounding like more than just people trying to put out the fires, though she wasn't quite sure how.

Onesimus angled his eyebrows in deep concentration, then finally said, "I believe it is a slave revolt. Not a major one, but not minor, either."

A slave revolt? She'd heard about those before, but had never witnessed one. The slaves in Rome, of which there were a great many, were generally well cared for, and penalties for misbehavior, once proven, were harsh.

"Does Ephesus have a lot of slaves?" She could sometimes tell if someone was a slave, but not always. She didn't remember noticing much in that regard when she had visited Ephesus with her family five years earlier.

He nodded, wearing a sad frown. "Yes, it does, unfortunately. Most, I believe, come from Parthian lands, and some from northern Africa as well."

"Where did you come from?" The question had popped out of her mouth before she could take the time to assess its propriety.

"Sarmatia, north of the Black Sea. Roman raiders took my parents, me, and my siblings, along with most others from our small village. We were sold for a fair sum to our first buyers, and were grateful to still be together. Several years later, though, we were separated and sold again. One of my brothers died in a freak accident trying to escape. My parents were taken to Spain, I think. My other siblings ended up in various places I cannot now remember."

"And you were sent to … Colossae?"

He nodded. "Yes. I had a good … master"—she could tell he didn't like saying that word, at least in that context—"and I have been far more fortunate than most, especially since we found the gospel."

"Through Paul."

"Yes. I miss him. I hope he is well." He turned his head in what Sophia guessed was the general direction of Carthago Nova, in Spain, where Paul now mostly resided. He didn't travel nearly as much as he used to.

"He's with his family again. I know how happy he is about that."

That brought a smile to the former slave's face. "Yes. And what is more, they are his eternally."

Her mouth spit out the next indelicate question. "You've never married, have you?"

He shook his head. "No, and I will not, unless the Lord directly commands it. I am too late in my years now, and I have other things to do. Don't worry, though. In the next life, opportunity will come. Brother Paul reassured me of that." He added an incongruous wink.

She had heard that said before, and not just by some of the priests and teachers. Her parents had explained it, as had at least one of the apostles. It often made her wonder if her calling was not to marry in this life, but to follow a different path. That option seemed both sad and exciting at the same time, and she couldn't quite square it.

She posed her third daring query. "What will you say to Philemon and Apphia when you see them there?"

His gaze became distant. "I don't know yet. I must learn not to have any anger in my heart. We are commanded to forgive. They treated me well, and they did eventually free me. I also have many fond memories of them and their family, and they died firm in the faith of Christ. As true martyrs."

Sophia's own eyes had unfocused a bit. "We have far too many martyrs."

"Do we?" The question jolted her back to full awareness, and she peered up at him.

"What do you mean?"

He shrugged. "This life is just a step, and a test, leading to what really matters. If we seek God, in truth, nothing can keep us from eternal glory with him. It doesn't matter the form our death takes, only how we live while he grants that we remain here, in his wisdom. And who is to say what effect those martyrs will have on others, not just now, but many years—even centuries—from now?"

Sophia pondered that concept in awe. "That is profound, Onesimus. I'm glad you are with me on this journey."

"It is my honor," he replied. "Philip stands close to God, and the Spirit confirmed to me that I should accompany you. This will be a marvelous adventure, even if we die." He settled his eyes on her and gave a small smile, accompanied by another wink. Until today, she had never seen him wink.

The docks weren't as bad as Sophia had feared. A pair of warehouses, two streets apart, still burned, but it appeared the flames were under control as water brigades doused them. Plumes of smoke rose in several other directions, though the picture they painted didn't seem as dire up close as from afar. Onesimus had insisted on helping unload the ship. Why, she had no idea, and she didn't ask. Instead, she wandered down their pier toward the dock, shouldering her personal bag. They would rent a mule, or procure a small cart, for the rest of their things. They hadn't brought much, despite Onesimus's occasional comment that they could have traveled lighter.

She found the captain speaking with one of the dockmasters, who had a perturbed look on his face. The fires would make things more difficult, and she knew the captain hadn't planned on spending any time in Ephesus. He had relayed his intention to pick up a few goods before continuing on. Hopefully, they weren't contained in either of the two burning warehouses.

"Excuse me, Captain?" He jumped as if stung by a bee, then beamed as he recognized her.

"Yes, Mistress Sophia?"

"I wanted to thank you again for the pleasant journey. You and your crew were wonderful."

He clearly hadn't expected that, so he fumbled for a response.

"Well, it was a pleasure having you and Master Onesimus," he said with a bow. "I enjoyed our conversations, and I look forward to seeing this majestic temple you described when I next dock at Ostia."

She wrinkled her lips. "I wish my parents still lived there, but they are in Verona now. They would have taken good care of you, but I can send a letter ahead to Rome. You will be welcomed."

He bowed again, and she noted a puzzled look on the dockmaster's face. She almost giggled, but reminded herself that she was a grown woman now, and grown women didn't giggle. Well, not much, anyway.

"That is gracious of you," said the captain. "You are a remarkable young woman, and your parents must be very proud. Chanah and …?"

"Barabbas."

"Ah, yes, Barabbas. My apologies. I told you I had heard that name before meeting you, though without many details. What a fascinating story."

She smiled wistfully. Her father didn't like talking about his past, especially the time before he married her mother, but she had wheedled a great many details out of him over the years. It was indeed a remarkable story, and another testament to the saving power of the Christ.

"Yes, but everyone's story is fascinating, and can become even more so with God's help. Remember, if you ever make it to Carthago Nova, seek out Paul and Miriam. They are well known there."

The captain chuckled. "I will, I will, but you've already given me such a long list of people to meet and places to visit that I'm not sure I'll live long enough to see them all—and I'm a ship's captain!" He laughed louder, slapping the dockmaster on the back. The fellow laughed along, but still looked perplexed.

Just then frantic shouts reached them, along with clashes, including metallic clangs. The captain and the dockmaster whipped their heads around as Sophia's eyes tracked the sound. Two piers down, several dockworkers were under attack by men with clubs and knives who seemed to be trying to access another vessel. At least a dozen men started sprinting toward the pier on which she stood, screaming a rage-filled challenge. The captain turned toward his ship, his bellowing voice booming like a wakening volcano.

"All hands, to arms!"

He put an arm around Sophia and hustled her back up the pier, the dockmaster having run toward the shore, shouting for the harbor guards, which would include Roman soldiers. Most of those, she imagined, were already busy fighting the fires.

Onesimus was the first to pass them, along with two of the sailors. He had obtained a spear from the ship's armory, and the two sailors carried long poles with sharp hooks at the end. In moments, Sophia was aboard the ship, and half a dozen more sailors had joined Onesimus as he directed them in setting up a defense halfway down the pier. He also sent a pair back to the ship, warning them some of the attackers might try to swim to it.

The wave of aggressors paused momentarily, wary of the bristling wall they faced, but then one of them roared, and they rushed forward. Even from a distance, Sophia could discern the desperation and rage in their eyes. She watched helplessly, concern for Onesimus spiking. Not only did she not want him hurt physically, she knew he would never want to kill another human being, especially a slave, and by the men's shouts, his assessment of a slave rebellion was confirmed.

Instead of stabbing with his spear, which would be deadly effective against men with short knives and clubs, he focused on batting their blows aside, stepping forward to push them back when he had opportunity. He was a strong man, and fit, despite his claims of getting old, and while the sailors didn't follow his non-lethal lead, they seemed to be energized by his courage. The battle was brief, with five of the attackers falling before the rest fled, searching for an easier target. They wouldn't find one, as several harbor guards and Roman soldiers rushed toward the scene, issuing blood-curdling warnings. The men finally halted, looked around frantically for a few moments, then dropped their weapons and let their shoulders slump, heads bowing in submission.

Sophia's heart quailed at their plight. Some of them, especially those found to be instigators, would be executed. Most of the rest would find themselves doing much harder labor, perhaps in a different place, and separated from friends and family. She was still crying as Onesimus strode up the gangway, carrying his spear limply in one hand. He found her along the port side and gently set the spear on the deck.

"I am sorry," he said. "Perhaps I should have convinced the captain to wait before bringing the ship into port."

She blinked at him in confused anguish. "No, this is not your fault. And thank you for protecting me—protecting us. You are a brave man." She desperately wanted to hug him, like she would her father, but she maintained her composure, turning to stare toward the docks, where multiple groups of men had been subdued and were having their hands tied behind their backs as they knelt on the ground. Occasionally, a soldier or guard would cuff one of them hard on the side of the head with an open hand or the flat of a sword, and each time Sophia flinched. The captain had returned to the docks, promising to get more information. She spotted him hollering for the dockmaster.

"This fell far short of what Spartacus achieved."

Sophia sniffled as she turned her gaze to Onesimus. "They all died."

"Not all of them. And they opened many eyes. From that time, many slaveholders began treating their slaves better. I am grateful for that. I owe Spartacus and his men a great debt."

"But slavery is wrong, no matter how well you treat slaves. Every person should be free to choose where to live, where to work, who to marry, how to worship. Spartacus didn't end slavery, and after the last battle—at Senerchia, I believe—the Romans crucified six thousand of the survivors, lining the road from Rome to Capua. It was evil and barbaric."

Onesimus nodded, his face hardening. "You know your history. I doubt slavery will ever be completely eradicated. It has existed since almost the time of our first parents, in all areas of the world. Men are so easily deceived by the Evil One to persecute and enslave each other. Some even claim placing certain people in servitude is a mercy!"

"It may appear so on the surface sometimes," Sophia mused solemnly, "but it is never the right answer … to anything."

"Indeed. Our Lord weeps for those so abused. But he comforts them as well, and he urges them to do good in their circumstances. I can personally witness to that. I don't know when it is right to rebel, but *he* knows. Perhaps he inspired Spartacus and the others who helped lead that revolt. They didn't know their Savior in this life, probably. Spartacus himself was Thracian. But they all came from the same God, the same place where he dwells. They all shared the same eternal, familial link."

The commotion from the docks had subsided considerably, though angry outbursts from the guards and soldiers still pierced the air at intervals. She placed a hand on his shoulder, knowing that was considered forward but intending only to convey her friendship and respect. "Yes. And you rebelled, too. You left Philemon and Apphia to find Paul and labor with him in his ministry."

He nodded, then took a deep breath, letting it out with a long sigh. "I did. I still believe I was right to do so, but Paul felt concerned about the consequences—for me, not him—of breaking Roman law. He knew how much my former masters valued me as well. He urged me to return, and whether he was right or wrong, I feel justified in trusting him. His heart is pure—the purest of any man I have ever met."

Sophia had no immediate response to that. Some people thought the apostles were perfect, but she knew that wasn't the case. They struggled with difficult decisions, and the Lord made them work hard to discover his will. She didn't always understand why, but she knew *He* was perfect. He didn't make mistakes, and his plans always unfolded in such amazing and beautiful ways—ways that aimed not at worldly success, but toward an eternal abundance.

She removed her hand from his arm. "Well, thank you again, Brother Onesimus, faithful of the Lord. It becomes clearer to me every day why we are traveling together to find the apostle John. Let us not keep him waiting."

CHAPTER 1

Sophia nodded in appreciation at the cart they had procured, weighed down now with their luggage. She had splurged on renting a mule as well, rather than asking Onesimus to pull it.

"Too many bags, and you even brought a crate," Onesimus commented.

"A small crate," she corrected.

He raised an eyebrow from across the mule's rump as they walked along the main road toward the city of Ephesus, just a few miles east of the port. The land was relatively dry, especially since it was fall, with stubby trees, thick brush, and hardy grasses, but they passed palm trees at semi-regular intervals. Since John's home sat on the eastern edge of the city, they would stop at Elhanan and Junia's house first. Sophia was especially excited to see their children, Alia and Ezra. Alia would be fourteen now—fourteen!—and Ezra, who was adopted, would be twelve. She wondered if he still had issues with his lungs and his left foot. Perhaps he had at least grown out of the lung issues, and maybe his misshapen foot had healed, too. Or been healed.

After following the decumanus to the center of the city, they traveled the cardo north for a stretch until turning off to make for the house. Anticipation grew as they neared, though Sophia had no idea, of course, whether any of them would be at home. The last time she was here, Elhanan's tentmaking shop was in a different part of the city.

The first thing Sophia noticed about the house was that it now had glass in the broad front windows. Elhanan's business must have done well over the last five years. The door was different, too, made of a darker, smoother wood. Sophia left Onesimus with the mule and knocked firmly on the door, then took a step back and waited. After several seconds had passed, and she couldn't hear any sounds from inside the house, she stepped up and knocked again, louder, cringing at the noise she made.

She stepped back again, then nearly jumped out of her sandals as Junia rounded the corner of the house, holding up her skirts in her hurry. She stopped, perplexed, then broke out in a huge smile, emitting a squeal of glee as she recognized Sophia, who did the same, grown woman or not.

"Sophia!" Junia dropped her skirts and dashed the remaining few paces to embrace her. Sophia squeezed her eyes shut in joy as she returned the hug.

"Junia, I should have written that I was coming." She separated herself a few inches so she could look into her sister-in-law's face. "We weren't sure where exactly we would be traveling first, but Philip recently received a letter from John, saying he was here in Ephesus."

Junia laughed as she let her go and took a step back. "It's all right. I'm so happy you're here. Elhanan will be delighted as well." She turned slightly, glancing at Onesimus. "And who is this?"

"This is Onesimus, a close friend of Paul. Philip asked him to accompany me, and, well, he's already had to protect us from some men trying to board our ship."

"The slave revolt?" asked Junia, her voice a touch breathless. Her eyes traveled up and down Sophia's body. "You weren't hurt, were you?"

"No, we're fine, but I'm afraid many men will die in the coming days as the Romans mete out punishments."

Junia's eyes reflected Sophia's own sadness at the thought. "Yes, you're right. It started, as far as we have heard, with two wealthy families who maintain palaces on the southern hills. They accused some of their slaves of stealing from them and demanded swift justice. They intimidated any who might witness for the accused, and the men were harshly punished. Things evolved quickly from there. The trial was only two days ago."

"And now it has ended." Onesimus had tied the mule's lead to a post and now stood near them.

Junia nodded at him. "Yes, it was futile."

Onesimus didn't respond to that, and Sophia changed the subject. "Where are Alia and Ezra?" She almost began bouncing on her feet saying their names.

"Ezra is with Elhanan at the shop. Timothy is there, too. Alia has apprenticed herself to an artist, if you can believe that. She sculpts, draws, and paints all kinds of beautiful things. Oh"—her hand shot up—"let me show you something Alia sculpted for us. Please, come inside." She motioned Onesimus forward, too, and they entered the house. Junia pulled the dark curtains back fully from the windows, allowing additional light to flood the room. Then she walked over to a narrow plinth with a small bust sitting atop it, turning and showcasing it with her hands.

"Alia finished this a couple of weeks ago. It's Jesus, and she says she based it on several other artists' work, including some who are, or were, saints." She beamed proudly, and Sophia's heart warmed as she approached to get a closer view. It was imperfect, clearly the work of a novice, yet somehow impeccable. Tears welled, and her throat tightened.

"It's beautiful. I've never seen him personally, either, but John has. Have you shown it to him?"

"Not yet. He has only visited us once, and that was several months ago. We go to hear him teach sometimes, of course, though he travels a lot. And Elhanan is so busy, both with the shop and with his responsibilities as bishop."

"Well," said Sophia, "I'll tell John about it, and ask him to come. Maybe he will, right?"

Junia's smile broadened. "Alia would be thrilled beyond measure. And Ezra adores his big sister, so he would be, too. I can't believe they get along so well."

"She takes care of him, right?"

"Yes. We've tried to heal his foot, but I think the Lord means for it to remain that way for a while longer, and he has his reasons. Alia helps Ezra cope with that, make the best of it. He is such a naturally happy boy. And she is a jewel, she really is. I don't know how we got so lucky. I mean, we're decent parents, but she came to us this way, I'm sure of it."

Sophia thought of her own sister, Marian. So innately good. Sophia had to fight a little harder for it.

"Please, sit," said Junia. "I'll get you some refreshment. You've had a long journey … and a bit more excitement than you expected."

Sophia thanked her as she found a cushion on which to sit. Onesimus remained standing, but leaned against the wall next to her. His back bothered him, and sometimes it was more comfortable for him to stand.

"When were you last in Ephesus?" she asked Onesimus. "I think you told me, but I forgot."

"About five years ago," he replied, crossing his arms as he gazed out the front window. "Paul sent me with some letters, including one for Timothy. I had been traveling with Aristotelis, the son of my former masters, and his wife Rebekah."

Sophia nodded, remembering. Paul had related the encounter briefly. "Mary Magdalene's daughter. They were traveling to Britannia, correct?"

"Yes. They made sure I knew they arrived safely."

"They know my sister, then, and Corun." She smiled wistfully, feeling both happy for Marian and sad that they were so far apart.

"Corun witnessed the siege, correct?"

Her smile faded, floating away like the ashes of Jerusalem on a burning east wind.

"Yes. Marian says it still haunts him. Members of the church want him to tell the story, but he doesn't like talking about it. I can understand. I mean, I know it was prophesied by Christ himself, and the Jews at Jerusalem had utterly rejected the gospel, but …"

"They had fair warning," he intoned.

She gazed at the floor. "Yes, but Titus was so brutal, so cruel. And he is likely next in line to be emperor. I don't know how to process that."

"He might be better than you think. It's his brother Domitian who worries me more. He is said to be crueler in nature, to enjoy seeing people suffer. And Titus spared Corun."

"That's true. Or maybe he had no choice. God didn't want Corun to be executed for desertion, and there was nothing Titus could do about it."

She looked up, and Onesimus gave her a slight shrug. "Yes, that may be so."

"What's this I hear about Titus?" said Junia, entering the room carrying a tray filled with dried fruits and aromatic bread, along with a small pitcher and cups. "And did I hear you mention Corun? How are he and Marian doing? Word takes longer to reach us here, and I'm sure they write to your mother more than to us." She winked, offering the tray first to Onesimus, then lowering it to Sophia before setting it on the floor and sitting across from her.

"They're doing well. No children yet, though they've been trying."

"Any miscarriages?"

Sophia shook her head. "No, and that concerns Marian more, I think. She fears she is barren, though she remembers the miracles of the past—not just people like Sariah and Abraham, but her own conception as well."

Junia took a sip of water, contemplating. "Well, she will have children. I'm positive of it. And not just by adoption."

Sophia had never heard Junia speak so prophetically. She blinked, searching her own heart. Yes, it felt right. She smiled, then popped a pair of dates in her mouth. At that moment, with her mouth full of fruit, Elhanan burst through the door.

"Sophia!" he shouted in delight.

She scrambled to her feet, chewing furiously and swallowing. "Elhanan, brother." She accepted his embrace, which lifted her off the floor, then spotted Ezra standing in the doorway. He had gotten so tall! He still looked shy, but not like he had before.

When Elhanan let her go, she greeted Ezra, then introduced Onesimus. She turned to Elhanan. "How did you know we were here?"

"One of our neighbors recognized you. She sent her son running to the shop. The boy is fast." He laughed. "Once Ezra and I heard, we came immediately. It's not far. *Why* have you come, by the way?"

She punched him in the arm. "To see *you*, of course. Oh, and John." In her tease, she made the apostle sound like an afterthought. He laughed again—a sound she loved to hear—but then gave a small frown.

"I'm afraid John isn't here."

"Oh? Where is he?"

Elhanan shrugged. "I'm not sure. Timothy might be able to tell us more. He's coming for dinner." He looked to Junia, standing a little behind Sophia, apology already creasing his face. "I hope that's okay."

Junia gave an exaggerated sigh, shoulders slumping, then laughed. "Of course it is. Your sister's here, and we always love having Timothy. When Alia gets back, we'll run to the market for a few more things. Dinner might be later than usual, but it will be good, I promise." She winked, and then Elhanan rushed to sweep her up in his arms, kissing her full on the lips in front of everyone, including Onesimus. It didn't feel inappropriate, though, and in fact, Sophia felt joy from it. Her brother was a good man, and he'd married a marvelous woman.

Timothy arrived early in the second hour of the evening. Ezra was quick to take his cloak, and the pat on the shoulders he received in return reminded Sophia very much of Paul. Of course, Paul and Timothy were close, and both wholly devoted to their Savior. Timothy's hair had become significantly grayer and thinner since last she'd seen him. His frame seemed slighter, too, though he appeared healthy.

No introductions were necessary, as Timothy already knew Onesimus and joyfully welcomed him. They all sat in the front room, except Junia and Alia, who sounded happily engaged together in the kitchen.

"You arrived at a sad time for our city," said Timothy. "I'm sure you've heard a few things about it already."

"We experienced it," said Sophia. "On the docks. Onesimus had to step in and rally the sailors of our ship so it wasn't boarded and taken."

Timothy's eyes widened. "Oh, my. I'm sorry you had to go through that. It must have been a frightening affair."

Sophia nodded appreciatively, but then said, "It was far worse for the slaves caught up in the revolt. I can't imagine how some of them are feeling, awaiting their punishment. I mean, maybe they shouldn't have revolted like that, I don't know, but—"

"But maybe they needed to," added Onesimus. He gazed at his hands, resting in front of him. She was glad he was able to sit for a stretch. "Paul and I have had this discussion more than once. I know it will take time to convince enough people that there is a far better way to advance society and take care of the poor than by enslaving them, but events like these can help, along with our missionary work." He finally looked up, eyes landing on Timothy.

"Indeed," said Timothy. "We are all alike in God's eyes, and his Son suffered for each of us, no matter our social station in this life. That is a radical concept for much of the world—not just Rome—and a great many powerful people feel threatened by it."

"But none of those people, nor all of them collectively, is more powerful than God," said Sophia.

She expected Timothy to respond, but instead it was Onesimus. "God's purpose isn't to prove he is the most powerful. His purpose is to save our souls, to reunite us with him so that we can achieve our eternal potential. He could send his angels and destroy every living slaveholder in an instant, but what would that accomplish? People would fear him, without seeing him as a god of love, and eventually new slave owners would arise anyway, driven by pride and greed."

During the pause that followed, Junia appeared, addressing Sophia and Onesimus. "Just a quick question. Light, medium, or heavy on the garlic? And do you like coriander?" She looked expectantly at the two, and Sophia had to switch tracks in her mind before responding. "However much you normally use of both is fine with me. Onesimus?" He nodded, and Junia thanked them before retreating to the kitchen.

"I think I understand," said Sophia to Onesimus, returning to their topic. "Satan's plan, buttressed by false promises of perfect safety, was to force us to obey him in every single thing, but we don't learn anything from coerced obedience, only by having to make difficult choices and trade-offs—and even by suffering. Many slaves have joined the church, but they are counseled to honor the law and be faithful servants, exhibiting the fruits of Christ to their masters so that their hearts might be opened to the good news of the gospel as well."

Onesimus nodded. "That is well said. When I fled to Paul, I considered myself a free man in Christ. And I *was*. As was Philemon. Paul counseled me to return—not just because of the laws of men by which I was bound, but because Philemon was my brother in Christ. He sent counsel to Philemon as well, advising him to treat me as a brother and not a servant, and that made a difference in both our lives—and in our understanding of the mercies of God. I was soon officially freed, and I gladly remained employed in the household of Philemon and Apphia."

He paused, his mien becoming more solemn. "If I had refused to return, I'm sure I would have become bitter and proud. Such feelings lead us away from God. I might even have ended up a participant in a slave revolt, and without the Spirit to guide me. Again, sometimes it is justified to rise up in rebellion against earthly authority, and it is Christ who can tell us when those times are. He knows far more than we do, and his purposes are always just, merciful, and true."

Timothy nodded in admiration. "And eternal. Paul—and Philip's—trust in you is well placed, Brother Onesimus."

"I do wish the church would make some official announcements regarding the moral wrongness of slavery," said Elhanan. "More stability can be found in freedom than in comfortable bondage."

Timothy smiled wanly. "John essentially did, right here in Ephesus, which is why he had to leave." He chuckled softly. "There is a reason the Lord called him and his brother James 'Sons of Thunder.' He is not afraid to call out the rich and powerful, and he certainly did that last week. He also doesn't believe in the Eleventh Commandment."

"What is that?" asked Sophia.

"That as Christians we must be nice above all else. That is not true, of course, at least from the perspective of true charity."

"But the second great commandment …"

"Is enabled by the first, which is rooted in God's wisdom. If someone you love is making decisions that are destroying their life—especially spiritually—do you withhold sound counsel from them for fear of offending them or appearing 'mean'? Of course not. Neither does the Lord. He respects our agency, but he will warn us, patiently and repeatedly, even though the truth is sometimes hard to hear."

Sophia nodded. She had taught such things before, but without understanding their true profundity. And now she was even more excited to learn from John. He was legendary. It was rumored that Mark was close to completing a history of Christ's ministry, and that Luke and Matthew were working on their own. Many members wanted John to do the same thing, though he had so far demurred. What would it be like to meet one of the Sons of

Thunder? Her disappointment that he had been chased out of Ephesus must have shown on her face.

"Don't worry, Sophia," said Onesimus. "It took me a lot longer to learn that than it should have, despite my circumstances."

"What? Oh, no, it's not that. I just wish we had found John here. I was really looking forward to meeting him."

"You might find him in Smyrna," offered Timothy, "if you don't want to wait here for him. He had been planning to go there soon, anyway, as Epaphras is visiting from Laodicea, and there are many saints in the area. I don't know how long he'll be away, but tempers here will cool down eventually."

Elhanan must have seen a signal from Junia, for he suddenly rose. "Well, you'll find him soon enough, Sophia, I'm sure of that. But let's help Junia and Alia get everything served so we can eat."

CHAPTER 2

*If we say that we have no sin, we deceive ourselves, and the
truth is not in us. If we confess our sins, he is faithful and just to
forgive us our sins, and to cleanse us from all unrighteousness.*

1 John 1:8-9

Sophia enjoyed hearing her brother preach that Sabbath. When he asked her to say a few impromptu words, however, she was less than ecstatic. She was usually comfortable speaking, but she liked to be more prepared, even if all he'd asked her to do was describe a little bit about their parents' time in Rome and share a brief testimony of the Savior.

Alia, it turned out, couldn't stop talking about how good her 'sermon' was. Junia confided to her later that Sophia's presence had already been a big help. Alia's art teacher had been pushing Greek philosophy on her, and while some of it was innocuous enough, and a portion even useful in some ways, the overall tendency was to discount the Christian religion as a mystical construct of the uneducated. Reliance upon God's help to understand his teachings was even more of a foreign concept, and so Junia and Elhanan had been struggling to help Alia become serious about how she approached her Heavenly Father in prayer and study.

"You're the smartest person she knows," said Junia. The kids had fallen asleep long ago, in their rooms. Onesimus had chosen to accompany Timothy to his house.

"Well, that can't be true."

"In her mind it is. You lived in Rome, and had good tutors there. And you've always seemed to understand things. Now that I think about it, you're one of the smartest people *I* know. Elhanan loves to tease you. That tells me something, too."

They both giggled, and she gave Elhanan a fake scowl. It was hard to believe he was forty-three years old. He had married later than most, so he had known her well when she was a child, but it seemed like he should be younger.

"I do not," he protested. "Sophia just takes things the wrong way." He smiled, giving away the lie.

Junia's face took on a serious cast. "What is it like traveling with Onesimus? He seems, I don't know, kind of somber and stern. That's only a first impression, of course."

"Well, he's a former slave."

"I figured that, because of his name."

"Yes, well, I was a little uncomfortable when Philip asked us to travel together, and Philip knew it was an unusual request."

"Is he a eunuch?" asked Elhanan.

Sophia thought he was teasing at first, which would have been in poor taste, but he looked sincere … and genuinely concerned.

"No, I don't think so. And so far, it's been like traveling with an uncle. He's very kind, and he's a good conversationalist. I can tell he has a sense of humor, too, but I haven't been able to draw much of that out yet. He's been a lot of places and met a lot of people. And I was grateful he was there when the men tried to force their way down the pier and onto our ship. He's clearly a brave man."

"Where is he from?" asked Junia.

"From Sarmatia, he says. He was taken by Roman soldiers when he was a young child. Barbaric, to raid villages for slaves. How depraved can people be?"

Elhanan gave a heavy sigh. "Very, unfortunately. We have several members of the church here who are slaves, and whose masters are not Christians. Some of those masters, while they pretend to be gracious and tolerant, are most definitely not. A few, in fact, are pure, unadulterated evil, driven by so much greed and pride they've tossed aside almost all their humanity."

Sophia shivered as a remembrance came, startling her with its starkness.

"Are you okay?" asked Junia.

"Yes, I mean … well, yes." She looked at Junia and Elhanan in turn, both of them intensely focused on her. "I had an experience with pure evil in Rome. I haven't told anyone about it yet, not even Mother and Father, or Philip. I haven't known how exactly to describe it."

Elhanan narrowed his eyes. "You don't have to tell us, either, unless you feel like you should."

She tilted her head, pondering that a moment. Yes, she did feel like she should. Why, she wasn't sure.

"Well, I was confronted by a man as I walked along a street near the Forum. He was possessed by a demon."

Junia put a hand to her mouth, gasping.

"What do you mean, 'confronted'?" asked Elhanan.

"He knew who I was," she said, trying to sound nonchalant. "And then he tried to kill me with a sword."

Junia's hand went to her belly, and her eyes popped. "What did you do?"

The memory became warm, and the lights in the room sparkled through her tears. "I didn't do anything. Another sword appeared, in an instant, blocking the demon's swing. The demon screamed as he fled, and then I looked to see who had saved me, expecting a Roman soldier or some passing guard."

She paused, until Elhanan asked, "And?"

"And he said his name was Raphael. He was an angel." She left out the part where he had told her she might need him again. She didn't like to think about that.

"The angel Raphael?" asked Elhanan in wonder. "Are you sure?"

She nodded, grateful she had finally told somebody. "Yes. I'm alive because of him. And I'm here. And now I'm supposed to find John, but Philip isn't sure why. He says John will know."

"Cryptic," said Junia. "Why are the apostles so mysterious?"

"Because the Lord's ways are so much higher than ours that it's impossible for us to fully understand them," mused Elhanan. "He holds back, giving us only what he knows we can deal with … until we can handle more. He has to hold things back from the apostles, and sometimes they have to hold things back from us, because we can't deal with them properly."

"Yes, I've thought about that," said Sophia. "Jesus himself, as a boy, increased in stature, line upon line, until he grew into his fulness as the Only Begotten. I wish I knew what else I could do to be ready—and to deserve—more knowledge."

Elhanan closed his eyes, nodding slowly. "We all do. But if we remain faithful and obedient, and exert every bit of energy we can toward serving him and trusting him, the spiritual rewards will come. And they'll keep coming, even beyond this life."

Elhanan had become so wise and eloquent. She knew he and the flock in Ephesus had faced persecution. Nothing too serious, thankfully, but that could change. Things were always changing.

———————

The short trip north to Smyrna passed quickly. Sophia and Onesimus had left the cart and mule—along with most of their belongings—behind, thinking they would be back that way soon. She had probably overfilled her pack, but she wasn't about to complain to Onesimus about it. He never offered to carry any of her things in his pack, either. That was good.

They found the house where Epaphras was staying easily enough. It was a little off the main roads, surrounded by trees announcing their bold fall colors. It was the middle of the day, and Epaphras was working in the large garden in the back with several other people, harvesting various vegetables and fruits.

When the lady of the house announced them, Epaphras stood and stretched his back. Then he strode over, looking more spry than his at least sixty years.

"Sophia, did you say? Daughter of Barabbas? Yes, I've heard of the good bishop, but have never met him." He held out a hand, and they clasped forearms. Then he turned to Onesimus. "Dear Brother Onesimus, it has been a long time. You look well."

They also clasped arms as Onesimus replied, "As do you, brother."

"Come, let us go inside, out of the sun," said Epaphras. "We can enjoy some refreshment. I'm dying of thirst." He winked, and they followed him inside.

After they situated themselves in chairs near the kitchen, Epaphras asked, "What brings you to Smyrna? Are you passing through, or do you intend to stay?" By the way his eyes studied them, he seemed to be trying to figure out why they had arrived together.

"Philip sent me to find John, and assigned Onesimus as my traveling companion. We just came from Ephesus, and Timothy said he had come here."

"Ah, yes, well, I wish I could give you good news on that front. You narrowly missed him. He has gone to Philadelphia, saying he needed to make a visit and personally deliver a letter. I asked him when he might be back, but he couldn't say. He is an energetic one, I'll give him that. I don't know where he gets all that vigor. I know he was the youngest original apostle, but he isn't young anymore." He chuckled, then took a long drink from the cup in his hand.

Sophia glanced at Onesimus, who nodded.

"Well, then, we'll be heading straightaway for Philadelphia. If you can give us a couple of good places to stop along the way to sleep and get something to eat, we would be grateful. We left most of our things in Ephesus."

"Of course, my dear, of course. I travel these roads often enough, and know most of the members along the way. Many are eager to assist in the labor of the Lord's ministry in any way they can."

"Thank you, Brother Epaphras. The Lord bless you."

"Ah, you're welcome, young one. It is fine to receive such a blessing from one so full of the fire of the Spirit. Thank you, Sophia, daughter of Chanah and Barabbas."

Such an effusive compliment buoyed her spirits, and after a brief meal at the same house, she and Onesimus set off on their nearly week-long journey to Philadelphia, hoping to reach the home of one of the saints Epaphras had listed before full dark.

The first part of the trip was pleasant, with fair weather and plenty of hospitable, even excited hosts. The second half became more difficult, with a sudden storm assaulting them on the fourth day, bringing copious sleet and hail. Sophia might have laughed that off, but they had a hard time finding a meal and a place to lodge that evening. Two of the members whose names Epaphras had supplied were not at home, and most of the other people they talked to exhibited strongly held suspicions of the Christians. Finally, though, a middle-aged widow who swore Sophia was the spitting image of a departed daughter let them in, fed them, and helped them dry out. She even let them talk with her about the teachings of Jesus, which she had never heard. They left the next morning with great gratitude in their hearts.

Besides some of the now soggy roads they had to travel, and Sophia's feet becoming sore, they made it to Philadelphia without incident. They quickly located the bishop there, a man named Georgios, who welcomed them into his woodworking shop.

"This area is beautiful," noted Sophia as she sat on a stool. Onesimus preferred to stand.

"Yes," agreed Georgios, maybe a year or two older than Elhanan. He was definitely of Greek stock, his prominent nose joining with his name in revealing that. "This is the most beautiful part of the valley, in my humble opinion. Very fertile as well. My great grandfather moved here many years ago, and he claimed it was the most important decision he ever made, including marrying my great grandmother." He chuckled, then began working a piece of wood that looked like part of a chair.

"Is this one of John's favorite places to visit?" she asked. "We heard he was here."

Georgios furrowed his brow in concentration, then shrugged as he continued to work. "I don't know. John seems content wherever he is. At least, that's what everyone who has traveled with him says. I, personally, have not, though I hope to." He smiled as he glanced up, then re-focused on his work.

"Does he normally stay with you when he's here?" asked Onesimus.

"No, he doesn't like to burden any one family too much, and despite his bold and even gruff reputation, he's incredibly personable and loves meeting all kinds of new people. That's my view of him, anyway."

"Do you know where he's staying this time?" asked Sophia.

Georgios paused, straightening. "Oh, he's not here. He left two days ago, heading north into Bithynia. He was planning to go all the way to Heraclea, I believe, on the shores of the Black Sea, though he wouldn't say why. Apostles can be peculiar, you know." He chuckled again as he continued shaping the chair piece using a small tool with a curved blade. He suddenly looked up, concern painting his face. "Was he expecting you?"

Sophia shook her head and gave her own light laugh. "No. We've been chasing him, though, on an errand from Philip; first to Ephesus, then to Smyrna, then here, and now to … where did you say?"

"Heraclea."

"I've never heard of it. What would be the best route, where we might find lodging and food along the way? We are traveling light."

"*I'm* traveling light," quipped Onesimus, which earned him a surprised glare. She refused to look down and compare the sizes of their packs. She already knew the answer, and she wouldn't give him the satisfaction.

He and Georgios laughed together, which earned them both glares. Then, Georgios put down his tools and raised his hands in surrender. "My apologies, Sophia. To answer your question, my wife is the best person to help you with that. She and some of the other sisters keep an active correspondence with many other sisters up and down this western side of Asia Minor, and even beyond a bit. They do a marvelous work, they really do, helping those in need. In fact," he leaned toward her and Onesimus with a conspiratorial expression, lowering his voice, "her job is more important than mine, but don't tell her I admitted that." He grinned, then led them out of the shop and toward his home.

They departed the next day for Bithynia, Onesimus's pack stocked with enough provisions that it bulged larger than hers in a quite satisfactory way. Georgios's wife Chryssa outlined two routes they could take, but warned that they could spend at least a couple of nights sleeping under the stars. They already had a pair of blankets, plus their cloaks, but she provided them with another set of blankets, given how much cooler the weather was getting.

Instead of traveling in a straight line from Philadelphia to Heraclea, they swung in a westward arc, keeping to the lowlands and the more moderate weather as much as possible. It was a longer journey, and Onesimus insisted they pace themselves better. Sophia knew he was concerned about her feet—about her health in general—and she didn't argue with him. She was tempted to head back to Ephesus several times. There was a chance they would miss John again in Heraclea, and then what? They'd have to return to Ephesus anyway, and wait until he returned.

But for some reason, she couldn't get herself to turn back. And so she kept trudging on. Chryssa had been right. They spent a few nights sleeping under or near any cover they could find, and the extra food they had brought was a blessing. Fortunately, they were able to hitch a ride on the occasional wagon, saving both time and her feet. Onesimus's joking comments about how it was easier to travel with a pretty young woman aside, she began to enjoy the journey. They saw so many beautiful places, and met hundreds of people.

As they sat on the back of a wagon, feet dangling above the road, she turned to him. "I didn't know you had such a sense of humor."

He smiled. "Because I tease you back? I've become better at doing that over the years, after I became a free man. As a slave I was generally quite reserved."

"I didn't mean *that*," she said, feeling a bit uncomfortable. "You're naturally clever. You pick up on things. The small comments you make in conversations to lighten the mood, or to help someone see an issue from a different perspective. You have a knack for humor and insight."

"So, what are you suggesting? That I perform, see if I can earn a few coins for us?"

He was teasing her again, and he truly did feel like a close uncle now. Philip's wisdom in pairing them for this journey continued to shine brighter.

"Yes. At the next town. We could perform together, come up with an act … you know, like a short, funny play."

He quirked an eyebrow, his smile tempering. "I don't think so. We will preach."

"But Jesus had a sense of humor."

"I have heard that," he conceded, "and even read about it. But his primary focus was the teaching, not the other way around."

She had to agree, so she shrugged. Then she scrunched her brow. "Do you think he still has a sense of humor? You know, in heaven."

Onesimus pondered that for a minute as the horses' hooves clopped and the wheels squeaked and clattered. Then he said, "I'm not sure how much time he actually spends in heaven. I'm sure he isn't resting, nor are his angels." Sophia immediately thought of Raphael again as he continued. "But yes, I do believe he has a sense of humor. In the first place, we share the same heritage. We are like him, and our Father, in many ways. In the second place, why would he stop having a sense of humor, especially since he knows we all enjoy it so much?"

Sophia gave him an impressed turn of her lips. "That's good logic. There's other evidence, of course, like sending us on this mad chase after John. I think John and Jesus will both enjoy a good chuckle when we finally catch up to him."

He laughed at that. "I suppose that's true. Let's hope we find out soon."

Even with the help of those few wagon rides, it took them almost three weeks to get to Heraclea, and by then fall was nearly spent. Snow already dusted the tops of the distant mountains to the east and south. They arrived on foot, late in the day, heading for the market first, hoping to find a few stragglers, whether shoppers or vendors. They also kept careful watch for Roman or city guards, as they might be a good source of information, too.

The Lord indeed had a sense of humor, because the first guard they encountered knew who John was but reported he had just passed through. Everyone else they talked to hadn't heard of him. They sat down dejectedly on some boxes near a vacant market stall, and within a minute Sophia nearly fell off her box as an apple appeared out of the growing gloom, arcing toward her head. She caught it, barely, and then heard a deep, hearty laugh.

"Onesimus, is this the daughter you never told me about?"

A man came into focus, walking toward them. From the descriptions Philip had given her, it looked like John. But how was that possible? Unless … of course.

Onesimus jumped to his feet and nearly knocked John over as he rushed to bear-hug him. "John, how did you find us?"

After he'd let him go, John acted like he'd broken some ribs, wheezing, coughing, and wincing in pain. Then he straightened, laughing, and made a slight bow to Sophia. "It is a pleasure to meet you, young lady. I hope this clumsy oaf hasn't bored you to death." He glanced at Onesimus. "And the question is, how did you find *me?*"

Sophia rose, blinking and swallowing. It really was John. She said a small prayer of gratitude, woven with great relief, before she responded. "My name is Sophia, and Philip asked me to find you. We went to Ephesus first, but, um …"

"But you had caused a slave revolt," supplied Onesimus, giving John a fake frown.

"Ah, that," said John, seeming to wince for real. "Well, certain nobles asked me what I thought, and I told them. You'd think they'd appreciate honesty more. They claim to. Now, let's let Sophia finish."

She blinked again. "Oh, well, Timothy said you went to Smyrna." He nodded. "You had already left when we got there, of course, and Epaphras sent us to Philadelphia. We met Bishop Georgios there, and he said you'd come here, but, um, he didn't know why."

John took a deep breath. "Well, you've had quite a journey. I apologize for that. I'm glad you didn't wait for me in Ephesus, though. You would have been waiting a long time."

Her eyebrows rose as Onesimus uttered, "Oh? Where are you going?"

John laid a hand on his shoulder. "We should talk about that. But let's get you two out of the cold air. I'm staying with a blacksmith here, in some rooms off his shop. If you don't mind some early morning clanging, it's wonderful lodging." He winked, then turned and motioned them to follow.

They soon arrived at John's rooms. At this late hour, the blacksmith shop was blessedly quiet. After John had fetched them some water, bread, and dates, they sat on the floor of one of the rooms, lit by a pair of large candles. A fire crackled in a hearth, and the windows were shuttered and draped.

"Did you go to the market to find us?" asked Onesimus.

John nodded. "It appears that way. I was only told I needed to go to the market. I usually don't question the why."

Sophia had witnessed many such miracles, especially around Paul, so she wasn't too surprised. She was also grateful for the room's warmth seeping into her bones.

"Well, we're happy you did," said Onesimus. "It would have been a cold night. Bless you for listening."

John rubbed his chin, gazing at Sophia. "Sophia, daughter of Barabbas and Chanah. You have a sister, correct, and two brothers?"

"Yes," she replied, surprised he knew that. "Marian lives with her husband in Nazaretum, in Britannia. He was a Roman soldier."

"The one who witnessed the siege, yes. Marian wrote down his account. I have seen it. Almost too horrible to believe, and yet it is true." His shoulders slumped a bit, but then he breathed in deeply. "And your brothers? One is in Africa, is that right?"

"Yes. Matthew lives with his family in B'Ashra. He is a Teacher there."

He nodded. "I remember now. With Cornelius, who is a Seventy. Their temple was recently completed. So many miracles have happened there, and they continue." A slow smile spread across his face, and then he added, "I'm almost jealous. I've not witnessed such quick success on so great a scale. Oh, that would have been wonderful to see. Have you been there?"

She shook her head, her desire to visit someday sharp in her heart. "I will, eventually."

"So will I," said John, eyes twinkling.

"My other brother, Simon, lives on Melita, where we all used to live."

John narrowed his eyes in wonder, slowly shaking his head. "Your family is as spread out as any I've seen. From Britannia to northeastern Africa; on an island of the sea; and you here. The Lord wasn't kidding around when he called you to the work. And now … you will go farther."

His words sounded … not ominous, but certainly portentous.

"What do you mean?" asked Onesimus.

John's look intensified. "What I mean, good brother, is that I am going north, across the Black Sea to Sarmatia. The Lord has called me there, and I would like both of you to accompany me."

Sarmatia. Sophia studied Onesimus's reaction to that. Did John know that was where he was born? Besides a flicker of surprise, though, Onesimus didn't react at all. Instead, he turned his gaze to Sophia, the question in his eyes. Before she could respond, John spoke again.

"Do you know what village you were born in?" So, John did know.

Onesimus lowered his head. Now she spotted a reaction. "No, I do not. My parents were commanded never to speak of it again, not even to their children. They died before they could work up the courage to disobey that order, I guess."

John's eyes glistened, his expression filled with compassion. "Well, we have a vital work to do among your people. There are many descendants of the lost tribes of Israel in Sarmatia and surrounding lands. You, by the way, are from the tribe of Asher."

Onesimus's head jerked up, eyes wide. "I am … how do you know?"

"The Spirit told me, just now. Mind you, your direct lineage to the House of Israel—and mine and Sophia's as well—doesn't make a lick of difference in our covenant progress toward eternal life. You are part of the body of Christ by choice, not happenstance, and you are responsible to follow the Lord and keep his command-ments. It does, however, link you with an Abrahamic promise."

Onesimus still seemed dumbfounded, and Sophia had nothing to say at the moment, either.

"Abraham was promised that through him and his seed, all the people of the earth would be blessed. You are of his seed, and you are one of his missionaries, called and empowered to bless God's children and guide them toward the light of their Savior. It is a magnificent opportunity and blessing."

Onesimus lowered his eyes again. Sophia wished she could read his thoughts. Then he looked up at John. "When do we leave?"

John smiled, then gave a soft chuckle. "Well, I don't propose traveling there now, and the Lord hasn't asked it of me. We can stay here through the winter, preaching and baptizing as we may, building a branch of the church that can sustain itself with minimal assistance from either Pella or Rome. And we can prepare ourselves for the great work that lies ahead of us in Sarmatia, where very few missionaries have been sent, and those for only brief periods of time. Do you remember the words of Joshua to the Israelites on the eve of their entrance into the promised land?"

Onesimus shook his head, but Sophia recited them. "Sanctify yourselves, for tomorrow the Lord will do wonders among you."

CHAPTER 3

*And with great power gave the apostles witness of the resurrection
of the Lord Jesus: and great grace was upon them all.*

Acts 4:33

Winter in Heraclea wasn't as bad as Sophia had feared. Yes, the nights could get cold, but it reminded her of Rome. She knew, of course, that it was much colder in Sarmatia, which received heavy snowfall, so she was happy they were waiting for spring to set sail.

John was a marvelous teacher. He wasn't as charismatic as Paul, and often more blunt, but he was just as full of the Spirit of the Lord, and she fed off his energy. He often asked her to speak, and gradually she became more accustomed to extemporaneous presentation, though she was sure she would never actually enjoy it. Well, probably not. She had plenty of opportunities to prepare her remarks beforehand, too, and the people didn't often see women preachers, of whatever religion they might profess.

Onesimus was effective as well, especially when he described his background and bore powerful testimony of how God views all individuals equally, no matter their earthly circumstances. When he spoke about the hope he felt in the eternal promises made possible by Jesus's willing sacrifice, it gave her shivers.

Nearly four dozen people were baptized, in the ocean and during the warmest times of the day. They drew many onlookers, including some officials of the city—there, they claimed, to make sure no laws were broken and nobody was coerced into anything. They had heard of the Christians, of course, and one had let slip that he knew of Vespasian's tacit favor, but they had never had to deal with any significant numbers within their populace. She understood. They didn't know what to expect. John reassured, them—quite tactfully, in her opinion—and besides the spreading of some odd rumors, they had no serious issues.

As they ate one evening, with the warmer months fast approaching, Onesimus brought up one of those rumors.

"I was speaking with a pair of city guards today, just outside one of their buildings, and several women approached. One of them claimed we were branding all the new converts."

"Branding them?" asked John around a mouthful of food.

"Yes. On the buttocks, so it wouldn't be seen."

"And what did you tell them?" asked Sophia, shifting her seat.

He blushed a little. "I showed them my buttocks, one at a time."

John nearly spat out his food, his eyes bulging—not in shock, but in mirth. When he had recovered, he asked. "And what happened then?"

"I think one of the guards got a hernia, he was laughing so hard. I made sure not to laugh. My purpose wasn't to embarrass them, but I fear I did. People need to know the truth, though." His serious mien cracked, and a smile emerged. John was still chuckling, shaking his head. He took a long draft of water and cleared his throat.

"Well, one man went to the mayor and accused us of stealing chickens and sacrificing them under a full moon while babbling in our own language. The mayor summoned me to answer the charges, and we ended up having a pleasant conversation. It turns out this man often accuses people of stealing things, but never with any proof. And now"—he slapped his thighs—"we should discuss some details of our trip to Sarmatia."

It seemed so soon. Sophia was beginning to like Heraclea, despite its quirks.

"When should we leave?" she asked, instead of voicing an objection which would have sounded like whining. She was speaking to an apostle, after all.

He seemed to have read her mind. "I wanted to get your thoughts on the matter. I know you enjoy it here."

"Well …" She pondered a few moments, searching her heart, glancing at Onesimus. It was to his homeland they would be traveling, even though he never mentioned it, and that sealed it. "As soon as possible, or practical. I don't know what the weather is like there."

John nodded, then looked to Onesimus. "And you, Brother Onesimus?"

Onesimus stared beyond them for a few seconds, then pursed his lips before responding. "We could probably find a ship within a week, but I believe we should wait until April, even the middle of the month." He looked at John, then lowered his eyes. "That's just my opinion, though."

John nodded thoughtfully, setting his hands on the floor beside him. "Mid-April. That sounds good to me. Let's pray about it, though, and see what the Lord thinks."

***

Mid-April it was, and they found a ship sailing under the sign of Castor and Pollux, going diagonally across the Black Sea, stopping in Panticapeum and then continuing through the narrow strait into Lake Maeotis and on to Cremni. Sophia remembered Paul making mention of a ship sailing under the same sign, but there were lots of them.

They soon discovered there were two Sarmatians on board—or rather, two *other* Sarmatians. They said they were trading scouts, but John let her and Onesimus know they were likely spies. Relations between Rome and Sarmatia weren't openly hostile at the moment, but beyond some of the normal trading, they weren't good, either.

One of the men clearly took a liking to Sophia. His Greek was good, and he was handsome in a roguish sort of way, but she had zero interest in him. Less than zero. In fact, she pretended to be sick for two whole days to avoid his attempts to talk to her. Finally, when Onesimus said both the spies were below and probably sleeping, she came out on deck in the early morning to enjoy the fresh air of springtime and the beauty of the sea. Onesimus stood with her for a while, then remembered something he wanted to speak to John about, promising to return soon.

She could have predicted what happened next. The spy seemed to pop into existence right next to her, hands on the railing.

"You are feeling better?"

She looked around. Several sailors, along with another passenger, were also on the deck, which eased her nerves.

"Yes," she replied, staring across the waters.

"You don't seem to like me."

She glanced at him, then returned to her sea watching. "Why would I like or dislike you?" It was a cold, sterile thing to say, but it felt appropriate.

"Hmmm …" he responded, his voice deep. "Is it because I am from Sarmatia, and you are Roman? Have you heard … stories?"

"No. I don't care where people are from."

"You don't?" he sounded genuinely taken aback. "I'm not sure I can believe that. We aren't on the best terms with Rome. We conquered the Scythians before they could; maybe that's part of it."

"That was four hundred years ago."

"You know the history. Where did you study?"

"In Rome," she replied, and left it at that. She realized part of her had said it to impress him, and she chided herself for her pride.

"Wow. So you are from Rome. The so-called 'Caput Mundi.'" He didn't say it with a sneer, but the 'so-called' gave away his feelings on it.

"No. I am from Judea." There, that should lower his estimation of her.

A long pause followed, but she refused to look at his face to see what he might be thinking. "Your people were slaughtered by Titus, and his father Vespasian before him, but mostly by Titus."

"Sadly, yes, but they brought it upon themselves. I wish it were not so." Unwittingly, he had carved a hefty slice out of her emotions. She had read Corun's reluctant first-hand account of the siege from a Roman soldier's perspective, several times. The suffering was unimaginable. And though she had told this man—whose name she didn't even know—that she was from Judea, that wasn't true any longer, because Judea was no more.

Another long pause followed. Finally, he broke the relative silence. "What is your name?"

She wouldn't lie to him. "Sophia."

"Sophia," he repeated. "Wisdom. And the taller man who travels with you, he is your slave?"

She couldn't stop her head from swiveling toward him, nor could she suppress the anger that flushed her face and infused her voice. "Not a slave. Never, *ever* a slave."

His eyes widened, and he gripped the railing harder. He tipped his head. "My apologies. I shouldn't have assumed. You are not a fan of slavery. Were you …?"

She turned her head back to the sea. "No, nor any of my family. It is evil, and it always has been."

"So … you have never owned a slave?"

How could he ask such a stupid question? She didn't look at him again, but her jaw hardened.

"I'm sorry," he said. Was he? He was a spy, trying to get information. "My name is Fyodor, by the way."

Sophia gave a slight nod.

"I live near Cremni. That's where you're going, right?"

"I don't know where we're going yet."

"You don't … who gets to decide that?"

She finally looked at him again, this time turning her whole body. "God." With that, she stepped around him and walked quickly toward the stairs, happy again to disappear belowdecks. As she went, she thought about the similarities with her older sister Marian's first introduction to Corun, on a ship, on this same Black Sea. He and other soldiers had been escorting some prisoners, all the way to the tin mines in Britannia. Marian had rejected Corun then, too.

The difference—and her sister had confided this to Sophia— was that she had immediately been attracted to Corun. Sophia was definitely on another boat.

The stop in Panticapeum was brief—less than a day—but it felt good to walk on dry, solid land for a bit. The rest of the journey wouldn't be long, either. One of the first things she noticed was that most of the houses and buildings had peaked roofs, some of them quite sharp. Snow still clung to the edges, and in some piles on the ground. To her youthful adoptive aunt Esther, way up in Trento, this would look familiar. The ship traffic was less than she expected, but they weren't traveling to any of the major ports along the Black Sea. Two good meals later, they took to the ship again, setting sail late at night. By mid-morning of the third day out, the captain announced that they would be docking in Cremni soon, and Sophia rushed up to the deck to see. Fyodor and the other spy were there, but she ignored them, happy that both John and Onesimus accompanied her.

"Cremni," John said with a thoughtful gaze. "What mysteries do you hold?"

Onesimus stared stoically at the city, but Sophia could tell he was deep in thought and struggling with some emotions. She certainly would have been.

"Will we start in Cremni?" she asked John, "or is this just where we're landing? You haven't said yet." She secretly hoped for the latter.

"I believe we can spend at least a few days here, if only to get to know a little bit about this land and its people. Then, we'll go where the Lord leads us."

"Do you know where we'll be able to stay?"

"No," he replied, then turned to her and smiled. "But I'm sure we can figure it out. I remember when Jesus first sent us out in pairs across Judea. We didn't take anything with us, not even any money. He's not asking us to do *that*, but we can trust him just the same."

Sophia didn't feel too worried about it, beyond the normal trepidation of an entirely new place and people, with their own culture and attitudes. How would these people receive them? She reminded herself that they were all God's children, so they had that in common. Then another thought came. In Cremni, as with other places along the coasts, most of the people would be conversant in Koine Greek, but what if they traveled significantly inland? What language would those people speak? Actually, the more she thought about it, the more excited she grew at the prospect of learning another language. Her Hebrew was almost nonexistent, but she knew Latin and Greek equally well. Adding a third good language would be a useful challenge.

Searching for a place to stay in Cremni turned out to be a little more dramatic than she had bargained for. As they entered one plaza, the strangled scream of a horse ripped through the air, freezing her footsteps. Her eyes tracked to the source, and through breaks in a small crowd she watched in shock as a man finished killing a horse by severing its jugular. The people had placed it within a low-walled, wooden structure, and several other men held tight to ropes keeping the animal in place.

"That seems like an odd way to put a horse down," said Onesimus, who had a better view with his height.

"They aren't just putting it down," said John. "It's an older horse, true, but they are performing a ritual sacrifice. I believe it's meant to draw the favor of their god of fire for the spring planting. Why they didn't use a younger, finer specimen, I don't know. Perhaps they think their god isn't paying close attention. My guess is that they will gather the blood to sprinkle in one of the fields, and then burn the body."

"Barbaric," said Sophia.

"Not uncommon," said John. "And most people think Jewish animal sacrifices mystical and backward. Of course, if the Israelites hadn't provoked the Lord one too many times after escaping Egypt, all the additional ritual sacrifices under the Law of Carnal Commandments wouldn't have been needed. They would have kept the original, higher Law of Moses, which Christ has now restored and fulfilled with the New Covenant."

Sophia refused to watch the rest of the horse sacrifice, and they moved on. By the time they found a room to rent, with the requested privacy partition, her stomach had settled, though she definitely didn't feel hungry.

John and Onesimus left her there to rest while they went to find the synagogue John had heard about in the city. There weren't many Jews in Cremni, but enough that John wanted to meet the local rabbi or priest.

They hadn't been gone more than a few minutes when the lady of the house knocked on the door to the room. Sophia rose and answered it.

"Miss, there is a visitor here to see you."

She was confused for a split second. Then her heart sank.

"Who is it?"

"A young man, from here. He says he knows you and your companions. He is waiting in our front room."

"Very well." She lifted her skirts and hurried down the short hall, wanting to get it over with quickly. The woman disappeared a different direction.

As expected, Fyodor awaited her, and again she thought of Corun's ardent pursuit of Marian—how alike and how different the circumstances were.

"Fyodor," she said coolly but respectfully, "we did not expect you."

"We? The two men you travel with left, so it is just you. Perhaps you will now feel more free to talk to me?"

"About what? My friends don't tell me who I can talk to, nor about what."

He looked a little crestfallen at that. "Ah, so, on the ship, you really didn't want to talk to me."

This was awkward, but she decided to be straightforward and brave, like John. "I enjoy talking to people, but I perceived you only wanted to talk to me because you thought I was pretty. I'm really not interested in such conversations right now—not just with you, but with any man. I'm not looking for marriage any time soon, if ever, so it's best if I avoid any pretenses."

He blinked, clearly surprised at her stark honesty. If he was really a spy, such behavior might seem anathema to him. "Oh, I see. Why are you here, if I may ask?"

She stood straighter, lifting her chin slightly. "If you must know, I travel with an apostle of the Lord Jesus Christ, known as Jesus of Nazareth by the Jews. He was crucified by them, but, as promised, he reclaimed his body and rose from the dead on the third day. He is the son of God, and the Savior of the world."

He cocked his head. "You are … a preacher?"

"Yes."

His gaze became thoughtful. "Does that mean you are not allowed to marry? I once heard of a small group of religionists far to the west who believed that."

"No, it does not. That is my choice."

He frowned slightly, then nodded. "Ah, then I am wasting my time here. I cannot convince you to even get to know me a little better?"

"No, and I do not have the time. Why would you be interested in a Roman woman, anyway?"

He shrugged. "That is a good point." Somehow, that seemed to sting him the most. "I will leave you now. Good night."

It was like she blinked, and he was suddenly gone. Wow, she had gotten rid of him. She felt proud of herself, and a little amazed. She returned to the room, said a prayer of thanks, then took out an old letter from Paul she had brought. She always loved reviewing his accounts of his travels, and his counsel to the saints. Every time she did, a window into heaven cracked open, and light poured through.

———

The next day they visited the local rabbi in his home, near the center of the city. His name was Nazrim, and he had reached the age where Sophia couldn't guess how old he was. He could be a hundred. His voice was soft and raspy as he addressed them.

"It has been a long time since we've seen any visitors from Jerusalem." Sophia wondered if he knew Jerusalem had been destroyed. He must. Perhaps he was becoming forgetful?

"We are glad to be here," said John, showing deep respect for the man. "We bring a message all Jews should rejoice in. Messiah has come."

The man's eyes widened, the number of wrinkles on his face exploding. "He has come? Finally? Ah, that is good, that is good." He nodded, over and over, whispering to himself so low Sophia couldn't understand.

"Yes, it is," said John softly. "He offers salvation to the entire world, and he sends his people to share that glad message.

Nazrim started rocking back and forth. "Indeed. I am too old to be of much use, but there are many here who keep to the old ways, not just the members of my congregation. They could be of help to Messiah."

That seemed to pique John's interest. "What do these non-Jews do? How do they keep to the old ways?"

The rabbi closed his eyes, smiling as he rocked, and it seemed he hadn't even heard the question. His hearing might be bad, too. But suddenly, he answered, eyes remaining shut.

"Some of the feasts and the sacrifices—using pigeons, I'm afraid, because they are pests—and ritual washings. I heard of a temple once, too, in Metropolis, similar to the one the Samaritans built on Mount Gerizim. They don't seem to understand much about the coming of Messiah any more, but legends still persist."

Legends. Some of those legends would be eight hundred years old, from the time the Assyrians carried away most of the people of the ten northern tribes.

"But you understand," said John.

"Yes, I do, and if you say he has come, then I believe you."

"You do?" Sophia couldn't help herself. She had expected some sort of pushback.

He stopped rocking, then opened his eyes and fixed them upon her. They were milky, and they wavered a little, but she still felt their strength. "I once made a promise to the Lord, many years ago, that if he would let me live to at least hear about the coming of Messiah, I would stay wherever he wanted me to stay, and do whatever he wanted me to do. I feel the truth of your proclamation. The Lord has fulfilled his promise to me, and I am happy now to go the way of all the earth." He turned his attention back to John. "I don't know how many of my congregation will believe your news. I have tried to prepare them well, but they are their own creatures. I wish you well."

Deep furrows carved John's brow as he brought his clasped hands under his chin. "You truly believe, don't you? That Messiah has come."

"Yes, I do."

"Do you know the name by which he is called?"

Nazrim shook his head. "No, but I dreamed once that it was a common name. That his circumstances were humble, unlike what many would expect."

"You are correct. He lived a life full of humility, even as the Only Begotten Son of Father Elohim. His name is Jesus, called the Christ, of Nazareth."

Nazrim breathed deeply, closing his eyes again. "Nazareth. Yes, the promised branch, springing from the root of Jesse. The salvation of all mankind." Tears leaked from the corners of his eyes, and then he arched his neck back, turning his face toward heaven. A smile spread across his face as the tears began to flow, and then, of a sudden, his head fell forward, and his whole body seemed to … collapse.

Sophia let out a small yelp as Onesimus and John got to their knees and grabbed his arms. They got his legs out from under him as well, then laid him reverently on the carpet. The old rabbi lived alone, so there was nobody they could call. John leaned down to check his breathing, then his pulse, at both wrist and neck.

Finally, he turned to Sophia. "He is gone, returned to God and his Savior. I have rarely seen such faith, and I am sure the reunion will be a happy one. I am not sure how we tell his congregation, but we must."

They all stared in solemnity at the body, until Onesimus finally broke the silence. "And so the work here begins."

CHAPTER 4

---

*Beloved, believe not every spirit, but try the spirits whether they are
of God: because many false prophets are gone out into the world.
Hereby know ye the Spirit of God: Every spirit that confesseth
that Jesus Christ is come in the flesh is of God: And every spirit
that confesseth not that Jesus Christ is come in the flesh is not of
God: and this is that spirit of antichrist, whereof ye have heard
that it should come; and even now already is it in the world.*

1 John 4:1-3

After the days of mourning for Nazrim, who had no living family in the area but was beloved by his congregants, two of the synagogue's members asked John to help them craft a letter to the nearest governing Jewish body, located in Byzantium, requesting a replacement. John was happy to do so, but also asked that they allow him to share with them and their friends and neighbors the message that had made Nazrim so happy before he died.

Since the synagogue was so small, it was arranged that they would speak in a more spacious outdoor setting, three weeks after the rabbi's passing, in the middle of the afternoon. The prescribed day turned out beautiful and nearly cloudless, the light breeze softening the warmth of the sun.

Onesimus began, relating his history as a son of Sarmatia, then a slave, then a freed man, and most importantly a follower of the Messiah, Jesus Christ. Sophia followed, telling her own story and raising a few eyebrows—and even a look of scorn or two—as she described her time in Rome and the close encounters of her family with high Roman officials, including two emperors. John then rose to address the group, which had grown to at least a hundred people, a few of them finding shade under white-flowering trees. Sophia had looked forward to this sermon with great anticipation, and she was even ready to take careful notes.

"My dear brothers and sisters, beloved of the Lord, and not just those of Jewish blood, I am honored to stand before you today as a witness of the greatest events this world has ever seen, without which none of us could ever be redeemed in the kingdom of God."

That was a sound opening, and she scribbled furiously to get it all down.

"As many of you know, my name is John, and I am an apostle of the Lord Jesus Christ, one of twelve called to declare his coming. Long have the Jewish people awaited their Messiah, Rabbi Nazrim among them. Over many hundreds of years, however, the expectations became distorted. Many came to believe that Messiah would arrive with great fanfare, perhaps even descending from heaven among concourses of angels, with a sword in his right hand and the balm of Gilead in his left. He would violently overthrow the oppressors of his people—most recently the Romans—and restore Israel to the might and majesty it enjoyed under King David and King Solomon. All the world would reverence and fear this kingdom of God and his Christ.

"But the Savior, this long-awaited Messiah, had a mission much greater than that, encompassing not just the mundane experiences of mortality, but the vast eternities that await each and every one of God's children. The Christ's name was Jesus, and though he was born among the Jews, in fulfillment of prophecy, his power and grace extends to all people, everywhere, without variation."

He gestured toward Onesimus. "This man is Sarmatian by birth, as you have heard, and as much a son of God as I am, born Jewish. He was taken as a slave by evil Roman raiders, but that makes him no less a son of God, nor does it reduce his eternal potential. If he believes in the Son of God, keeps his commandments, and follows his example of faith and service, he will be welcomed into heaven one day, to dwell with God, who is the Father of light and truth."

He turned toward Sophia. "This woman, too, is no less beloved of God, and no less useful in his kingdom. Every boy and girl, every man and woman, can find ways to serve, if they are willing, and thereby enjoy the precious fruits of discipleship.

"Now, it is not easy to follow in Jesus Christ's path. We face physical, mental, and emotional challenges. We are tempted from every side to give in to our natural passions and prioritize the pleasing of our flesh over the nourishment of our spirit. Jesus himself faced the same hardships. He not only overcame them all, leading the only sinless life in the history of the world, but he understands perfectly how we feel in any circumstance, and he shows unbounded compassion.

"He is just, too, of course, because he is God. He seeks every opportunity to help us and strengthen us, and he gives us every chance to repent and do good. But in the end, if we reject him, if we deny the supernal atonement for our sins that he willingly suffered, then we are left to ourselves, and to the master we have chosen, which is the devil, fallen from the presence of God, without hope of redemption, miserable beyond our imagining, hungering to steal our souls and make us his. None of us wishes to be a slave, and slavery is and always has been evil. Why, then, are we so often willing to enslave ourselves to the master of lies, through our passions, our greed, our jealousy, and our anger?

"If you would try to connect personally with your Maker; if you are willing to exercise a particle of faith in him and in his Son; if you can find the determination to turn away from your lustful desires and place the welfare of others before your own; if you can profess the name of Jesus Christ as your Lord and Savior and open your hearts to his love … then you can begin upon the path that leads to eternal life, which is eternal joy, which is a multiplying of the seeds forever."

Sophia was writing as fast as she could, but there was so much, and it was terribly good. She caught herself a couple of times just staring—once at John, and once at the crowd, many of whom clearly felt something.

"Why are you really here?" asked one man near the front, arms folded, eyes narrowed in suspicion. He wasn't as ancient as Nazrim, but he would be soon. "Rome tolerates you Christians, and last time I checked, Rome had a lot more people than Sarmatia."

John gave him a frank answer, followed by a reinforcing question. "I do not know. God sent us here. Are you any less important to God than the Romans, even Vespasian himself?"

"Vespasian," grumbled the man, turning his head to spit, causing the man next to him to jump and lift his foot with a curse. He mumbled a half-hearted apology, then returned his attention to John. "You claim your God cares about us, and the next thing you'll do is ask us for money, which will make its way to Rome." He spit again, on the other side, eliciting a similar reaction from a woman, who hit him in the arm. He massaged the spot as he said to John, "Argh, we're not as gullible as you think!"

John stared at him for long moments, his face unreadable. Then he grinned. "We're not going to ask for money. In fact, if we can organize a group of followers of Jesus here, not only will you manage your own monies, but some additional funds may be provided from Rome based on your legitimate needs."

"We don't need Rome's filthy blood money."

John narrowed his own gaze. "None of us knows from day to day exactly what our needs will be, and if we let our pride rule us, we will become poor indeed. You have clearly seen enough years to know *that*."

Sophia couldn't tell if John had meant that to be insulting or not, but she presumed not. He was calling the man out for his obstinacy, and she doubted she could have come up with a better approach. Unexpectedly, it appeared she might have to. The old man pointed a finger at her, still addressing John.

"This girl here told a fair story, and I'm sure she was well coached on it. But she's here to bat her pretty eyelids and put us under a spell. And to make sure you and your tall showpiece here have all your needs met as well."

Sophia knew instantly what he had implied, and she couldn't help but jump up. Her feet didn't stop there. She approached the man, getting to within a foot of him, feeling the thunderheads on her face. The man clearly recognized them, too, and he tried to back up a step. Unfortunately for him, the crowd pressed in instead of giving him room, and she glared up at him.

"Your insulting inference is both pathetic and childish. I will not stand idly by and allow my honor to be dragged through the mud—especially not by a man who can neither see nor spit straight. Withdraw your comment."

"Or what?" shouted a man farther back, eliciting a few chuckles.

She intensified her glare, ignoring the snide remark. "Withdraw your comment."

The old man blinked a few times, alternating his gaze between her and John. Then he reached a hand up and ran it through his thin white hair, clenching his jaw once in defiance before his resistance collapsed.

"Fine," he said, but not loudly. "But don't expect me or any of my kin to believe a word you say about anything, especially about some mystical Roman god."

Her expression softened, though only a little. "He is not a 'Roman' god. Have you not been listening? Everything around us, in the earth and even in the skies, denotes there is a God. The entire world is his creation, and all the creatures who live upon it. Not just Rome, or Sarmatia, or the Parthian Empire. *All* of it. And you can never drive him out, no matter how hard you try. You can only turn your back on him, to your own detriment."

She folded her arms to emphasize her point, then felt a little foolish as she noticed all the intense stares. The old man folded his arms, too, cocking his head and grinning. For the first time, she noted his discolored teeth. The fetid smell of his breath, too, as the breeze had died down.

"It has been a long time since a child has lectured me. I didn't realize how amusing it would be. Now, you and your friends run along. We're fine without you and the stories of your god."

Sophia almost accepted the remonstrance and turned away. But then she tilted her own head. "You have your choice. God values that, just as he values the choice of each and every person here. And none of you are 'fine.' Neither am I. Each person here has their own battles with the vagaries of life, and with their own weaknesses. Some are in deep despair, though they are loathe to show it. Our Maker, our God, offers to help us through *all* the battles we face. That help is valuable, but he won't make you accept it. He respects you too much. Yes, God *respects* you. He doesn't just dance around in the heavens issuing edicts and laughing while we try to carry them out. His commandments, given through his chosen prophets, like Moses, whom you may have heard of, are designed to guide us in the paths most profitable for us, both physically and spiritually.

"We witnessed a brutish horse sacrifice to your whimsical fire god when we arrived, by the way. There was nothing useful, enlightening, or uplifting about that. God doesn't require blood sacrifices any longer, anyway. He—"

John had come up beside her and rested a hand on her shoulder. It was then she realized the man's grin had become a pasted rictus. Perhaps she had gone too far.

"As Sophia said, God respects your right to choose what to believe, and—within limits—how you express those beliefs. What you may not know about the Jews is that their own disobedience to God's commands, after he had delivered them from slavery in Egypt, caused him to institute additional rules and sacrifices to help them remember and be grateful for his great mercies. Even then, sadly, they so often strayed from the path, and the natural consequences are well known and recorded. At one time, Israel was a great kingdom, the envy of many kings and queens, but they rebelled against their God, and he withdrew his protections. Now the Jewish nation is gone, its people scattered. It is a mighty lesson, and not just for those of us of Jewish descent."

He gave a slight bow as he applied some pressure on her shoulder, drawing her back toward where Onesimus stood. As she turned to regard her companion, she noted his anxious expression, which was clearly linked to her. She went to stand beside him, while John spread his arms and addressed the crowd again.

"My brothers and sisters, children of the same God, I ask you to give consideration to our words, and to pray to God for his wisdom to distill upon you. More importantly, love each other. Serve each other. By so doing, you will abide in the light and will have no cause to fear; otherwise, you will face your battles in darkness. This world will pass away, as will our lives, but if we seek to do the will of God, and his Christ, we will overcome the world and obtain eternal life.

The joy we will then feel is beyond mortal comprehension, but we can glimpse it. I have. You can, too. That I promise, as an apostle of the Lord Jesus Christ, the Redeemer of us all. Amen."

It was a masterful close, and Sophia ceased worrying about how angry she might have made some of the crowd with her bold denunciation. She felt somewhat confused, however. John's audacity in Ephesus with regards to the evils of slavery had inflamed a great deal of anger and gotten him kicked out of the city. A horse sacrifice wasn't the same thing, but she certainly felt justified in denouncing it.

After the crowd dispersed and they made their way back to their rented room, she asked him about it.

He rubbed his chin as he contemplated an answer. "Well, first of all, I am not perfect. But secondly, each circumstance is a little different, including in ways we cannot see. But God sees, and if we are listening, he will guide us, in ways both large and small. As I reflected afterward on my biting words to the nobles of Ephesus, I realized that the Lord wanted me to condemn their cruelty, for his own purposes. I was willing to accept the consequences. Now, did I ever feel I was truly in danger? No, the Spirit assured me I wasn't. But I had to leave, and then … well, I was guided here, and miraculously, I get to be with both of you. The Lord's plans are perfect. So very, very perfect."

Sophia nodded, searching her mind and heart to better understand what she had said to that old man, and why. Had she followed a spiritual prompting? Had she said the right things? She couldn't be sure, and that was frustrating. In fact, she wasn't used to being so uncertain. Yes, she had encountered other situations that had rattled her or made her feel uncomfortable, but maybe she'd never felt the same obligation to get it right … without fully understanding how.

"It's all right, Sophia," said Onesimus. "None of us is perfect, and we did some good today, I'm certain of it."

"Yes, indeed," echoed John, but that only made her feel worse. In essence, they'd just confirmed she'd blundered. She trusted John's ability to interpret the Spirit far better than her own, and he had clearly felt the need to step in and smooth things over. What a disaster.

"Thank you both," she said after a few moments of anguished contemplation, "but I'm sorry. I guess I need to be more patient … and follow your leads more."

John laughed, lightening the mood. "You do well enough, Sister Sophia. Keep striving to know and do the Lord's will. That's all he asks. As Onesimus said, none of us is perfect, and that most certainly includes me."

That made her feel only marginally better. She spent the rest of the day and evening in deep introspection, trying to understand how she could improve. She also worried about what damage she had caused, and that spike in her heart didn't dull a whit during the night.

———

By mid-morning of the next day, she knew why. Two city officials showed up at the door to the house, asking for them. Two city guards accompanied them.

"What is it, good sirs?" asked John when they stepped outside. The day had dawned overcast, but most of the clouds had dispersed. She and John and Onesimus had just finished some studying together, and had been making plans for their preaching that day.

"It appears," said one of the officials, a balding man who looked more Roman than Sarmatian to her, "that you caused a serious disturbance yesterday. Two major complaints have come in against you, and I'm afraid we must arrest you and place you in our prison for now."

Sophia's eyes widened, her heart quailing. *Prison?*

"The first complaint relates to the so-called 'disturbance' we caused?" asked John, utterly calm.

"Yes," said the official.

"And what is the second?"

The official glanced at Sophia in distaste and fear, lifting his hand partway to point at her. "That she is a witch, and practiced her witchcraft in public yesterday, confounding and befuddling many with a spell."

"A spell," deadpanned John as Onesimus gave an amused huff. The apostle glanced at Sophia, then addressed the official again. "She's no more a witch than I am a pomegranate. We have done nothing but speak the truth as we see it and try to serve the people of this city. We have harmed no one, and whatever powers of persuasion we might possess most certainly do not come through witchcraft, or any dark power. And you could never show that they do. Who accused her of being a witch?"

"Two people," responded the official, lifting his nose. "An old man … and his grandson, recently returned from a trip to portions of the Roman empire."

"Fyodor?" asked Sophia, flummoxed. "He thinks I'm a witch because I resisted his attentions?"

"His … attentions?" asked the other official, quirking an eyebrow.

She nodded. "Yes. We met on the ship that brought us here. He took a liking to me, but it wasn't mutual. I let him know that. And now he thinks that if I didn't fall for him, I must be a witch? That's rich." Her tone was challenging, and she didn't care how that sounded.

"Well, I … um, that is …" The second official didn't appear comfortable with any of this.

"It's all right," said John. "We will go with you without incident. It won't be the first time I have been imprisoned for being a Christian and letting people know about it. We have broken no laws, and that will become clear. If you will allow us to gather our things, we can all be on our way."

Sophia's heart stopped for a moment. The guards looked at each other in some confusion, as did the two officials, but they nodded their assent. A few minutes later, after John had settled their account with the woman of the house, they marched in the middle of the group toward the center of Cremni, with its administrative buildings, including the prison.

"Neither of you seem worried," said Sophia as they walked. The drumbeats inside her chest were deafening.

John gave her a reassuring smile. "If I were worried, it would be for you and Onesimus. But I am not. This is just as the Lord planned it."

"It is?" She tried mightily to let that comfort her, but it was still difficult.

He chuckled. "Yes. Is that so hard to believe? Wherever we are, even in prison, we are witnesses. I have a feeling that our access to people won't be as limited as one might normally expect. This is an opportunity and a blessing."

"I just hope they have good food," interjected Onesimus.

Sophia wasn't sure whether to express horror or humor. Her face must have been an odd mixture of both, because her companions laughed, and then John laid an arm lightly around her shoulders. "Do not worry, Sophia, daughter of Chanah and Barabbas. You are my special charge, and the Lord has assured me you will be all right. Do you believe me?"

She blinked, staring up into those mysteriously colored eyes. Were they hazel? Light green? Sometimes they looked blue, sometimes dark gray. She wasn't sure how she felt, but what else could she say but, "Yes?"

"Good, good. You will see. Have faith, daughter."

She would try, but she had never been in prison. She'd heard many stories about horrendous prison experiences, though. And she was a woman. That often brought worse things than just physical deprivation and solitude. She swallowed, and John caught her worry. He didn't say anything more, though, just removed his arm and kept walking, engaging Onesimus in a brief conversation, something about an experience they had shared in Colossae. And chickens. She didn't follow the conversation too closely.

Their arrival at the prison struck the ominous chord she had imagined. It was an ugly, two-story building, gray stone streaked with darker gray, splotched with black. Luckily, it didn't appear that any of the cells were underground. Perhaps the water table had something to do with that, and she was grateful.

Sophia was given her own cell, while John and Onesimus shared one two doors down. With that cell in between, she instantly felt isolated. And worried.

"Pray, Sophia," said John before they closed her cell door. "And keep praying."

There wasn't anything else for her to do besides imagine horrible things, so she followed his advice, praying well into the afternoon as she knelt—and then sat—on the thin sleeping mat. A chamber pot sat on the other side of the cell. As evening came, she felt calmer, and not so alone, though the guards had warned John not to talk loud enough that she could hear him clearly. She jerked to full alertness as a guard appeared at her cell door in the evening. It was somewhat early, as light still penetrated her cell through a small, barred window.

He held a plate of food, with a cup set in the middle. After unlocking the door, he stepped inside and offered her the plate. He didn't seem afraid she might be a witch. She was intrigued by that … and she was bored.

"I might be a witch, you know."

He blinked, appearing startled for a moment. But her tone had been unmistakable, and he smiled. "I doubt it."

"Why? Don't I look the part?"

He blinked again, clearly wondering why she would question him about it.

"Well, I don't know, I guess—"

"Have you ever seen a witch?"

He shrugged. "Maybe we all have but don't know it."

"Ooh, that's a good answer." She tapped her lips with a finger. "I wonder if I've ever seen a witch. I have seen an angel, though."

The guard jerked his head back, still holding out the plate, which she finally reached up and took, setting it on the floor beside her. "An angel?"

"Yes," she said, "a being from the other side of the veil, where we all go after this life. He saved me from a sword-wielding demon. I'm not sure why, but I'm grateful. His name was Raphael."

She was no longer bored, and remembrances of that miraculous encounter gave her renewed confidence.

The guard straightened, then cocked his head slightly. "You saw a … god?"

She shook her head. "No, an angel. Angels serve God, doing good things for people. Except the angels of Satan, of course. He is the Father of Lies, and his angels are evil. None of them have bodies, though. Raphael does. A sword, too."

The man stared at her a moment more, then broke into a grin. "That sounds like an interesting story. Maybe you should write it down. Sell it as a fable for children."

She pursed her lips. "That was rude. I'm actually telling the truth. Do you want to hear the full story? Then you can talk to John the apostle. He wasn't there, but he's seen similar things—even greater, actually. His stories will make your toes curl, and your soul fly."

The guard shook his head, still grinning. "I'll do that. Maybe tomorrow, though. My shift is ending."

"Oh, okay. What is your name, by the way?"

"I'm not supposed to give it."

"Why, and says who? You know I'm not a witch, so I can't torture you with it." She let a small grin creep across her lips. It had only been a few hours, and she could already tell how much she craved this small bit of human interaction.

"Hmmm," he replied, studying her. "It's Shayvin."

"Well, it's nice to meet you, Shayvin. And thank you for the food. Please thank the chef for me."

"You haven't even tasted it."

"I'm sure he … or she … tried."

He laughed at that, shaking his head. "You are an odd one. Good night." He retreated from the cell, but remarkably didn't lock the door. She held her breath as she realized it, waiting until his footsteps had receded before breathing in again. Wait, had he done it on purpose, to trap her? If she left the cell, would she get in more trouble?

After eating her meal, which wasn't half bad, she finally decided it was worth the risk. She rose, tiptoed to the door, then opened it slowly, wary of any creaks. Fortunately, it was well oiled. She padded down the short hallway to John and Onesimus's cell, presenting herself at their barred door in the dim light of a pitiful torch.

"John, Onesimus," she whispered. She didn't even know how many other people occupied cells on the second floor, though the cell between was empty.

"Sophia?" said John, clearly surprised. "How are you out of your cell?"

"The guard left the door unlocked. I don't know if he forgot, or if it's a trick."

"Hmmm … well, I think he will appreciate it if you point it out to him tomorrow. You'll be able to tell by his reaction."

She hadn't thought of that. "Yes, that's a good idea. Um, did they feed you?"

"Not yet, but we're fine."

She scowled. "Well, it's still not right. They already brought me some food. It was decent, too."

"I'm glad," said Onesimus, "but don't worry about us. I'm sure they'll bring us something later, or in the morning. Either way, we're all right."

"Okay, well, I guess I should stay in my cell. I really don't like it, though."

"I know," came the compassionate response from John, "but praying helped, right?"

"Yes."

"Keep it up. Trust in the Lord. These are valuable tests, and, like I said, opportunities."

"I will, thank you." She still had a hard time seeing opportunity in all of this, despite stories from Paul and other disciples, but she retreated toward her cell. Then her consternation about John and Onesimus not being fed yet flared, and on impulse she proceeded past her cell, turned left, and approached the door at the top of the stairs. She knocked, trying not to be too loud. At first she detected no response, so she knocked again, slightly louder. When she heard some murmurs, and then a man's boots hitting the bottom steps, she backed up a pace, folding her hands in front of her.

A different guard opened the door, widening his eyes as he beheld her calmly facing him.

"What are you—"

"Shayvin forgot to lock my door after he brought me my food, but that's not why I'm here. My companions have not had anything to eat yet. Is their meal expected soon?"

She had been as polite as possible, remembering many lessons from her time in Rome … and with her family, of course, particularly her mother. It seemed to work.

The man studied her, seeming unsure what to think. "Um, yes, it will be here soon. You … should go back to your cell."

She couldn't help but bat an eyelash at him. Maybe it was immature, but she needed to maintain whatever advantage she could—within reason and propriety, of course. "I will. Thank you for bringing them food. Mine was good, by the way." She smiled, giving a small curtsy that came out of nowhere, then turned and walked back to her cell, closing the door behind her. The guard didn't follow, strangely, and she was glad. She felt less lonely with the door unlocked.

Her cloak and the small amount of heat vented up to the second floor from the fireplace below warded off the worst of the chill that night, despite the lack of a decent blanket—those they had brought sat uselessly in the guard room downstairs.

She slept better than expected and was awakened by Shayvin opening her door to hand her a tray with some bread and dried fruit on it, plus a cup of water. She sat up, accepting the tray graciously.

"Thank you for leaving my door unlocked."

He stared down at her, face unreadable. A thought struck her, stemming from a dream she'd had that night, and she tilted her head. "Were you ordered to do that? Did the officers believe I would try to escape if I were guilty? I'm not familiar with what constitutes guilt when it comes to witchcraft, but this sort of test is infinitely better than dousing me with oil and lighting me on fire to see if I burn, or dumping me in the ocean to see if I can float with a bag of rocks tied around my ankles. I've heard of such being done in some societies; it's both illogical and highly paranoid."

He still didn't reply, so she took a small bite of bread and added, "Thank you for not lighting me on fire or drowning me. You would have seen I'm not a witch, but ... well, I'd be dead."

His eyebrows came together in a mixture of confusion, consternation, and relief. Did he believe her? She hoped so, and not just for her own sake.

"How are my companions? I heard the guards bring them some food last night."

He finally spoke, face returning to a semblance of normal. "They are well. We would take you all to meet the judge today, but he is traveling to some other towns. He'll be back in the next couple of weeks, though."

She stopped mid-chew of some fruit. "So we have to stay here until *then?*"

He nodded, looking a bit uncomfortable.

"Can we at least have our things, including our blankets? I know the weather is warming, but the blankets would make a big difference. And maybe stools to sit on?" She realized she had just asked a lot—probably too much—and she chided herself for thinking her feminine charm would get them preferential treatment.

And why would she even *want* preferential treatment? Wasn't she supposed to be gladly willing to suffer for Christ's name's sake?

"I'll see what I can do," he said, surprising her with what sounded like earnest willingness.

"Thank you," she replied, matching the earnestness. "You realize I'm not a witch, right?"

"I doubt you are, but your circumstance is still … strange to me."

She nodded in understanding. "Ah, yes, I agree. I hadn't planned this, either. I mean, our prophet, he sent me to be of some assistance to John, who is an apostle of our church, but I didn't know what exactly that might be. I expected to find him in Ephesus, by the way, but he is *very* opposed to slavery of any kind, and that made some upper crust Roman nobles there pretty angry, and so Onesimus and I chased him all the way to Heraclea … and then he said we were coming here to preach!"

She barely realized she had stood. Shayvin's face became thoughtful as she continued. "I mean, I've preached before, in Rome and a few other places close by, but not quite like this. I know you probably don't see a lot of women teachers, but if you think about it, we can teach as well as men. That's just one reason mothers are so important, including yours, I imagine."

He nodded at that, folding his arms. "My mother was a great teacher."

She caught the way he emphasized 'was.' "She has passed?"

He nodded, eyes lowering.

"I'm sorry. I'm fortunate to still have my mother, who now lives in Verona with my father. She might be the most powerful teacher I know, except maybe Paul, another apostle. He lives in Spain."

She noted with a small smile how talkative she was. Lock or no lock on the door, it was good to converse with someone, and her subconscious mind ran with that.

He scrunched his brow. "Paul. I've heard of a man named Paul, who has traveled many places across the Roman empire. Some traders and ship captains have mentioned him."

"And their impressions of him were positive?"

"Not all of them."

She shrugged. "Oh well, that's not surprising. What he teaches—the same thing my companions and I teach—challenges people, not just in their thinking, but in their way of life. The Savior of the world is very patient and forgiving, but he is also demanding—for our own good. As you can imagine, many people react negatively to that, and God gives them agency to act as they wish. He still tries to teach and encourage them, though."

He pondered as she ate more of her food. "I worship a powerful god, but I don't know much about him."

"The god of fire?"

"Yes."

"Well, the one true God is not only all-powerful, but he is your father. That is, the father of your spirit."

"My spirit?"

"Yes. Do you believe you go somewhere after you die?"

"My essence, yes."

"Well, your essence is your spirit, and it looks like you. When you die, your body returns to its mother earth for a time, but then, eventually, spirit and body will reunite in a perfect form that can never die again—the same kind of form God has."

"That is blasphemy."

She shrugged again. "Is it? After Jesus of Nazareth in Judea was crucified by the Romans—at the insistence of the Jewish leaders, by the way—he reclaimed his physical body after three days, as he had promised he would do. There are hundreds of witnesses to this fact. Hundreds. Not me, of course, I'm too young. Nor my parents—they weren't followers of his at the time. But I've personally listened to the testimonies of many of those witnesses, and the Holy Spirit, which comes from God and testifies of him, has also assured me it is true in ways my heart *and* my mind could never deny, unless I chose to rebel for some short-sighted reason or another. You could threaten to burn me in oil, by the way, and I still wouldn't deny."

Her determination in that moment warmed her soul, both spirit and body. It felt good to share testimony so firmly. It felt good to be bold.

He hummed deep in his throat, alternately studying her and the wall behind her. "Well, you are convincing, and you are definitely a good teacher. You would make a fine mother."

Oh, my. That was *not* what she had intended. She put on a kindly frown. "I don't know if I will get married in this life. My sister and three brothers are, and maybe that suffices for our family. I want to see more of the world, meet more people, teach them and learn from them. Like you. I'm sure you could teach me some things."

He unfolded his arms and raised his hands, palms out. "I doubt that. Not I. And I must attend to my other duties now, including feeding your companions. Would … would you like the door to remain unlocked?"

She blinked in delighted surprise. "Yes, of course. And the door to John and Onesimus's cell, too, if you don't mind."

He barely paused. "Sure, why not. None of you are dangerous. That's one thing I *am* good at … detecting dangerous people."

CHAPTER 5

Wherein I suffer trouble, as an evil doer, even unto
bonds; but the word of God is not bound.

2 Timothy 2:9

Following breakfast, John called to her, inviting her to come talk to them. She left her tray and cup on the floor, then exited her cell. She was delighted to find that, indeed, John and Onesimus's door had been left unlocked. How extraordinary. Again, she tried not to feel too proud of herself.

"I overheard your conversation with the guard," John said as she sat down across from them. "What is his name?"

"Shayvin."

"Shayvin, yes. You taught him some crucial doctrines. If he chooses, those will allow him to lay a firm foundation for much more."

She felt her cheeks warming. "Well, um … I've had lots of good examples to follow."

John nodded, glancing at Onesimus. "Indeed, you have. Paul, I know, is one of those." Lines creased his forehead as he studied his hands for a moment, and then he looked back up. "I've been thinking about some of the good Paul has done with his letters to the various churches. Many of them are deeply doctrinal, and important in helping to maintain the purity of Christ's teachings against constant attempts to modify or adapt them to other social or even religious cultural traditions.

"So far, the few I've written have been shorter and more focused on solving specific problems I've become aware of. Not that Paul doesn't do some of the same, but … well, Mark has been compiling some of the recollections and reflections of Peter when he walked with the Savior during his ministry. I've heard that Matthew is thinking of doing the same thing, and Luke has already started producing some remarkable histories."

He paused, and Sophia spoke her thoughts. "You should write an account of the Savior's ministry as well. Plus some of the other experiences you've had as an apostle."

The corners of his lips curled down. "I'm not good at writing. Not only is it far easier for me to speak than to write, but I'm not disciplined enough to do it often. I don't enjoy it. I would much rather just be speaking and working with people, and let others do the scribe work."

Sophia nodded in understanding. Most people were like that, actually. She didn't mind writing herself, but she didn't love it. Her sister Marian, however … she was passionate about writing, whether fiction or non-fiction. She was also really talented at it.

"Well," she said, "I guess we have a little time right now, and I think the guards will let us have our things back. We have some writing implements."

Onesimus's eyebrows shot up. "Why do you think we'll get our things?"

"You heard. I asked Shayvin. He said he would see what he could do. And I think it will happen. The guards know we aren't dangerous, and that we're innocent."

"We don't know if all of them do," cautioned John.

"True, but there are two now I'm pretty sure of."

John and Onesimus shared another glance, and then John gave her a considering look. "Well, then, I think my idea can be implemented right away."

"What is your idea?" she asked.

"You already know, it appears. I would like *you* to help me record my testimony of the Savior, based on my experiences with him. Not only can you help me stay disciplined, but I know you are a better writer than I am; I've seen some of your work."

"You have?" she asked in some surprise. Very little of what she had written had gone anywhere, though she knew her mother had sent a few things to other churches over her objections. That included … well, Ephesus, where Elhanan was bishop.

He chuckled. "I have. I even suggested to Philip that you might be useful to me, though I didn't explain to him exactly how. He prayed about it and agreed. Now you're here, and, as you said, we have some down time."

"I … um … this is why I'm here?"

"Primarily, yes. But I know the Lord had other reasons, too. He didn't need to divulge them all to me. They will come forth in time. In fact, that is already happening."

She gave him a concentrated stare, searching deeply her own thoughts and feelings. Predictably, they were muddled. Was John really asking her to help him like Mark assisted Peter? Based on the way he continued to gaze at her, the answer was clearly yes.

"Well, okay, I guess, but are you sure?"

"Yes, I am. And we don't need to wait for something to write with. I'd like to review some stories and impressions with you first. We can begin writing them later."

"All right," she said, scooching back a few inches so she could lean her back against the wall.

He stared at the ceiling for a few moments, then set his hands on his knees. "I'd like to start the account of my witness with who Jesus was, from the very beginning, and why he came. He was with God, as were we. He created this earth, and everything in it, according to God's own plans and perfect wisdom. He agreed to take on the role of the Redeemer of all mankind, becoming, even from the days of Adam and Eve, the light and the life of the world, a light that those who opposed him, led by Lucifer, could neither comprehend nor defeat, try as they might to extinguish it."

Sophia had to keep her jaw from going slack. She had felt the power of the Spirit in those words. "That was … beautiful, Apostle John. Why don't you just write that down?"

He shook his head. "I told you. That is not my talent. When I go to write something I've said, I can't get the words down quickly enough, so they escape me, and I have a difficult time recapturing the essence in a way that is … satisfactory."

"I see." She did, actually. His mind must be moving very fast, all the time. He was older, too. Could that be part of it? No, she decided. There were no signs she could discern of declining mental acuity, or even physical activity. He was in remarkable shape for a man closing in on seventy years of mortal existence.

They heard a soft knock on the door, which stood open. Shayvin and another guard occupied the hallway, bearing three stools and their packs. Sophia gave a very un-Sophia-like squeal of delight as she jumped to her feet and grabbed one of the stools, thanking the two guards profusely.

John invited the guards to stay, but only Shayvin did, or could. He remained standing in the doorway, leaning against the frame. After Sophia, John, and Onesimus were settled, and she had a wax writing tablet and stylus ready, she asked John to go back to the beginning, so she could capture it all.

He did, offering additional details of Jehovah as faithful First Son of the Morning, chosen to implement the Father's plan. He talked about Mary, the woman who accepted the call to be his mother with extraordinary faith, and his kinsman John, who became the Baptist, born at nearly the same time and destined to be the crucial, long-prophesied forerunner of the perfect man who would become Messiah.

He continued by describing how Jesus's mission was to give men and women the power to become exalted sons and daughters of God, provided they chose to believe in him and follow in his ways. For the Jews, he would fulfill the Law of Moses while expiring the lesser set of statutes and performances meant to point them toward God's higher law, restored and renewed by himself, the Great Jehovah, come to earth and born the Christ.

Many Pharisees had, apparently, believed John the Baptist to be a prophet, and even an Elias. They asked him if he was Messiah, but he proclaimed that a greater was coming after him. When Jesus was ready to be baptized, as an example for all to follow, he came to John, who objected at first. John the Apostle had been a disciple of John the Baptist first, along with Andrew, Simon Peter's brother. John had witnessed Jesus's baptism at the hand of the Baptist. He described in vibrant detail how the Spirit had descended upon Jesus then, as if it had happened just that morning.

A beautiful sweetness filled the cell, making it difficult to remember they were sitting in a prison, far from home, outside even Roman lands. Shayvin stayed silent, but Sophia could tell the apostle's words were impacting him. They were affecting her as well; she felt like an empty pitcher being filled with fresh water. She furiously recorded as much as she could, enough so that she could go back later and fill in any blanks in the grammar.

Later that day, Shayvin and another guard returned. Even the guard who had answered the door to the stairs, whose name was Nicolai, made an appearance for about half an hour. He didn't seem as impressed by John's stories, but at least he didn't act offended or upset.

That night, after dinner, she, John, and Onesimus moved their stools to her cell, which was both warmer and a little larger, though they still wrapped their blankets around them. John had asked her to put away her writing materials a couple of hours ago.

"Can you tell me again what happened at Cana?" she asked him.

"Yes, Jesus's first public miracle."

"Public? You didn't mention that earlier."

"Yes. He had performed miracles prior to that, and even at age twelve astounded some of the doctors and scribes with his knowledge. He grew step by step in his wisdom, as we all do, but of course at a much faster pace. He had greater access to the Spirit, too, because of his perfect obedience to the Father's will, which enhanced his understanding and abilities further. Much further. His mother Mary had seen him perform miracles before that marriage feast in Cana, many times, though always in private. So, when the host lacked for wine, she immediately turned to her son, knowing what he could do. And he took care of it.

"But which do you think was more astonishing—this miracle or his second public one, in which he healed the son of a nobleman from Capernaum who was at the point of death?" His eyes twinkled a little as he watched her mull that over.

Finally, she responded, "Neither, though the son's life was more important. God knows all the physical laws perfectly, so it wasn't any more difficult to do one miracle or the other."

John's eyebrows rose slightly. "That is a remarkable answer. And very true."

Onesimus chimed in with another question. "Why did he cleanse the temple so soon after beginning his ministry?"

John nodded thoughtfully. "Well, there are two parts to that question. The first is why so soon? The answer is that he was not shy in proclaiming who he was, from the very beginning. Yes, there were times when he asked people, like the leper he healed early on, not to tell anyone what had happened—which in that case didn't work—but remember what he said when he visited his home town of Nazareth? He quoted Isaiah, then declared that the prophet's Messianic prophesy had been fulfilled in their presence that day. They wanted to cast him off a cliff for blasphemy. Many other times he clearly identified himself; it was just too difficult for most people to believe."

He took a deep breath, eyes wandering in remembrance. "The second part is why cleanse the temple at all, especially when those who presided over it—and who would later have him killed—defiled it daily with their greed, arrogance, and lustful abominations? The answer is that the Law of Moses had not yet been fulfilled, which law Jesus himself obeyed, and the temple was not wholly defiled. It was still his Father's house, and a valuable resource for his children. He needed to remind the people of that, for their sakes.

"Now that temple is gone, as he had promised, never to be rebuilt until the time of his Second Coming. We have other temples now—holy, consecrated places where the Lord and the Father can dwell. Their Spirit can abide in righteous homes, too, and in our hearts. We are never without the Comforter—again, as he assured us—though we can turn away in our grief or our pride. I have some thoughts on the Comforter that I would like you to record, but they can come later."

Suddenly, Sophia felt exhausted. They hadn't done anything physically strenuous, though John had suggested they walk the upstairs halls of the prison at several points throughout the day, just to stretch and loosen their muscles. But the Spirit had been so strong, her soul filled so fully, that her mortal mechanisms craved rest. John must have noticed her body begin to slump, for he slapped Onesimus on the back and then rose.

"Come, Brother Onesimus, let's all get some sleep. This was a good day, and tomorrow will be, too."

They departed her cell, and it didn't take long for her to find her mat and fall fast asleep.

———

John slowed the pace a bit over the next couple of weeks as she scribed and they waited for the magistrate to return. Two additional guards began listening in from time to time, which made four including Shayvin, as Nicolai never returned. Shayvin acquired some additional parchment for them, using money John gave him from his pack, so that Sophia could transcribe from the wax tablets onto something more permanent … and reuse the tablets. She had visions of great scrolls filled with John's words of testimony regarding the Savior of the world, with the Word of God traveling the length and breadth of the world, being read and shared everywhere, filling souls with light and hope.

At dawn of the beginning of the third week of their soft imprisonment, which now included a daily walk around the center of town with two of the guards, Fyodor showed up at her cell door, sending a shiver down her spine. He scowled as he pushed open the unlocked door, but then his face showed some hesitation as well. It looked odd on him. He was a spy. Was he also an assassin?

She stood and backed up to the wall with the window. She didn't call out, knowing it wouldn't do any good. On the contrary, it would only endanger her friends. The guards had obviously let him in. Had Shayvin stepped away for a moment? Would he return? It was a slim hope.

He took a step into the cell, but only one. "You look healthy and clean for a prisoner." She couldn't decide if his voice was cold or neutral.

"For which I am grateful," she replied, maintaining her posture and trying not to lean against the wall.

He grunted. "You have not tried to escape. Why?"

Her shoulders twitched. "Because I am not guilty of breaking any of your laws, and I trust that justice will be done, even for a Roman."

"You are still a witch." Coldness had definitely entered his tone, but also … anxiety.

"I am a child of God, like you. I seek to honor him, and if his protection seems like witchcraft to you, you've confused the source."

His eyes narrowed, jaw hardening. "I was not able to kill you, to make sure justice truly was done. Three nights past, I had arranged with one of the guards to let me inside. But I couldn't get within a block of this building. My legs froze, even my arms. At one point, I couldn't even look this direction."

She blinked several times, then swallowed hard. He had intended to *assassinate* her? After a few moments, her heart stopped racing, and then she knew.

"Raphael."

"What?"

"Not 'what,' 'who.'"

"What are you talking about, witch?"

Either bravery or annoyance surged—she couldn't tell which. "For the last time, I'm not a witch. But you experienced the power of an angel of God. That same angel saved me once in Rome, and he said I might need him again. Clearly, he was right." Her brow stiffened. "Wait, how are you here now?"

"I don't intend to kill you … and I had to leave all my weapons below."

"The guards made you hand them over?"

He shook his head, his expression a mixture of anger and fear. "No. I … just couldn't bring them up."

She nodded. "So, God showed you he didn't trust your intentions. Though you still have your hands."

He placed his hands behind his back and studied her for nearly a minute, his shallow breathing the only sound she could hear. "My grandfather and I will withdraw our claims against you, but you and your friends must leave the city."

"Or what?" she challenged him.

His lips pressed tightly before he answered. "Just leave. It will be better."

She was sharply tempted to dress him down for being such a cruel liar … and a particularly rude pig. Then some of John's words began resonating in her mind, along with images of how Jesus must have appeared as he healed and taught.

"I will need to ask John first."

"But you are the—"

"I am not a witch!" Oh, it felt good to let that out at such volume, but she cringed as she realized everyone within a mile must have heard it, including John and Onesimus. Sure enough, in seconds the two men stood behind Fyodor, just outside her cell, wearing anxious expressions.

Fyodor didn't respond to their presence, just dropped his hands to his sides and glared at her. The fear was gone. "You would have made a fine warrior, perhaps one of the finest of our females. The charges are dropped. Leave the city. The guards can escort you."

She caught John's eyes, and he nodded.

"Very well," she said. "But don't follow us. Remember Raphael."

The farmlands and forests beyond Cremni offered everything Italy could and more; they were just flatter. John said he wished to stay among the more populated lowlands close to the coast, moving northwest and then slowly arcing until they traveled southwest and ended up in Odessa, which was technically in Roman lands, though warmly disputed from time to time. Their first major destination was Stalitza, which the Romans called Metropolis for some probably pompous reason. Shayvin alone escorted them out of town, and he assured them that along the main road toward Stalitza they would encounter many villages, some of them quite large. John seemed especially happy about that, and before they parted, he pulled a parchment from his pack and handed it to the erstwhile guard.

"For you, friend. You treated us with dignity and respect. God is well aware, and he will bless you. I hope these few words from a humble servant can help guide you through the storms of life. Other Christians will come to Cremni in the years to come, some from surprising directions, and a few will even stay. Keep your eyes, your mind, and your heart open."

He patted him on the shoulder, and Shayvin seemed at a loss for words. He took the parchment, rolled up and tied with a string, staring at it for a time. When he looked up, his face conveyed sincere emotion. He glanced at Onesimus and Sophia, then gave John a nod.

"I will. May your god prosper you on your journey." After another glance at Sophia, he began marching back to the city, quite rapidly, as if he didn't want to be reminded they were there.

John turned, staring up the road with its moderate traffic. He took a deep breath, then set out with long strides, especially for one so old. Onesimus and Sophia hurried to catch up, then matched his pace.

"A fine day," John remarked.

Sophia looked up. The sky was mostly clouds, some of which threatened rain. The wind had picked up a bit, too, though it was warm.

"How far do you want to go today?" she asked.

He glanced at the sky, appearing to see through the clouds. A contented smile creased his face. "I have no idea. But the Lord does. I can't even say if we'll stay on this main road or not. God has been preparing some of his children to hear us, and we'll find them, wherever they are."

She was already used to cryptic apostolic declarations, and she certainly wasn't worried. She felt a little guilty, though. She had just 'endured' her first time in a prison. She hoped never to see another prison from the inside, but she had been relatively spoiled. It could hardly have been called a travail. So many other saints had truly suffered in the Lord's name. Wait, was she … jealous? That seemed silly on one level, but logical on another. Complaining either way wasn't acceptable, though, so she lifted her chin, took her own deep breath, and fell into the rhythm of their journey.

It wasn't long before they came to a minor crossing road. John stopped, looking to the right. A mile or two that way lay a small village, maybe two dozen homes. He glanced skyward again, then headed toward it. Sophia looked at Onesimus and shrugged. They could still see Cremni in the far distance, since it was at a slightly lower elevation and no hills obscured their sight. She couldn't tell where the sun was, but it had to be about noon.

John's pace quickened further, and they soon reached the village. Smoke from a few indoor and outdoor cooking fires wafted up to be scattered by the wind, and some of the smells made Sophia hungry. There must have been a creek nearby—the land was bursting with them—because a few women and older children carried baskets of laundry both ways along a path out of the village. She was glad there wasn't a tanner nearby, but she caught the sounds of a butcher at work, out of her sight. A few smaller children, most without shoes, played a game with long sticks and an uneven ball in the single street, or sat in doorways playing pretend with various toys. One seemed to be an elephant, though what they would know of elephants this far north she couldn't imagine.

A lone boy, maybe nine, sat on a stool by the stone coping of a well, watching all the play with a somewhat forlorn smile. John made a beeline for him.

"Young man," he burst out in greeting, "I understand you can offer me and my companions a drink of water."

The boy hadn't even noticed them until John spoke, and he nearly fell off his stool. As he tried to right himself, Sophia could tell one of his legs was withered and misshapen. A birth defect. Her heart went out to him. Did he come out to watch the other children play every day? Did he have any friends?

"Oh … um … yes, yes," he stuttered as he got up on his one good leg and lowered a small bucket down into the well. It didn't have to travel far. They probably got most of their water from the nearby creek anyway, Sophia reasoned.

After pulling up the filled bucket, he magically produced a ladle and offered it to John, who smiled graciously as he took it, filled it, and drank.

"Ah, thank you." He handed the ladle back, and the boy re-filled it so that Sophia, and then Onesimus, could quench their thirst. He seemed eager for the attention.

"Where is your house?" John asked. "Is anyone there?"

The boy blinked, then turned his head and pointed. "Just down there. My mother is home, and my baby sister. My father is out in the fields, directing some horses."

"Ah yes, you have many fine horses in these parts, I hear. And good for many things besides farming. What is your name?"

"Tedric," he replied, beaming up at the apostle. He could probably sense he was in the presence of someone special.

"Can we go see your mother?"

Tedric shrugged. "I guess so." He retrieved a crutch leaning against the well, then led the way down the dusty street, likely soon to be mud, until they entered a modest, wood-framed home with just a single room separated by curtains for the sleeping areas. A woman sat near the front window on a stool in the best light, mending a pair of heavy men's breeches.

"Mama," said Tedric, startling her. She surveyed the strangers with a wary eye, then stood, still holding the breeches.

"What can I do for you?" she asked. "I have a lot of mending yet to do today, but I could probably fit you in tomorrow."

John took a small step farther inside, allowing Sophia and Onesimus through the door; and none too soon, as large droplets began splatting into the dust of the street, slowly at first, but with increasing frequency.

John motioned toward Tedric. "Your fine boy here helped us at the well, and we wanted to meet his mother."

She gave him a confused look. "He helped …?" She glanced at Tedric.

"They asked for some water, and I got them some," he supplied, then looked shyly down.

"Oh." She returned her gaze to John. "So … you don't have any mending for me?"

John cocked his head, looking thoughtful, then raised his voice as the sound of the rain increased. "Mending … well, we could all use some mending, every day. This life is not easy, and it isn't just physical disabilities that ail us, but spiritual ones as well." He glanced at Tedric's lame leg. "Your son was born this way?"

The woman nodded, resuming her stool. "Yes," she answered softly.

"And you kept him." Sophia noticed a glistening in John's eyes as he continued. "Many would have … well …" He glanced at Tedric, voice trailing off.

"He is my son," she said, her tone tinged with pride and defiance.

John nodded. "Indeed, and he is God's son, too, just as precious as any of his other children. Tedric clearly has a good heart as well. I'm sure that comes, in part, from you."

She didn't respond to that, just stared at her son.

"I am an apostle of Jesus Christ, the Son of the living God. I have certain authority from him to bless the lives of his children. Do you believe God can heal your son?"

Her eyes snapped back to John, hope warring with disbelief. "*Heal* him? Some witches and sorcerers claim to have such power, but I have never sought any of them out."

John clasped his hands in front of him, studying her intently. "You are wise. Unholy powers walk the land, trying to mimic holy influences. They can be deceptive. Would you like your son to be healed?"

She returned his gaze with a flat one of her own, wariness returning. "What would you require in return?"

"Me? Nothing. But the Lord Jesus Christ will make a request of you—that you express thanks to the Father for the healing, and that you open your heart to the spirit of truth."

She considered that, eyes turning to her son. She swallowed, and her chest heaved. She looked up at John again. "I believe you can. I don't know how."

"God is helping you, though you already had some faith that perhaps you weren't even aware of." He reached a hand toward Tedric, still focused on his mother. "Tedric, take my hand, please."

After shifting his wide-eyed gaze briefly to his mother, the boy did so, and then John closed his eyes, bowing his head. "Father, this is why you brought us here. Thank you. Please heal this beautiful boy, in the name of your Only Begotten Son."

Sophia had instinctively shut her eyes as well, but they sprung open of their own accord as a sharp wind seemed to blow right through her. She focused on Tedric's legs, and suddenly she couldn't remember which one had been lame. They looked the same. She blinked, refocusing, as Tedric's mother cried out in joyous surprise. The woman bounded off her stool to sweep her boy up in her arms, swinging him around with such force that his feet nearly clipped John's legs.

Tedric was soon laughing and shouting, then asking his mother to set him down. She finally relented, her breath coming in heaving gasps amid sobs and tears. He tested his legs, jumping up and down on both, then on each in turn. He looked up at John, wide eyes brimming with wonder. "How did you do that?"

Tears streaked John's cheeks. Sophia knew her own face was a mess. "I didn't. God did. He just let me participate, for which I am grateful. And that is *my* payment. Now, if you will let us sit for an hour or two and share some important truths with you and your mother, we will be on our way. We have more ground to cover before the end of the day, after the rain lets up."

"But where are you going?" asked his mother.

John chuckled. "God only knows. And it is wonderful."

By mid-afternoon they departed, leaving an ecstatic Tedric racing around the rain-soaked streets of the village with the other children, laughing so happily Sophia thought her heart would melt completely and spill out through her toes.

When they reached the main road, John commented, "Not every visit will be like that, of course, though it would be nice. That woman had great faith, even though she didn't recognize it. Remarkable. I could never have figured that out on my own."

They walked on, discussing the experience for several miles, until it was starting to get dark. The twinkling lights of another village greeted them from not too far ahead.

"Onesimus, you've been quiet for a while," noted the apostle.

Onesimus gave a soft grunt, then added, "I feel uneasy about something."

"Oh? Do you know what it might be?"

Onesimus stopped, looking all around them, then shook his head. "No, but I—" In an instant he had placed himself on Sophia's left, feet apart, hands ready, facing a line of trees along the edge of the road, the spaces between them quickly darkening.

Sophia backed away a step, toward John, senses heightened. "What is it?"

"Listen," said Onesimus.

There was no traffic nearby, and most of the animal and insect sounds had somehow abated, so an eerie silence descended, lasting several seconds. Suddenly, a crashing sounded from the trees, and a form burst toward them, stopping just short.

"I know you!" said a grotesquely shaped man, his face and arms covered in scars, some of the wounds fresh. He pointed at Sophia.

She struggled to focus on him, much less try to recognize him, until it dawned on her. The man who had tried to kill her in Rome! He didn't carry a sword this time, but his fingernails looked like claws.

John stepped around her, eyes alight with a holy fire. He stood next to Onesimus, then stretched out a hand.

"In the name of Jesus Christ, you will depart this man and leave him in peace, never to return." He said it with such authority that Sophia's breath caught. Then she watched as the man's body contorted in unnatural ways. He screamed in fully fettered agony.

"Why must you take this from me? I found him and claimed him!"

"He is not yours. You have no rightful claims on him, nor does your master. The true master of this world has so decreed. Go. *Now.*"

Another shriek froze Sophia's blood, and then the demon departed the man's broken body. Sophia thought she could almost see it. The man collapsed onto the grass, and Onesimus rushed to him, hands recently prepared for defense now searching for ways to assist. John stepped toward the body, then kneeled by it, laying a hand gently on the man's chest. Sophia couldn't detect it moving, even as she moved closer.

"He is gone," John pronounced.

Onesimus sat back on his heels, hands on his thighs. "Just like that?"

John nodded. "Just like that. He chose to be free of his earthly confines, and now he moves on to the world of spirits, where he will have an opportunity to embrace his Savior if he so chooses. The work proceeds apace on the other side of the veil, as Christ organized it and directs it."

Onesimus nodded, seeming satisfied with that answer. Sophia understood it, too. It was part of the reason her father and mother had been called to oversee the construction of such a magnificent temple in Rome. It linked them to their ancestors in a glorious eternal chain.

"How did he get this far? This is the man who tried to kill me in Rome."

John's neck twisted as he looked up at her. "Are you sure? The very same?"

"Yes, I'm sure. Did he somehow follow me?"

John stood, then shrugged. "Who is to say? He may have, driven by the demon who possessed him."

She shivered as Onesimus also got to his feet, looking up and down the road. "I've never seen the casting out of a demon. He was very … angry."

"Frustrated, for sure," said John. "He rebelled before anyone came to earth, and lost his chance at gaining a physical body. All the demons are even more frustrated now that Christ has fulfilled his mission. They imagined they could stop him. It wouldn't have helped them, anyway. They just hate those who have surpassed them. Now, every son or daughter of God who comes to earth will receive a perfected body in the resurrection, owners of it forever, while the demons will continue without. So very sad. But they made their choice, using their agency, allowing themselves to be deceived by Lucifer, former Son of the Morning and now the Father of Lies, who will also forever remain in his self-imposed misery."

For an instant, the eternal plans of their Heavenly Father were laid bare before Sophia. For the briefest of moments, she could comprehend them. But then the glimpse dissipated, leaving her with just the warm vestiges of knowledge and endless joy which accompanied her peek at the great Plan of Happiness.

John stared at the body of the man, and Sophia gasped as it began to fade into the ground. She had never seen or heard anything of the like. In seconds, the body—tattered clothes and all—was gone, leaving no trace.

"How did you do that?" she asked.

John stared at the spot a few seconds longer, seeming suddenly tired. "The Lord allowed me to. We didn't need the complication of being discovered here in the vicinity of a dead body, now did we."

Just as he finished, Sophia heard the sounds of a wagon approaching, heading in their direction of travel. John turned and hailed the driver, who stopped. After a few words of discussion, they procured a ride. It was a hay wagon, and John took advantage of the opportunity to lie back and close his eyes. Onesimus followed soon after, but Sophia couldn't keep her mind off that poor, bedeviled man.

CHAPTER 6

*There is no fear in love; but perfect love casteth out fear:
because fear hath torment. He that feareth is not made
perfect in love. We love him, because he first loved us.*

1 John 4:18-19

That next village was a little farther away than it had appeared, but by wagon the trip passed quickly enough. Plus, their feet got a rest. John thanked the driver, whose destination was a farm a good distance off the main road, then led the way toward a tiny inn. Sophia had often wondered what it would be like to own and manage such a place. On the one hand, she would meet so many fascinating people passing through on various business; their house in Rome had sometimes been like that. On the other hand, crowds could become unruly. However, if she could get Raphael to be her bouncer …

She dispelled that silly, frivolous thought as they stepped inside. Two tables, each with four chairs, barely fit into the small front room. Two weary travelers sat at one of the tables, holding a low conversation. They glanced up, frowned, and resumed talking.

A woman with a wide, dirty apron appeared from the kitchen in the back, wiping her hands on her skirt, not the apron. "You all need a meal, I gather?"

"Indeed, good woman," said John. "Whatever you have. And a room, if one is available."

She eyed Sophia for a moment, and Sophia didn't appreciate the expression. "Just one room?"

"We can afford but one. What do you suggest?"

"She sleeps with me."

John turned to Sophia. "What do you think, Sophia?"

She wasn't too keen on spending the night with a stranger, but she nodded. "That's fine with me."

"Sophia. A fine Greek name. You are Romans. Your Greek is too good for it to be otherwise."

"You are perceptive," said John. "But Onesimus here is Sarmatian, taken as a slave when he was but a babe."

"By the Romans," spat the woman.

John turned to Onesimus, a clear encouragement for him to answer her. "I am a free man now, and I travel with a man who opposes slavery everywhere he goes. It gets him in trouble sometimes."

She narrowed her eyes at John. "Well, slavery is not good, unless the slave is Roman. Then it's justified, because of what they have done over the centuries."

John frowned, shaking his head. "Slavery is never good. Criminals need to be tried fairly under the law and punished, which might include labor to keep them busy or teach them a skill while they serve their time, but enslaving someone based on where they're from, or what they look like, is pure, unadulterated evil." His stare became a stony challenge. This truly was a sore point for him.

She finally threw up her hands and huffed. "Sit down at the other table. I'll bring you some food. When you're done, I'll show you two to your room, and the girl can come with me."

"Woman," said Sophia, correcting her.

The woman's eyebrows rose. "Really? How old are you?"

"Twenty-three. I know I look young, and I'm not married, but I'm also not a girl."

"Right. Very well, then. I'll be back in a few minutes with your meal."

———

Sleeping in the woman's room wasn't horrible, even though she snored a little. Sophia wanted to ask her what it was like to run the inn, but the woman didn't seem to want to talk, falling asleep almost instantly. The night passed slowly but peacefully, and by the morning Sophia felt ready to continue the journey … after a good breakfast, of course. She offered to help the woman prepare it, and finally found out her name: Irena. She also got in a few questions about her work. It turned out her husband had loved taking care of the inn, but he had died after getting very sick. She herself didn't love the work, but it was a living, and she had no children.

Before they left, she felt impressed to make a promise to the woman. "We'll be back through here, I'm positive. I'd like to talk to you about your husband, and about the good you do here. I admire you."

The woman gave her a funny look, halfway between stunned and annoyed. "You can if you wish. Don't expect to learn much from me."

"I think we can learn from each other," Sophia insisted. "We're traveling to Odessa, but I'll convince John to come back this way."

A cocked eyebrow accompanied a snort. "That's a tall promise, lass. Now let's get this breakfast served, and you all can be on your way."

Sophia refused to be disheartened by the dismissive tone, and she said a silent prayer that the Lord would prepare Irena for their return visit. She already looked forward to it.

The trip to Stalitza took almost two weeks. They stopped often to engage people in conversations about Christ and his gospel, and the randomness became a fascinating guessing game. The city was about the same size as Cremni, but given it wasn't a port city, the look and feel was shockingly different. Everything seemed calmer, and while the people acted a little more suspicious—like Fyodor and his grandfather—they were also more grounded and ultimately easier to engage in substantive conversation.

They found a small, somewhat dilapidated house to rent near the center of the city, but only for two weeks—John said they would need to move on to Odessa after that. They also discovered a tiny Jewish synagogue, presided over by a half-Jewish man who they heard had made some modifications to the standard ordinances and performances. He seemed wary as he welcomed them into his home, motioning his wife out of the room.

His eyes darted between Sophia and John. "So, you are Jews. We see very few Jews pass through here. We are not treated well in Stalitza, owing to some things my predecessor did to anger some city elders."

John didn't ask what those things were, and curiosity gnawed at Sophia.

"How large is your congregation?" asked John instead.

"Just ten of us. My wife and I run a bakery, and I make sure we remain in good stead with our neighbors."

"The people who told us where you live described some of what you do in your services. It sounded … unorthodox."

John's small smile seemed to unnerve the much younger man, who said, "We are devoted to the Lord, but we are poor. We do our best, and we are happy. You … will not report us to the elders, will you?"

John's laugh was probably meant to be reassuring, but the man's face fell. "Of course not. Our relations with Jewish leaders are, I dare say, far worse than yours could ever be. Besides, they are still reeling from the loss of Jerusalem, and indeed, a cohesive Jewish state. I doubt they will pay you much mind, for good or ill."

The rabbi scrunched up his face, eyes darting again, among all three of them. "What have you done?" he finally asked, leaning back slightly from his position on the floor on the other side of a low table.

"Hmmm … it is as much who we are as what we have done. We follow the greatest prophet to have ever lived, Jesus Christ, the Messiah himself, raised from the dead as foretold. And I was one of the first to see him after he was resurrected."

"We are all Christians," added Onesimus. "I am from Sarmatia, but was taken as a slave by the Romans. I am free now, and I go wherever the Christ directs me."

The rabbi let his eyes rest on Onesimus. "Sarmatian, truly?"

After Onesimus nodded, John said, "He is descended from the lost ten tribes, many of whom settled in this area. The Lord seeks to gather them back to him."

The rabbi spat to the side in surprising boldness. "They are traitors. They brought their fate upon themselves."

"As did those of the tribes of Judah and Benjamin," noted John. "And they compounded their unfaithfulness by crucifying their long-awaited Messiah, even Jehovah, who condescended to live among them, teaching and healing, doing many mighty works and wonders. I was witness to many of those as well. They rejected him, and now our blood is scattered. It will be a very long time before we will gather in great numbers again."

The rabbi blinked at John several times, clearly shaken by his intensity, then leaned forward again. "There are no Christians here in Stalitza; none that I know of, anyway, though several have passed through. You will find some in and around Odessa."

John leaned forward, too. "We aren't here to find existing Christians, though we will seek to strengthen all we come across—and learn from them, too. No, we are here to help any willing to accept their Savior's invitation to come unto him and find peace and eternal salvation through the higher law, not the lesser law instituted by Moses."

"That is blasphemy."

"How is it blasphemy? Moses was given the higher law in the sacred mount, then returned to find the Israelites whoring after the gods of the Egyptians. God then retracted his great gift, giving them a lesser law of outward performances to point them toward a time when they might achieve the higher law … and to remind them of the coming of Messiah. They provoked him again when the first spies were sent into Canaan to scout the land and its peoples. Only Joshua and Caleb were faithful … and only they survived of that generation of men to enter the promised land. This is not a mystery. This is part of our history of betrayal. We are a covenant people, but blessed of God only if we keep that covenant and serve the inhabitants of the earth as we have been commanded to do. Our non-Jewish brothers and sisters have the same opportunity to receive the blessings of the covenant, for all are God's children, equal before him."

The man shook his head fiercely. "I cannot listen to this. You would cause me to stray off my path. So I must—"

Sophia spoke for the first time. "The Lord calls you to *his* path."

He raised his hand in a warding fashion, then got to his feet. "Please, you must go. I will say nothing of this, if you will say nothing to the Jewish elders."

John nodded, then slowly rose, Onesimus and Sophia following suit. "I have nothing to say to the Jewish elders that they have not already heard. You need not worry about them. But worry about your soul, and those of your family and your small flock here. Thank you for meeting with us."

And that was it. No great miracle had occurred. Sophia had felt hopeful one would. Other missionaries had passed through. The rabbi struggled with a tiny congregation. She didn't see or hear any children around, and he and his wife were both fairly young; they may have faced some harsh challenges in that regard. They weren't well liked in the city, but becoming Christians wouldn't necessarily fix that. It could help them deal with it better, though.

With a glum feeling, she exited the house with John and Onesimus. It was late in the afternoon. John gave them both a cheerful smile. "That was good. Thank you, both of you. We are planting seeds. Come, let us continue. I cannot say how many of those seeds we will get to harvest, but the harvest will come." He bounded like a deer down the street, searching for the next person they could talk to. Sophia shared a look with Onesimus, and neither could help but smile, then shrug, then chase after their fearless, indefatigable leader.

———

John was right about planting without harvesting, at least in Stalitza. People remained friendly as long as they didn't feel threatened, but most were happy with their fire gods and shamans and occasional aging horse sacrifices. They loved their horses, and they knew their husbandry and training extremely well.

They left Stalitza on schedule, following the arc that would take them to Odessa, stopping frequently. Summer came, and the climate was so pleasant, the air so clean, that Sophia wondered why more people didn't flock to this place. The amount of well-watered arable land was tremendous—they could feed the world if they needed to, just from this place!

Just a few miles from Odessa, near the end of a long day of mostly walking, they entered a larger village. John stopped the first person he saw, a woman carrying a large, covered basket, probably filled with food. Sophia thought he was about to ask if she could spare a few morsels for them.

"Pardon me, ma'am, but do you know the young couple who recently lost their children?"

Sophia stared at him a moment, then noticed the woman's reaction. She nearly dropped the basket, emotion washing across her face.

"It was horrible. So sad. Yes, I know them."

"Where do they live?" asked John gently.

She gave them directions, then hurried on her way, apparently trying to outrun a new wave of grief.

John led the way, then knocked on the door to a sizeable house set in a haphazard cluster of similar homes. The wood on the roof clearly needed some repair, but it was an impressive home—nearly as large as the one her parents had been given next to the temple in Rome.

"Come in," came a frail female voice.

John glanced at them, concern in his eyes, then pushed open the door and entered. The room was dim. A woman sat on a chair, rocking back and forth, holding a multi-colored bundle of cloth in her hands. She glanced up at them as they entered, then stared at an indeterminate point on the wall opposite her. A man walked in from another room, wearing the beginnings of a protective glower.

"Who are you?" he asked, his voice not quite gruff.

"We are here to help, if we can," said John, studying the young man for a moment before resting his eyes on his wife. "You have experienced a great tragedy. I am sorry."

The man gazed at each of them in turn, then let his shoulders slump. "I doubt you can help. Nobody can."

John turned to Sophia, eyebrows rising slightly. She took the hint.

"What happened?" she asked. "We have just heard, and we are new here."

Her voice seemed to soothe him a little—the wife, too, for her rocking lessened. "We lost our triplets. They …" his voice caught "… they drowned in a shallow pool of water after a hard rain. They had just learned to crawl."

"And I wasn't watching closely enough." The woman's scratchy voice caught Sophia by surprise, but her look of intense anguish didn't.

The man moved immediately to her side. "It wasn't your fault. You were a wonderful mother."

"Were," she wailed, then started to weep bitterly, burying her face in the cloth. The man held her closer, tears leaking from the corners of his eyes as well.

Sophia swallowed hard, blinking rapidly as she let them vent their grief.

"How long ago?" she finally asked, her tone reverent.

"Three days," said the man.

"And they were all healthy?" That was amazing. Healthy triplets—with a living mother—were extremely rare.

"They were a miracle," said the man, "and then they were gone. It doesn't make sense."

Sophia felt his pained confusion keenly. "What are your names?" she asked.

"Helmer and Rena."

"I am Sophia. This is John and Onesimus. We are Christians, come from Ephesus. John is an apostle." She knew John must have received some sort of communication from the Lord, perhaps even a vision, so she added, "God led us here."

"God?" said Rena, face emerging from the cloth. Helmer looked skeptical.

"Yes, God. Your children are back with him now, and they are happy. We can't know why they could only stay with you on earth a short time, but you can see them again."

"Please, don't," said Helmer. "That doesn't help. They were taken from us. It was cruel."

Sophia tilted her head. "It seems so, I know. I have three siblings—Hannah, Joel, and Miriam—who didn't even live long enough to crawl. My mother thought she would die of grief, three different times, especially with Miriam, born after she had been declared barren."

There. That seemed to have an impact. Rena's eyes widened, and she straightened on her chair. "She had a miracle baby, too."

"Actually, several. I'm one of them. My mother treasures all seven of us, plus another my parents adopted, and rejoices in the time when we will all be together."

"That is not possible," said Helmer, squeezing Rena's shoulder tighter. The protective mask came into full view.

She met his glare with all the determination she could muster. "How do you know?"

His eyes narrowed, and then he looked down at Rena. "It just isn't."

"I was pronounced barren, too," said Rena, her tears spent, "after they were born."

"What were their names?" She knew that was a risky and tender question.

"Pyotr, Esak, and Coren," she replied. "Three precious boys, as alike as three perfect acorns." She sniffled, but didn't start crying again.

"And you live here alone?"

Rena shook her head. "No, both our parents live here now. They are away today visiting friends. Helmer has acquired a strong reputation as a horse trainer, and we are close enough to Odessa that he attracts some wealthy foreign clients as well."

That sounded impressive. But no number of rich horse owners willing to pay top prices could make up for the loss of three cherished children. She glanced at John to see if he wanted to take over, but he just gave her a slight nod of encouragement.

"Well, I am no expert on horses," Sophia continued, "though I have ridden, and for some long distances. If you will allow me to tell you how I know you can see your children again, we will depart, leaving you with whatever blessing we can."

Helmer began to shake his head, but Rena's voice lost its raspy quality as she perked her head up. "Yes, please." She grasped her husband's hand on her shoulder, then gestured for them to sit. Onesimus chose a stool, but there were two chairs as well. Helmer remained standing by his wife's side.

After one more glance at John, who seemed perfectly content, Sophia did her best to describe the grand arc of life, happiness, and salvation through the One who had made it all possible.

———

Rena took great comfort from Sophia's message, and over the next several days—after insisting they stay with her and Helmer in their home—her faith in Jesus blossomed. She began leading some of the prayers, and her energy level exceeded even John's. Helmer remained somewhat aloof, but he occasionally expressed gratitude for the changes in his wife's demeanor and outlook. He was able to return to his work full-time, which included some travel in the local area, so they didn't see him much.

John made several trips into Odessa by himself, and on one occasion he carried letters for Philip and Timothy which he arranged to send from there. Onesimus began accompanying him, leaving Sophia with Rena, her fast new friend. Normally, it might have bothered Sophia that she wasn't traveling to Odessa and meeting more people, preaching with the apostle, even conversing with members of the significant Jewish population there. But she realized how comfortable—and useful—she felt spending the days with Rena. They began visiting people in the town, called Vrisla, including those who were sick or who had suffered tragic losses of their own. Sophia couldn't help but be impressed by Rena's sincere desire to help. In fact, it made her re-evaluate her own genuineness. That was good, of course, but often unpleasant.

Somehow, the days passed into weeks, and before she knew it, three months had passed. She had written several letters of her own, to the various members of her family, and she and Rena had taken a few trips into Odessa with John and Onesimus. The harvest moved into full swing, and Sophia again marveled at the richness of the land. No wonder Rome wanted it, and the Sarmatians fiercely contested for it. She encountered a few of the strange female warriors, and they didn't look like the depictions of goddesses in their war paraphernalia. They were generally taller and thicker than she was, and they dressed much like the men, without useless skirts and low-cut blouses. They usually wore flexible types of light armor, and the spear seemed to be their favorite weapon, including long horse spears.

As fall came to a close and colder weather began to bite, John returned one evening from Odessa bearing several letters. Helmer was home, and John asked them all to gather at the table near the kitchen. Helmer didn't seem interested, but he came anyway.

"I've received some letters—two from Philip, one from Timothy, another from Barnabas. Mary Magdalene also deigned to write to me from Armenia. She is a treasure. She sent her letter to Ephesus, and Timothy forwarded it on."

"Anything for me?" asked Sophia.

"Nothing yet. I'm sorry, though I have a feeling you'll see some correspondence soon."

She tried not to look crestfallen. "That's okay. I'm sure you're right."

John let his gaze linger on her a little longer, then continued, his cheeks drooping a little. "I'll start with the bad, or less happy news, first. Thomas, it appears, has been killed while teaching in India, near Mylapore. I believe he knew it was coming, and he was faithful to the end, but it is still sad. He was a dear friend."

John might have mentioned Thomas in a previous conversation with Helmer and Rena, but they didn't know him. Rena, at least, still seemed sympathetic.

"And Matthew is not doing well. He is in Rome, where he has been meeting with Philip and other leaders—including, apparently, your mother, Sophia. He is resting, being attended by the best doctors. He says he is willing to stay if that is the Lord's will, but he is also willing to pass on. I understand that sentiment, though I would rather stay myself. I do not know how much pain he is in, of course." He paused, gazing at his reflection in the polish of the table, which was an expensive piece, given as payment for Helmer's services by a wealthy customer, according to Rena.

John looked up, his face brightening. "The good news is that the Spirit is moving across the face of the land in many, many places. It truly is a wonder to contemplate. From Britannia to B'Ashra, from India to Spain, and from, well, here to Morocco, the Lord's Church continues to prosper. We still struggle, of course, with how to keep the teachings pure, but much good work is being done in that regard. Paul has been key in those efforts."

Sophia thought about Marian in Britannia and her brother Matthew in B'Ashra, both contributing to the work. And here she was in Sarmatia. If Simon were to travel to Morocco, they would have the current extent of the church cornered!

"Philip and the councils are pleased with our decision to labor here. It has been too long since missionaries preached in these lands, including this disputed area around Odessa. He asked that we stay for a time and establish a regular presence, with local leaders and priesthood authority. I am delighted to receive that assignment from the prophet of the Lord. Onesimus, Sophia," he looked at each of them in turn, "I hope you will consider staying with me."

Onesimus immediately consented, while Sophia asked, "How long does Philip think that will take?"

John gave a slight shrug. "Three years? That would have been my estimate, too."

Three years. That was long time. She hadn't pictured such a lengthy mission. But as she thought about it, she couldn't imagine anything else she would rather be doing, or that she *should* be doing.

She nodded her assent. "It feels right to me, though I'm not sure what my parents will think about it."

John nodded. "Yes, they will miss you dearly. Perhaps they could travel to Odessa for a visit? It's one of the few places in the world they haven't seen yet, right?" He winked.

Sophia smiled. "They're getting older, and they don't like to travel as much as they used to. I think my father feels a little like

Matthew now, though he wouldn't want to leave this life without my mother."

"Hmmm … yes, I picture them dying within days of each other. Some couples are like that. Too rare, probably. My wife, as you know, passed many years ago. We had a son and a daughter. Both joined the Lord's Church, then later left the faith. They and their families were lost in the siege of Jerusalem. I had tried to warn them."

Sophia had heard rumors of that, but had never heard it confirmed. Nor had she felt comfortable asking him directly. Her heart went cold.

"It's all right," he added. "We are all free to choose, and we can only do our best. I look forward to seeing all of my family again. And I believe there is still a chance for my children. We shall hope, anyway."

He seemed genuinely at peace, and Sophia marveled at that. Yes, a few years had passed, but talking about it must bring up the most awful of memories. What had his children and their families suffered during the siege? The stories were horrific, even mind-numbing, nearly enough to erase all hope in humanity.

John proceeded to offer more details about the church's progress—and its challenges—in various areas of the world, and it took a while. The letters were long. When he finally finished, Sophia noted that Helmer had fallen asleep in his chair. She almost laughed out loud, especially when Rena slapped his arm and he tumbled to the floor. It was all good. He would come around.

That winter wasn't particularly bitter—so Rena informed them—but it was plenty cold for a girl from Jerusalem and Rome. Sophia saw a great deal of snow, too, which drifted at times to nearly reach her height. She was effusively grateful to be staying in a nice, warm home, and while they didn't get out much, nor receive many visitors, John took advantage of the time to recite more of his experiences for her to record, which she happily did. At times, she felt like the finger of God wrote the words for her, and it was impossible to describe the experience.

Spring came, travel became much easier, and John announced they would set off into the countryside to preach the gospel. His excitement was contagious, and she and Onesimus did their best to match it and support him. If it were possible, the aging apostle seemed even more spry than the year before! She knew the Lord was helping him. It was too obvious not to notice.

They zigzagged all over the countryside, staying within about fifty miles of the coast and making it all the way east to Tanais Emporium, at the mouth of a winding river that fed the Maeotis Palus at its northeastern-most point. That sea, which hosted Cremni, spilled into the Black Sea.

The Jewish rabbi in Stalitza didn't want to talk to them, and Irena, to Sophia's profound and confused disappointment, had sold her inn and moved north, but they found many other people willing to listen. They avoided Cremni, though John promised they would return eventually. Tedric, the boy whose leg John had healed, nearly burst with joy when he saw them again. He, his mother, and several others in the village eagerly absorbed what they taught. Some were baptized, and John appointed one of the men and his wife to conduct prayer meetings and administer the sacrament, promising to pass through again to check on them and provide further instructions.

Sophia already knew how complex the administration of the church could be, even among a few people in a small village. The Lord's house was a house of order, and there were very good reasons for that. Various philosophies and traditions always sought to intrude, blunting the effects of the Savior's gloriously simple gospel. Both individuals and groups had to be vigilant and wise. What was it Jesus had said once? Yes, wise as serpents, and harmless as doves. And bold, too, for sometimes a temple needed to be cleansed of moneychangers.

By the time they passed through that same village on the way back toward Odessa, several more villagers wanted to be baptized and join the church. John carefully taught them and assessed their sincerity, asking Onesimus and Sophia to provide their opinions as well. Most were indeed baptized, and then John trained the man and his wife who led the small flock, along with a few others, based on instruction he had received himself on many occasions, including directly from Jesus. He ordained the man an elder, taught him how to confer the Holy Ghost—the 'baptism of fire'—and charged the couple to make sure they did everything with the Spirit's guidance. Sophia also recorded all their names.

It was the middle of fall when they returned to Helmer and Rena's home. It was good to be back, and John soon returned from Odessa with some letters for Sophia, mainly written by her mother. One came from Marian, though, and another from Reyanza, Matthew's wife in B'Ashra. Sophia treasured those updates on her siblings' families and their lives all the way through winter. They might have been what got her through that brutal season, which was less snowy but much colder. She hadn't thought it conceivable that the earth could get that frigid anywhere, though people kept telling her it was mild compared with places farther north and east. Impossible.

They set out again in the spring, revisiting many places they had seen the prior year, and discovering new ones. More seeds had started to sprout, and nurturing them was an exquisite gift.

So many people turning toward Christ, welcoming his light and love into their lives, healing in a multitude of ways, and sharing their newfound strength, knowledge, and joy with others. John performed more physical healings, too, and Sophia and Onesimus participated in some of those. Faith was growing, and the miracles flowed naturally. If Fyodr and his grandfather knew what was happening in their country, they would flip. Hopefully, they would at least learn some respect.

They ventured a little farther north this time, but not too far, so they didn't penetrate the true hill country. They observed massive herds of horses and cattle, though. In some places, the beasts seemed as numerous as the insects—an exaggeration Sophia thought Marian might enjoy for her literary pursuits. She determined to make sure she mentioned it in her next letter.

Again they returned to Vrisla at the end of the season, and, joy of joys, Helmer asked to be baptized. He and Rena had adopted a pair of orphans, too, a three-year-old boy and a two-year-old girl. Sophia had started to dread another long winter, but the children made it more than bearable. The next spring, John announced that this would indeed be their last year ministering in southern Sarmatia. Part of Sophia felt happy she could return home, while a growing portion would miss the people tremendously. They had been teaching the church members to keep records, and when they passed through places they had visited and baptized before, she was astounded at the size of the harvest. John sent regular updates to Philip, but she imagined their final report would open more than a few eyes in Rome. By the end of the summer, they would easily be able to count a thousand members of the Lord's Church in Sarmatia. More missionaries would need to come. Many more.

Their final winter was perhaps the shortest in terms of actual time, but it seemed to last the longest. Sophia was anxious to embark for home and share the success she had found with her parents, so most of the frigid days couldn't pass fast enough. That was good for her, though, she decided. She needed to learn more patience.

Still, as the snow and ice began to melt, she could hardly contain herself. At breakfast one morning, with the sun shining brightly through the windows, she expressed her eagerness to John.

"We'll be able to sail soon."

John's eyes twinkled, and he stared at her while he chewed on some bacon. He hadn't grown up with bacon, but he sure seemed to enjoy it now.

"What if I told you we aren't returning by ship? At least not for the first leg of the journey."

Her mouth dropped a little. "What do you mean? You haven't mentioned that before."

He gave her an apologetic look as he swallowed. "I know, and I'm sorry. I just figured it out myself."

She glanced at Onesimus, who shrugged. He wasn't the sheepish type, but this was one of those times.

"You knew?" she asked, narrowing her eyes.

"Just a few days ago." He glanced at John. "John asked me to let him break the news."

She took a deep breath, trying to figure out how angry she should be. Her plans had just been tossed in the air. Over a cliff. Into a tidal wave. Yes, she was being overdramatic, but it had been *three years*. She didn't want to complain, not after remembering what many others had gone through, but she fixed John with a glare.

"You should have told me earlier."

John maintained eye contact, his mien humble. "I can see that. I apologize. You do not, either of you, have to accompany me, though I would love for that to be the case. We could easily find you a place on a ship."

He was serious. She could depart, and certainly Onesimus would join her. Or would he? As she studied his face, she was unsure. He talked little about Sarmatia being the place of his birth, and she couldn't tell if he felt a real connection or not. It was strange, and yet not. He didn't know his original name, and couldn't even say where among the vast reaches of Sarmatia he had been born.

"Our destination is Rome, by the way," John added, "and we will pass through Verona after crossing Dacia, part of Pannonia, and Dalmatia. I have never met your parents, and that will be a singular honor. It will take longer, and our feet will be sore by the end, but we can do much good together. You have a gift, Sophia, which is quite useful to the Lord."

He was flattering her … and it was working. She looked at Rena, who smiled and nodded. Why would she do that? She wasn't the one who would be walking for months on end, and across mountains instead of plains all the way. The warmth from her eyes melted Sophia's opposition, though, and she finally nodded to John.

"I will go with you. The Lord knows better than I do."

John let out a breath, slowly. "Thank you, Sophia. The Lord will bless us, and we will arrive safely at our destination. That I can promise you."

CHAPTER 7

*Know ye not that ye are the temple of God, and
that the Spirit of God dwelleth in you?*

1 Corinthians 3:16

The Carpathian Mountains were stunning, so gorgeous it nearly made Sophia cry. They stopped a little more often than she would have liked, but her feet didn't complain, and she enjoyed the opportunities to preach and serve. For several weeks, they crossed and recrossed the amorphous borders in the area, but she could tell when they neared a firm border with Rome. For one, she saw a lot more soldiers, and those soldiers actively scouted in large groups. Secondly, people became more suspicious of them, especially when their speech clearly betrayed them as Romans. It hadn't been like that near Odessa, but she knew how much more volatile these inland borders had been. Why, she didn't understand.

When they presented themselves at a broad stone fort alongside a major road, Sophia became nervous. Another fort stood not fifty yards farther on, of Roman design, with more crenelations and rounded towers. The border obviously lay between.

A trio of Sarmatian soldiers casually moved to block their path.

"You are about to cross into Roman lands. What is your business?"

Sophia wondered what the proper response might be.

"We are Christian teachers, recently come from near Odessa," said John. "We have no other business."

Whether that was the right answer or not, an old man, a middle-aged man, and a young woman, traveling on foot with neither pack animals nor wagons, represented the least of their potential worries. And they were leaving, not entering.

One of the guards scowled, then eyed Sophia. "I have heard of Christians. Is she—"

Sophia's eyes must have burned with the heat of the sun, for his face blanched. "I am not a witch," she growled. "If you people can't get that out of your heads, you're beyond help."

That guard raised his hands in apology, while one of his companions laughed. "Witch or not, that made my day." He laughed harder, joined by the third guard, while the first one turned a bright red. He wouldn't be embarrassed for long, she was sure. He would turn angry.

"Go on along," he said, waving them past, his voice already steeling. They hurried past, and behind them one called out, "Our greetings to the Roman guards. Make them cry; it shouldn't be hard." More laughing ensued, and Sophia felt warmth in her own face. She glanced at John.

"I'm sorry. I should have controlled myself better."

John chuckled. "I think not. That was perfect. We're supposed to be meek, but there's a strength in true meekness. And they'll not soon forget the word Christian."

———

"Have you seen Patavium?" asked John as they descended the western foothills, aiming generally southwest.

"No," replied Sophia, "though I know it's very near Verona. It's also a lot colder than Rome in the winter, with the winds off the Adriatic."

"Well, I've been there, and I found it to be a beautiful city, though not large. If we keep traveling this direction, we'll get to Salonae, and we should be able to find a ship to take us to Patavium. From there, it's a short walk to Verona. After visiting your parents, we can travel to Florentia, and then Rome. I wish we had time to head north, into the Alps, but alas, that will have to wait."

"They are spectacular," agreed Sophia. "I think Onesimus has crossed them as well."

"Once," said Onesimus, pounding a long walking stick into the ground beside him. John never seemed to want to use one. "Breathtaking, for sure, but also treacherous if you don't know them well."

"That's true. John, you said you'd been to Britannia, but we haven't talked about it much."

John nodded slowly, eyes scanning the landscape. They walked a minor road, barely wide enough for a small wagon, but people were already plying it with their wares to trade. The weather was warm enough now, the snowline receded.

"Britannia. Yes, I'll make sure to tell you some stories from my times there. Jesus encountered the isle as a young man, too, with Joseph of Arimathea, who owned some tin mines. He visited a lot of places … knowing, of course, that his mission would extend to all of them."

"When did he know?" she asked.

John stopped, turning toward her. "Know in his mortal mind that he would need to atone for our sins and die?"

She nodded.

"I'm not sure. It is an insightful question. I asked him once, and he gave a vague answer. He commented that he knew he needed to be about his Father in Heaven's business from a very early age—before twelve, certainly—and he went where he felt the Father needed him to go, learning everything he could as fast as he could. That has always fascinated me, by the way. He was already a god, and yet passing through the veil to take on a new mortal body affected him like it affects us, at least in most ways. He couldn't be killed, of course, and he had his agency, as we have ours. He could have decided it was too hard, or not worth it."

"But he didn't."

"No, he didn't. When do you suppose, by the way, that the Father told him, Sophia?"

"The Father wouldn't have told him until his mortal mind was ready," she replied.

"I think that is right, too. Anyway," he put on a cheery smile, "however the victory was ultimately won, it *was* won. Such a miracle, and the only thing that gives us real hope. Satan's false promises offer us nothing, and it has always been so, even before the earth was formed."

They continued on that topic for some time, passing several people on the road, hailing a few who looked like they might like a short rest and some conversation before continuing to travel uphill. Sophia had been copying some tracts over many months, using parchment provided generously by Helmer, and they handed out a few of those, which included words from Jesus, Peter, Paul, John, Mary, Joanna, and others.

They soon entered areas that had been traveled more frequently by the apostles, the Seventy, and other missionaries. They were able to find homes of members to stay in for several nights as they progressed. The closer they drew to Italy, the more excited Sophia became. They faced some moderately difficult travel near the coast before dropping into Salonae, but her legs felt fresher, the soreness in her feet fading.

They waited less than a week to find a boat to carry them to Patavium, and the sailing weather was perfect. They made good time on a trip that was already short. She leaped onto the docks when they arrived early in the morning, as John and Onesimus both chuckled behind her. Neither said anything, though. She led from that point, until they reached Verona in the middle of the afternoon. Her parents had acquired a nice home on the southern outskirts, with a fair bit of land surrounding it. Much of it was planted in various crops and fruit trees. The front door was thick and recessed, and she opened it with a flourish.

"I'm home!"

She had expected an immediate answer, and the pause made her glance around uncertainly. Were they not home? Of course that was possible. They had many friends, or perhaps they needed to go to the market. Her father still made a few tents, though he had slowed down on that considerably.

Her mother suddenly appeared, sweeping into the front room. "My precious Sophia!" Tears were already starting, and Sophia felt her own floodgates open. They embraced for several seconds as John and Onesimus found a place to stand off to the side.

Chanah finally asked them all to sit while she retreated toward the kitchen to gather some refreshments. It was a warm day, and now that she was home, Sophia felt decidedly thirsty.

When Chanah returned, she looked at John. "Thank you for taking exceptionally good care of our daughter."

John winked at her. "I believe it is the other way around. She took good care of me and Onesimus … and many other people as well. We enjoyed a fruitful missionary assignment."

"Well, I still appreciate it," said Chanah.

"And I am grateful to finally meet you," added John. "Where is your husband?"

"Oh, he's off talking about a crazy new design for a tent with someone. He's excited about this one, because it's different. Less boring, anyway." She smiled, taking in Onesimus and Sophia as well.

As if he had heard his name called and magically transported himself home, her father walked through the front door. His face lit up when he spotted Sophia, and she bounded to her feet so he could trap her in a powerful hug. He wasn't much for crying, but she could tell when he was extremely happy.

"John, Onesimus?" he ventured as he let her go.

The two men stood, John extending an arm, which her father took. "Yes, that is us, just arrived in your marvelous home. I feel the Spirit here."

Barabbas dipped his chin to blunt the compliment, gesturing toward Chanah. "Thank her."

Warmth filled John's face. "Yes, without the women of the church, and in our families, this would be a cold, desolate, desperate world. Which leads me to say again that your daughter has been a tremendous boon to the missionary work in Bithynia, Sarmatia, Moesia, Dacia, Pannonia, and Dalmatia. She has shown much courage and fortitude as well."

Her father blinked, and Sophia saw the beginnings of tears. He embraced her again, then sat with the rest of them, next to her mother.

"How is Philip?" asked John of Chanah. "You were with him recently, I gather."

"Yes, I was. He conducted some important meetings. The church is growing so fast, and there are so many needs, both physical and spiritual. It's hard to keep up. We are setting up stronger regional organizations, which should help."

John nodded. "Yes, we have tried to do that before, but with only moderate success. Given a greater number of members now, perhaps we can achieve more. Did he say anything about Vespasian?"

"He did. He meets regularly with the emperor, who remains in good health. Vespasian recently began construction of a grand colosseum in Rome for some of the gladiator games. He is locating it next to that awful hundred-foot statue of Nero."

Sophia suppressed a rebellious giggle. Her father had remarked more than once that the statue of naked Nero was far more impressive than the actual naked Nero. She didn't blame the artists, though. They had made him look strong and virile on pain of their own lives.

"Interesting," said John. "Though he was promised by Philip that he would die of natural causes, Rome is still a city of a thousand sharp, spinning knives. He must feel he needs to maintain—or increase—his popularity."

"I'm glad not to be involved in those circles any longer," said Barabbas. "Dealing with Nero was enough for me."

"I can imagine," said John. "According to Paul, he started out a promising young man, but the power and paranoia overwhelmed him. That was sad for him and so many others. I, too, do not relish the thought of dealing with Rome's emperors, though I'm sure I won't be able to entirely escape it."

"Why do you say that?" asked Chanah, leaning forward, eyes suddenly intense.

John shrugged. "Just a feeling. And, well, I tend to get myself in trouble." He glanced at Sophia. "Your daughter knows that well. I was supposed to be in Ephesus when she came to find me."

Sophia nodded wholehearted agreement, adding a teasing eye roll, then wondering how she had become so comfortable in the presence of the apostle to do that. She felt like they were actual friends. She even blushed a little.

Onesimus laughed, but then took a serious tone. "You stand for the right things, and you're bold in doing it."

"Thank you, my friend. It won't kill me, but I'm sure I will face more difficulties. Rome has been reasonably kind to us, but it won't always be so."

That put a damper on the previous ebullient mood, but her mother rescued them.

"We just learned that Matthew and Reyanza had their fourth child, a healthy baby girl they named Aziera."

"Oh my," said Sophia, placing a hand on her chest. "They are busy, she with the city administration, he with the trading business, and now a fourth child?"

Her mother beamed. "They have plenty of help. They love the people there so much, and they are loved in return."

"Cornelius is not in good health at the moment, unfortunately," said her father, adding another wet blanket to the conversation.

"Is he recovering?" asked John, concern in his eyes.

"Yes, at least Matthew seems to think so. He still presides in the temple some days, so that's a good sign."

John nodded, sighing. "What a good man, and a powerful family. What they have helped build in Africa will last for many generations, blessing millions of lives." His eyes had gone distant, redolent of prophecy.

"Marian is finally pregnant," said her mother, and joy surged through Sophia. They had been trying for so long.

"When will she deliver?" She couldn't help the high pitch in her voice.

"Near wintertime. She says she is feeling well. She continues to write wonderful stories, and many people enjoy them. A few have even been turned into plays. They have a small theater in Nazaretum now."

Wow. Actual plays, with thespians in costumes, and maybe even some sets. "That's wonderful. So now, with Elhanan's two,

Matthew's four, Marian's baby, and Simon's two, you'll be the grandparents of nine."

Her mother's look of deep contentment lasted several seconds, but then Sophia thought she detected some anxiety. Concerning her, of course. She hadn't married yet. Or might not ever. She braced for the question, but it didn't come.

"I do have some unfortunate news," said her mother, glancing at her father before settling her gaze on Sophia. "Simon and Porcia have divorced. Or rather, Porcia requested it, influenced heavily by her parents, who have become highly critical of the Lord's Church, and Simon isn't the type to try to fight it."

Sophia frowned, her lips tight. "He's also the type to get really down on himself about it."

"I know. Your father and I will visit him soon. We'll leave within the month, in fact. The members on Melita have been very helpful, but … well, she took the children and moved back to Rome."

"That's kind of like what happened to Paul," said Sophia, "though at least Simon will know where they are."

Her mother's eyes saddened further. "But he won't be allowed to visit them. I can't imagine the heartbreak. Maya and Zipporah are such angels. They—" her voice caught as she began to weep, and her father placed a comforting arm around her shoulders.

"Keep the faith," said John. "Those girls have a Heavenly Father, too, and he will never abandon them. Your faith and prayers will work wonders as well, I promise. You might not see it until much later, but you can do much more good than you think. So can Simon, of course. Especially Simon, as their father."

"Thank you," said Chanah, wiping away tears, "that is helpful. We have been praying for them, night and day, and we will continue." She took a deep breath. "We want to hear all about your missionary journey, though. How long can you stay?"

After much cajoling, Sophia's parents convinced John to stay for an entire week. That gave Sophia plenty of time to tell the stories of her missionary journey, plus visit with several friends in the area. She looked forward to returning to Rome—she had many friends there, too—but Verona was so beautiful in the early summer. And the views of the northern mountains gave her constant joy.

Before they left, she made sure to write a careful, encouraging letter to Simon. Her heart ached sharply for him, and his children, and it frustrated her how some people could be so cruel. People like Fyodr, too, who had wanted to murder her. She hadn't told her mother that full story. Maybe someday.

With regard to what was next for her, she wanted to get Philip's opinion on it. She knew her parents' desires for her to marry, have a family, and serve locally in the church, and it might be presumptuous to think that the prophet would or could take the time to help her figure out her future, but it felt important that she speak with him, in addition to wrestling with the Lord over it, a little like Father Jacob had described.

They were able to secure passage with a swift caravan, so the journey to Rome took less than a week. When they arrived at the temple grounds, John found them rooms in the visitors house, though they could easily have stayed at Senator Manius Aviola's palatial home on the Aventine. He hadn't spent much time at his own house since becoming governor of Asia Minor—which was a great boon to the church—but some of his family still lived there.

As it turned out, the first person she saw that she knew was Luke, who was now an apostle, having replaced James the son of Alphaeus. He nearly started dancing when he recognized their group, giving them each enthusiastic greetings. He then informed them that Philip was in the temple, preparing to meet with the apostles and sister leaders. John hustled off with Luke, leaving her and Onesimus to settle into their rooms. Part of her wanted to go see their old house, but others occupied it now, and it seemed rude to intrude on them, especially after several years had passed.

Instead, she went to the library. True to Paul's vision, the temple site not only boasted many notable books now, but also a primary school. Many members of the church in and around Rome sent their children to the school at least three days a week. Sophia had met some of the first teachers who had been hired, and while not all were Christians, they were excellent instructors, and they adhered to the moral codes required.

Tall shelves and cubbyholes filled with documents and scrolls lined the walls of the library's main hall, labeled helpfully by topics and subtopics. She found a section on philosophy, narrowing in on some writings of the famous Greek philosophers. She spent the next several hours reading Aristotle, Thales, Socrates, Democritus, Epicurus, and Plato. It was fascinating to place herself inside their heads, in their times and places. They were keenly aware of what went on in the broader world around them—including the Jewish kingdom—and they offered astounding insights into life and progress, including a few ideas that sounded very much like some of Christ's teachings. Of course, Jesus was the ultimate philosopher—and scientist, doctor, diplomat, general, and … well, king. What would it be like when he returned again, as he had promised? Would she still be alive? Not likely, but that was okay. Maybe she could descend with him from the heavens, as one of his angels. Maybe she would even have a sword like Raphael's.

She didn't realize she had started daydreaming. John's voice startled her back to reality.

"Sophia? I thought I might find you here, among some of the great writings."

"What? Your meeting is already over?"

"It has been four hours."

"Four … hours?" Her eyes darted among the various scrolls, papers, and parchments scattered around her on a broad table, and it dawned on her how much she had read.

John chuckled. "The students left long ago. Few others remain, as it is getting dark. Shall we return to the visitors house? I could use a meal."

Her stomach growled in agreement, and she began gathering and replacing all her reading materials. What a treasure trove this library had become! God encouraged the pursuit of all truth, except for those few subjects, like the occult, which trafficked mostly in lies anyway and tended to lead one toward certain trouble. Satan was real, but one need not obsess over him and his teachings to understand how dangerous he was.

A good brother and sister in the kitchens were only too happy to fix the three of them something to eat. Onesimus had arrived back at the visitors house just before them, after a long walk around the countryside. Sophia didn't ask him why he felt like walking. She had experienced enough walking for the time being, thank you very much.

By the time they had finished, the common room had emptied, their only companions a few lit torches in wall sconces.

John patted his belly. "That was delicious. I had forgotten how good the food is in Italy. I'm not here often."

"So what did you talk about?" asked Sophia, having kept the question bottled up all through dinner, trying not to be rude.

He chuckled. "Many things. My, so many things. My mind is still spinning, and I'm not sure where to start. One thing we discussed was how to compile Jesus's teachings, along with those of some of the apostles and sisters, like Mary, Joanna, and Mary Magdalene, into a list of approved documents that the churches can use in their teaching and ministering. Efforts are already underway, but the Hellenists are making alarming inroads with many of the saints, introducing distortions to the Savior's clear and simple teachings, and we need to address the problem as quickly as possible."

That interested her, and she bobbed her head in agreement.

"Organizing the continually growing missionary effort is always a challenge as well," he continued. "Between the sending out and the receiving back of missionaries—including us—there is far too much for the leaders here in Rome to keep track of. So, a committee has been formed of strong brothers and sisters who will manage and keep track of everything, taking in and vetting recommendations for new missionaries and area assignments and passing them to the apostles for approval. Which leads me to another key point."

He paused, until Sophia asked, "Which is?"

"The new headquarters of the church is officially Rome now, not Pella. This is a hinge point for the growth and progress of the Lord's kingdom on earth, both now and far into the future."

Sophia nodded thoughtfully. She had suspected that would happen. The saints in Pella, mostly Jewish Christians, might want the headquarters to be there, since it used to be at nearby Jerusalem, but the membership of the church was so much greater in other parts of the empire, and even beyond. Rome made sense.

John stared at Onesimus for a moment. "We also talked about making an official statement on our opposition to all forms of slavery. As you know, it is a delicate political issue, but we have to keep pushing for progress. I'm probably not the one to say how bold we should be, but collectively we are trying to seek the Spirit to guide us. Heavenly Father wants his children to be free—not just for their dignity, but so they can accept without any fetters his Son's invitation to learn who they truly are and why they are here. We reviewed the first draft of such a document. I'm sure many revisions will follow."

Sophia studied Onesimus's reaction to that. He seemed grateful. It was good to have such wise, faithful people as the apostles and sister leaders guiding them by the Spirit.

"And one more thing," said John, "which I found to be quite good news." He looked at Onesimus, then Sophia. "Philip has asked us to continue together, if we are all willing. He wants us to sail for northern Africa, starting with Leptis Magna, one of the great Tripolitan cities on the coast. We need not leave until the spring, which is perfect, because we have more writing and studying to do, if you're amenable."

Sophia wasn't anxious for another extended trip so soon. Even Paul had rested between his major missionary journeys. But for a long time she had wanted to visit Leptis Magna, with its massive, famous hippodrome and other great architecture. Had Philip somehow known that? Well, the Lord did, of course, and he must have inspired Philip with the call.

"I'm willing," she replied, "but I want to visit Naples, Pompeii, Herculaneum, and a few other places in that vicinity."

"That is a splendid idea," said John, looking then to Onesimus, who nodded.

"I will go wherever the prophet points me, and I actually enjoy your company … an added miraculous bonus." He chuckled, and Sophia and John laughed.

"Well," said John, "my meetings here will last a few weeks, but then we can be off to do some exploring."

The next day, Sophia convinced Onesimus to take a stroll up to the Aventine, both to see all the gaudy palaces and to check on the construction of this new colosseum. He admitted he didn't much like standing anywhere near the most powerful parts of Rome, since they supported and proliferated the practice of slavery, which some even called an art—an *art!*—but he distracted himself by making amusing comments about the actual art and architecture along their path.

"Only an ugly god with an embarrassing past could inhabit such a building."

"If they're traveling up a mountain, why aren't they wearing any clothes?"

"How much larger would that cupola have to be to fit Augustus's ego?"

Sophia couldn't help but laugh at some of them, and while she understood that mockery, strictly speaking, wasn't a good thing, the opulence of the Roman hierarchy was truly astounding.

After descending the Aventine, she led them along the Tiber, enjoying the peace of the river and its beautifully dressed banks. Long barges languidly plied its course, contributing to the largesse they had just inspected.

As they neared one of the bridges, Sophia heard a whispered voice. "Stop."

She halted, turning to Onesimus. "Why?"

He quirked an eyebrow. "Why what?"

"Why did you tell me to stop?"

He shook his head. "I didn't." Then he looked around, clearly wary.

Was it the Spirit? She studied their surroundings, noting they were alone for the moment, which was decidedly odd. This path was heavily traveled, day and night. Rome rarely slept, and never in the middle of the day.

"What's happening?" she asked Onesimus, unable to mask her nervousness.

"I don't know," he said, "but it doesn't feel right. And you are a target of the Evil One."

Earlier memories of that truth had largely faded, but they came rushing back. Suddenly, a man stepped out from behind a tree. He didn't seem crazy; he wasn't foaming at the mouth or anything. He just walked calmly toward them, hands behind his back, a knowing smile teasing the corners of his mouth. He wore a strange brown hat, along with a finely tailored tunic and pants—not the Roman robe and toga.

He paused just a few feet from them, directly in their path, dark eyes studying her.

"Good afternoon Sophia, Onesimus." Onesimus seemed an afterthought, his attention focused on her.

"Who are you?" she asked.

He gave a thoughtful look. "I am the true master of this world. Its true heir. And as you can see, I've arranged for some privacy."

Her eyes narrowed. "You have some power. I see that."

Those twitching corners turned up sharply. "You haven't seen anything yet. You know so little, and yet … you could be great. One of the greatest. You could control kingdoms with millions of people. You could make their lives better with your enlightened approach to their welfare."

She knew he was lying, but she was curious. "And how would I control kingdoms?"

The man puffed out his chest. "Oh, that's easy, almost ridiculously so. Rome hasn't had an empress yet, but Sarmatia has had queens, and the powerful are so easily manipulated. Say the word, and you will be Queen of Sarmatia. As a start."

"Queen of Sarmatia …" She pretended to be considering it. "And how long would I be queen?"

"For as long as you want!"

She tilted her head. "For as long as I want, or as long as you want?"

"Providing our goals remain aligned … forever."

"Forever. And what are the goals?"

He pursed his lips in slight remonstrance. "You know them. An end to war, to violence. An end to hunger and fear. Prosperity for all, freely taken."

She couldn't pretend any longer. "You realize none of that can actually be achieved by force, right?"

His smile faded, his dark eyes glowing with fiery intensity. "To the near-sighted, that is true. But I have high hopes in your ability to see beyond the mundane and fruitless."

"Fruitless? I have experienced more joy than you will ever know, because I realize that people cannot be manipulated into achieving perfection. In fact, the attempt is always disastrous. And you abandon your agents in the end, without fail. Your true goal is our misery, is that not correct?"

He sneered, then snarled. "You know nothing, little girl."

"And you have no body, nor will you ever. Even Cain will be greater than you."

"Do *not* mention that name."

"Why not? Is he not one of your supreme successes?" She wondered at how she could continue this conversation. She was clearly receiving some help. Was this Satan himself? Or one of his top lieutenants? And why her?

"He is nothing."

"You tried to make him so, yes. And you largely succeeded. But you failed spectacularly with Abraham, and with Moses, and with Jesus of Nazareth. They all rejected your silly temptations of unlimited power. And they all transcend you as the sun outshines a firefly. Especially Jesus, of course."

"Say *that* name again, and I will destroy you." He said it with fierce malice, but a small shuffling of his feet belied his uncertainty. And that shuffling displaced a twig fallen from one of the great trees bordering the path. Which meant there was a physical body involved. Someone who had been possessed.

"Did the man whose body you inhabit put up much resistance, or did he invite you in?"

The demon blinked, then clenched his jaw. "You have not accepted my invitation. You have one final chance."

She almost said, "Or what?", but that would have been both immature and needlessly provocative. She also felt a prompting, which came with an urgency. She raised an arm, palm toward the demon.

"In the name of Jesus the Christ, Lord and Savior of this world, I command you to depart that body. It cannot be yours, now or ever."

The man began to shake in rage, hands clenching in fists at his sides, face taking on a reddish hue. A spike of fear caused her to take a small step back. Onesimus moved closer, his arm touching her shoulder as she said a silent prayer.

"You will serve me, and we will rule this earth! You cannot deny the power!"

Sophia calmed. Her arm was still raised. "I follow a power far greater, and perfectly faithful. If you could cause a mountain to fall upon me, and it was Jehovah's will that I die, I would leave this realm happy, while you would remain miserable. Again, I command you to depart. You cannot triumph."

The demon—or Satan—roared, arms outstretched, back arched, feet lifted off the ground a few inches. Then a column of light flashed from the heavens, causing both Sophia and Onesimus to shield their eyes.

When the glow had faded, she opened hers, lowering her arms. A man lay in a crumpled heap near her feet, dressed as before, minus the hat, which had disappeared. She couldn't immediately tell if he was breathing, but then he stirred. When he looked up, she saw that his true eyes were green. He looked to be in his late thirties or early forties.

"What have you done?" he asked in a raspy voice.

She blinked at Onesimus, who wore a deep and worried frown. He wasn't speaking Greek or Latin, and yet she understood him perfectly. She turned back to the man.

"I … freed you. Or rather, God did, through me. I can't explain exactly how."

"Why?" he asked, studying her intently as he tried—and failed—to get to his feet.

"Because you had been deceived and manipulated, and that devil was trying to do the same to me."

"That … devil? But he said he was an angel from God."

"Do you believe he was so now?" asked Onesimus, moving a step forward protectively, even though the man still sat on the ground, seemingly helpless.

The man looked down, blinking rapidly. "No, I suppose not. How could he have been? An angel could not have been defeated by a mere girl."

"A 'mere' woman," said Sophia. "But still a good point. You're thinking at least somewhat logically. Now, who are you, and where are you from?"

He made another attempt to rise, and this time succeeded, though he wobbled a bit. He reached up as if to settle his hat, which of course was not there. That seemed to annoy him. "Giofred, and I do not recognize this place."

"You are in Rome," offered Onesimus, "the capital city."

The man cocked his head. "Rome? Capital of what?"

Sophia and Onesimus glanced at each other, and suddenly the world seemed to resume its normal motion. They heard people moving up and down the path, conversing, laughing, even conspiring. The sun must have emerged from cloud cover, too, for everything seemed brighter, more vibrant.

But Giofred was gone.

CHAPTER 8

*By this we know that we love the children of God, when we love
God, and keep his commandments. For this is the love of God, that
we keep his commandments: and his commandments are not grievous.*

1 John 5:2-3

As unsettling as her latest encounter with a demon was, her dream that very night left a dark, foreboding taint. It started out innocuous enough. John was riding a dragon, or what she imagined a dragon might look like, at an elevation higher than the tallest of the Alps, while she and Onesimus each clung to a flapping wing, miraculously without the urge to vomit every few seconds. The air was cool, but the sun was bright, and they were heading … somewhere important.

That's when things became alarming. The dragon dove, almost straight down, and while John didn't seem concerned in the slightest, smiling all the while, she and Onesimus fractured the air with their screams, hanging on for dear life amid what looked like certain death. Instead of impacting the ground, however, they entered a great cavern. It went deep, so deep she wondered if they might come out on the other side of the world. The dragon suddenly cut its speed, and she couldn't tell how she hung on. They were crossing a great underground lake filled with bubbling oil, and when they reached the middle, the dragon spun, turning upside down and dumping John into the oil!

Again, the apostle didn't seem alarmed. In fact, he executed a perfect dive into the flaming liquid. A few seconds later, he burst from the surface, arcing through the air like one of those famed flying fish, to reenter and reemerge once again. In that fashion, he made his way to the shore, without even a hair singed, and he gave a great clap, at which point the dragon flung her and Onesimus off its wings. Sophia panicked, looking down to see where she might land, but in the way of dreams she found herself standing next to John, with Onesimus, both of them unhurt.

Without a word, John turned and began walking down a broad tunnel leading away from the boiling lake. He shouldered a pickaxe, and strange beasts with various numbers and configurations of heads, horns, eyes, and other parts began to appear, some approaching, some following, without coming too near. None threatened them, but they seemed wary of John. Or maybe it was respect they showed.

They walked a long time through that tunnel, until the last of the light from the lake disappeared completely. She stopped, and everything went silent. She called out, but nobody answered. And then she awoke.

It was the darkness at the end of the dream that bothered her most after waking. It hadn't just been complete absence of light. It was something more; thicker, carrying a taint of malevolence. She could almost taste it, and it made her want to retch. As she went throughout the day, which included another trip to the library, the essence wouldn't leave her, and it didn't lessen. She resolved that she needed to ask John about it, first chance she got. He was in constant meetings, so it could be a while.

Finally, many days later, late in the evening, he declared the meetings over. Sophia and Onesimus had just finished their meal in the dining room of the visitors house. John sat opposite them after making his pronouncement, and a woman hurried over with a plate of food and cup of water for him. A few other people sat at different tables, but the crowd had already thinned considerably.

After taking a long drink, John set the cup carefully on the table, glancing at the food but not yet partaking. As his eyes passed between her and Onesimus, his small smile drove her mad with curiosity.

"So, what did the quorum accomplish?" she asked.

"Well," he said, popping a grape into his mouth, "I'm glad we had a quorum, though just barely. Besides me and Philip, Luke, Silas, Matthew, Barnabas, and Decimus were present, so we had seven."

"Does Paul ever come to these meetings?" she asked, thinking about who else was missing: Matthias, Judas Barsabbas, Bartholomew, and … "And who is replacing Thomas?" she added.

John swallowed before answering. "Prochorus, though that must be unanimously agreed. Letters will be sent to the others to get their affirmation … or objections, though I doubt there will be any of those. The Lord's will on this seemed quite clear."

Prochorus. She had never met him, didn't know much about him, either. She had thought it might be Timothy.

"I originally put forward Timothy's name," said John, as if reading her mind, "and others agreed he would be a good choice. But as our discussion progressed, the Spirit made it clear that the time for his calling to the apostleship was not yet, though it will come. My guess is that Matthew will need to be replaced soon, but … sorry, I shouldn't speculate like that, especially in such casual fashion."

He looked down at his food, picking at it, eating little. The silence lengthened as Sophia readied her next question.

"The official position on slavery, was it finished?" asked Onesimus, beating her to it.

John's eyes snapped up to him, his forehead creased. "I believe so. It, too, must be unanimous. We crafted something that is bold in its principles while judicious in its approach to civil authority. The Lord taught us to be wise as serpents but harmless as doves, as we have discussed before, and which I am still learning. If we can get members of the church to fully espouse it, and we continue to grow and spread our influence, slavery will eventually collapse. In fact, I can guarantee, under a sure word of prophecy, with which Philip agreed, that Christians will lead the efforts to eradicate this evil practice in the years to come."

"Long years," said Onesimus, his anxiety on the topic clearly visible.

John's tone carried both sympathy and confidence. "Like you, I wish it were today, but I trust the Lord's wisdom. If he gave us a legion of angels to take over the governing of the world so we could announce an end to slavery and every other unholy and impure practice, where would that leave us? The angels would need to stay permanently, swords out, constantly enforcing the edicts among many millions of people. In the end, that would look very much like Lucifer's plan. Freedom would suffocate, our progress stagnate. We cannot collectively become like God. Though we can help each other, ultimately that can only be achieved individually. And without choice, it is impossible."

Onesimus nodded, staring at the table. He seemed both satisfied and resigned. It was another conversation they had all had before, and yet it was still difficult to fully abide the conclusion.

John continued. "Officially sanctioned and enforced slavery isn't the only way we abuse each other. Our selfishness and cruelty take so many forms, and we often judge others for what we are guilty of ourselves. This world is difficult … so very, very difficult."

Sophia agreed, but she desired to turn the conversation to something lighter. "You mentioned regional headquarters being reorganized and expanded. Have those all been decided upon?"

John took a bite of thick, moist bread. After a few thoughtful chews, he answered. "Yes. We'll have ten, though I know that seems like a lot. Each will be the charge of a specific apostle, with me and Philip being the two without such an assignment. Philip, because he is the prophet, and me because, well, I will be traveling the most."

"You will?"

"Yes. And for a long time."

"But you're over seventy now!"

She didn't mean that to sound harsh. He just chuckled in response. "Do I look like I'm slowing down yet?"

She glanced at Onesimus, then shrugged. "Well, no, but … how *do* you have so much energy?" She caught Onesimus smiling out of the corner of her eye, but he didn't say anything.

His expression held deep mystery, stoking her curiosity again.

His answer didn't reveal anything. "I have my call from the Lord, and I rejoice in it."

She wanted to press, but schooled herself to be calm. She did let a small frown slip, however, before returning to the subject of the headquarters. "So, where will these regional offices be?"

His eyes began to move around the top of the wall behind her. "Let me see if I can remember them all … Ephesus, Damascus, Alexandria, Kainepolis, Byzantium, Corinth, Lugdunum, Carthago Nova—Paul will preside over that one, of course—Nazaretum, and Carthage."

She thought about the list for a moment. Lugdunum was in Gaul, Nazaretum in Britannia where Marian lived, Kainepolis in Armenia.

"What about Pella?" she asked. "There are a lot of saints there."

John nodded. "That was an interesting discussion. Pella was never intended to be permanent. Many saints have decided to stay, but Damascus, which isn't far away, seemed the more logical choice, in part because Pella is seen as an exclusive Christian enclave by Roman officials and most of the nearby communities."

She supposed that made some sense. "And what about B'Ashra?" She thought of her brother Matthew, and Cornelius.

"Another valuable debate. It may very well become one. For now, it will reside within Alexandria's sphere, though travel between the two is neither easy nor swift. We thought about other locations as well, but … we can only run as fast as we have strength. These ten will meet our needs for now, and the Lord seemed pleased with our efforts, paltry as they are compared with his brilliance."

He continued eating, and after a minute Onesimus spoke.

"I would like to leave for Pompeii tomorrow. Would that be all right?"

John responded around a mouthful of food. "Of course. I am ready." He swallowed. "Rome is too stuffy, anyway. Philip seems to like it here, but I really don't. A good tour of the countryside will be good for all of us."

John roused them early the next morning … a little too early. The sun wasn't even up!

Grumbling a little, Sophia prepared herself, making sure she packed enough for a trip of several weeks. They would be on horseback, meaning she could carry more, and that improved her mood a little.

When she emerged from the building, she found John and Onesimus already standing with the horses. She and Onesimus would ride the two magnificent B'Ashran mounts given to her parents several years ago, while John seemed happy with his smaller but still sturdy horse, which sported shaggy, dirty white fur.

A few people emerged from their homes to see them off, including Luke and Philip. Luke demanded a hug from Sophia, causing her to dismount to accede to the request. She liked Luke, and he was a good friend of her family.

They headed south to meet up with the Via Appia, which would take them to Three Taverns and Forum Appius first. They would take their time, and Sophia had brought several scrolls and parchments she could read along the way. Her horse was well trained; it would just follow John's.

She had a hard time getting into her reading, though. The experience with the demon and her strange dream about John and the dragon amplified anew in her mind. So, as they left the populated areas around Rome behind, she moved her horse up next to John's.

"John, it's true the Lord gave his twelve apostles the power to cast out demons very early on, correct?"

John gave her an inquisitive look, then focused on the road ahead. "Yes, he did, and I can testify it was quite daunting. At least as much as the healing. Can you imagine? Being asked to heal someone of a serious malady, with their loved ones watching on anxiously? It was not easy, but we learned to trust in the Lord's promises, and we most certainly felt God's power. I still wonder sometimes why I didn't go screaming into the hills, unable to cope with the stress."

She could hardly picture that scenario. It was impossible to imagine John being so uncertain.

"Did he … give the women the same power?"

He didn't look at her, acting as if he had expected the question.

"It's all the same power, fueled by faith in Jesus Christ and willingness to obey his commandments. For men or women, its effect is the same."

"I know, but I mean—"

He smiled. "I know what you mean. Jesus didn't send the women out to teach and heal the same way he did the men. But opportunities still came to them, and they exercised their faith in remarkable ways. I know we focus a lot on the men, since they're ordained to the priesthood and carry most of the administrative burden, but women are every bit as important, especially within their families, where the next generation of saints is nurtured in the ways of the Lord. In fact, their impact cannot possibly be overestimated, now or in the eternities."

She mulled that over, trying to figure out how to proceed. She didn't feel he was being patronizing, but they hadn't gotten to the heart of her concern yet.

As usual, he could tell where she was headed. "Have you had a recent experience you'd like to tell me about?" He turned his head, his gaze locking with hers for a moment.

She swallowed, suddenly feeling nervous. "Well, Onesimus and I were walking in Rome a few days ago, along the Tiber, and we encountered a very powerful demon."

John nodded, jaw clenching slightly. "Yes, Onesimus alluded to it, but said I would need to speak with you. I've been waiting for you to bring it up … and I have to say, the wait has not been easy."

"I'm sorry, you've been so busy. I just—"

"Don't be sorry. Just tell me what happened."

"Okay. Well, he had made all the people around us … I don't know, go away. We were alone with him. He tried … to convince me to join him, promised me great powers."

He didn't look at her, but she could sense his intensity. "Like he did to Moses, and later to Jesus. Others, too."

"I didn't agree, of course," she added quickly. "And then … well, I commanded him to leave the body he had taken, which I could tell was physical, in the name of Jesus."

John nodded, seeming relieved. "That is good. And he departed that body, I presume? Did the man live?"

She swallowed again. "Yes, and he appeared fine afterward, though weak at first. It was strange, though. His name was Giofred, and not only did he not know where he was, he hadn't even heard of Rome."

"But he spoke Greek?"

"No, something else. But I could understand it. So could Onesimus."

"Interesting."

She waited for him to elaborate.

"Satan is clearly wary of your influence. He made a powerful play, bringing that particular demon and the man whose body he possessed a long way. There's no way to know how far he must have traveled. I wish I could have spoken to him, though."

"We tried to, but then he just kind of … disappeared."

"Hmmm … well, I'm sure your mother would be interested to hear that story. She is one of the most faithful among us. She has performed miracles herself. As did Mary, Jesus's mother, and Mary Magdalene." His gaze became distant, a small smile indicating pleasant remembrance.

They rode on for a short time, Sophia still staying even with John. "I also … had a remarkable dream. It was so vivid, and it hasn't faded. It involved you."

"Oh?" He regarded her with intrigue. "What was it about?"

"Well …" It sounded strange to mention, even if it was from a dream. "You were riding a dragon, and not a friendly one, but you didn't seem concerned."

"A dragon? Well, that's interesting. How could you tell it wasn't friendly?"

"It dumped you into a lake of boiling oil."

"Oh, my." He laughed. "That's rather morbid, don't you think?"

"But you didn't die. You burst out of the oil like a flying fish, making short jumps until you reached the shore."

His eyebrows rose. "And where were you?"

"Onesimus and I were on the wings, and then somehow we were with you on the shore."

"I'm sure you appreciated not getting dumped into the boiling oil. Was that all?"

"No, you put a pickaxe on your shoulder, and we started walking down a tunnel. All kinds of strange creatures approached us. They didn't attack, or even come too close. I think they were afraid of you. Well, maybe not afraid, but … I don't know."

"And you didn't recognize any of the creatures?"

"No, well, parts of them, I guess. And some had more than one head, and multiple eyes and crowns."

"Hmmm … some of that sounds symbolic."

"You think my dream meant something?"

He shrugged. "Maybe. Probably, actually. And I can tell you I'm not looking forward to dragons and boiling oil." He chuckled.

She couldn't tell how serious he was. He was probably teasing her, at least a little. Suddenly, he said, "Thank you, Sophia, for sharing that dream. The Lord communicates with us sometimes through such means, though it isn't always easy to tell when it's him and when it's just our fantastic imaginations. You live close to the Spirit, though, so if you felt it was important enough to tell me, it probably was."

Somehow, that answer eased her fears, even though he hadn't discounted any of the dangers her dream might portend. She was finally able to return to her reading.

—————

After staying in Forum Appius the next night, near the coast, they angled due east for a bit before following two valleys southeast. Three days later, they approached Pompeii, passing through Capua, where many of the gladiators trained, then skirting around Neapolis and the tall volcanic Mount Vesuvius, majestic in its protective overwatch position.

Pompeii was beautiful, but most buildings they passed elicited a frown from Onesimus.

"What is it, Onesimus?" she asked. "Have you been here before? You hadn't mentioned it."

He shook his head. "No, but it's clear they employ many slaves here—more than in Rome or Ephesus, in proportion."

"Oh." She looked around, trying to notice what he saw and feeling a little embarrassed.

He must have caught her expression.

"Don't worry. You don't know what to look for. I do."

"Rotten fruit," said John.

"What?" asked Sophia.

"There is a lot of rotten fruit here. Great wealth, along with stubborn indifference to the laws of God. Many slaves, as Onesimus pointed out. This is a beautiful area, but it doesn't feel that way. I'm sure there are some good people here. Our challenge is to find them." He gave a wink, and Onesimus seemed to relax.

The sarcastic wit in Onesimus's next words bit, though. "If I find one, I'll know the Second Coming is near."

———

They stayed just a single night in Pompeii, then traveled south over the low mountains to follow the magnificent coastline. The area took Sophia's breath away, and she made sure to thank her Heavenly Father for the opportunity to witness its beauty. Once the land leveled out again, they turned east, up into the southern ranges of Italy. If they kept due east, they would arrive at Tarentum and the heel of the boot, but John turned them northeast, wanting to visit some particular saints in that direction.

While not bathed in as much splendor as the Carpathians, these mountains certainly offered their own allure. At various times, Sophia wondered if it might not be nice to pick a town there and just stay … forever. The weather felt perfect, and the peacefulness defied description. They continued their languid journey, stopping often and enjoying the people, including many saints. After reaching the eastern coast, they followed it northward until they were almost opposite Rome. They rested the horses for a few days, and then began the trek west, traversing the higher central mountains. Again, she wished they could just stop and stay, but while they took their sweet time, they eventually found themselves descending the foothills and approaching the area around Rome.

Strangely, the closer they got, the better she began to feel. She had expected the reverse. Perhaps, she realized, it was because Rome now hosted the headquarters of Christ's Church, and several of the apostles lived there on at least a semi-permanent basis. The Lord's temple graced its environs as well—a resplendent reflection of his abundant love. Plus, she had lived here for several years. It was … yes, it was home, crazy deadly politics notwithstanding.

"So," said John as they neared the temple grounds, "are you curious to know what we might have missed? We've been gone more than a month, hard as that is for me to believe."

She gave a smile and a quick shake of her head. "Not really. But I've come to enjoy the food at the visitors house. We have some talented chefs."

John and Onesimus both laughed, while also encouraging their horses to move a little faster. Sophia joined them.

CHAPTER 9

*But sanctify the Lord God in your hearts: and be ready always to give
an answer to every man that asketh you a reason of the hope that is in
you with meekness and fear: Having a good conscience; that, whereas
they speak evil of you, as of evildoers, they may be ashamed that
falsely accuse your good conversation in Christ. For it is better, if the
will of God be so, that ye suffer for well doing, than for evil doing.*

1 Peter 3:15-17

The winter months passed uneventfully. Sophia's parents had decided to tarry in Melita, but she would hopefully hear from them again sometime in the spring, when the ships could sail safely. She continued to study, marveling at the number of items in the growing library. She also visited the rising colosseum in the heart of the city again. It would be breathtaking, holding tens of thousands of people. And they could house animals and gladiators underground, moving them to the surface of the arena using elevators and trap doors. Amazing. Also primeval and cruel. The people seemed to love it, though, so the emperor and senators gave it to them—mainly to keep them distracted, of course.

John waited until April to find them passage to Leptis Magna, but still no letter had arrived from her parents. She wrote them one, though, catching them up on everything she had seen and was learning.

On the docks at Ostia the day of their departure, two men wearing sizeable packs approached them. John squinted for a moment, then expelled a loud greeting of recognition.

"Rufus, Alexander, I haven't seen you in ages!"

After accepting his embraces, the men stepped back, and Rufus—well, she thought it was him based on descriptions of the well-known sons of Simon the Cyrenian—spoke. "Well, we were living peacefully on our farms, just a little north of here … and then the call came. Luke delivered it in person. We are to be missionaries among the Tripolitan cities and Cyrenaica. We've never traveled to the land of our parents, so it is a great honor for us."

"Wonderful!" exclaimed John. "And your families will be all right while you're gone?"

"Yes," replied Alexander. "The barley will be more difficult than the grapes, but they'll have plenty of help."

"Including from the Lord," added Rufus.

John smiled broadly. "Well, I'm sure the Lord himself remembers the burden your father carried for him, even though the Romans commanded it. He passed recently?"

Rufus stared away toward the bay. "Yes. Peacefully and gratefully. He will still be missed, but now he can be with our mother again. She has been waiting several years."

"Those are happy reunions," agreed John. Then he gestured to Sophia and Onesimus. "These are my traveling companions, Onesimus and Sophia, who is the daughter of Barabbas and Chanah."

"Ah, yes," said Rufus as he and his brother bowed. "We have heard of both of you."

"We returned recently from a three-year trip to Sarmatia and some surrounding areas," John continued. "The harvest was very good, and several pairs of missionaries are traveling there to continue the work."

"We heard tell of the recent successes in Sarmatia," said Rufus. "If we can do half as well, we'll consider our journey an astounding success."

John chuckled, clapping them both on a shoulder. "You will do wonderfully. The Lord will bless you. I promise that."

Their eyes widened in obvious awe at his pronouncement, and they thanked him profusely. The three conversed for a few more minutes about the city of Leptis Magna, until the captain of their ship approached, a broad man with a slight paunch.

"We are ready to take on passengers now," he announced, hands behind his back. John had mentioned he was a Christian, and his tone carried respect for them … or at least for John; in her experience, ship captains were always at least a little prickly.

"Excellent, thank you, good brother," said John. "Lead us aboard."

After they and a handful of other passengers were settled, the captain gave the orders to cast off and get underway. Low clouds tumbled across the ocean before them, but no storms threatened, and as soon as they were turned, the winds became favorable. Sophia stood at the railing, breathing deeply the brisk sea air, trying to picture where Melita was. The island carried many fond memories, along with a few frightening ones. She recalled the time Simon had run away; the Spirit had guided her father to find him in the caves. Paul's shipwreck and the miraculous rescue of everyone on board was both harrowing and marvelous to think about. And there was the deadly viper that had bitten him, with no effect. She had cast out a demon, but if a highly poisonous snake bit her, what would she do? It seemed different, somehow.

Onesimus broke her reverie, coming to stand next to her. "I'm glad you agreed to come, Sophia."

She turned. "I hope I will be of use."

He smiled. "Is that humility or uncertainty?"

She shrugged, turning to stare at the sea again. "I don't know. I've never been to Africa, not even the Roman parts."

"But you've seen plenty of other places. You're going to set a record soon for travel by a woman."

She pondered that a moment. Was it something to be proud of? At least satisfied, right? "I don't need to set any records, Onesimus. But this trip feels … I don't know, important. I mean, I know our last trip was significant, too, but … I can't explain it." She let go of the railing to raise her hands, looking at him.

He nodded, taking a slow breath. "Yes, it feels important to me, too. And I've come to love John. Until he sends me away, I'll continue with him."

"I love him, too. I didn't anticipate the great blessing Philip's original assignment would be to me. It's been incredible writing his story, too."

"Which isn't done yet," noted Onesimus with a low chuckle. "He seems like he could live forever. I know we shouldn't bet, but I'd put everything I have on him outliving me."

"Well, you're no spring chicken," she teased, "so it's not the worst bet you could make."

He laughed, grasping his chest as if wounded. "All too true, daughter of Barabbas. All too true."

Her first good view of Leptis Magna wasn't all she had built it up to be in her head, but it was indeed an impressive city. She wasn't used to so much lifeless sand and rock, but in the midst of that vast expanse had arisen a city full of fabulous buildings and thousands of palm trees. She spied the famous hippodrome in the background, along with at least one large theater and a dozen or more major temples to various gods.

As the boat bumped gently against the pier, the sailors busied themselves securing the rigging and making the ship fast in her mooring. Sophia always marveled at their agility and swiftness, and they hardly ever seemed to make a mistake. She didn't feel like she was anywhere near as physically coordinated.

John led them toward the home of the bishop of the city, having requested that the captain arrange delivery of their luggage.

Antiomnah, a trader, was away, but his wife Lydia welcomed them graciously. They had been expecting additional visitors from Rome, though John was a surprise. She told Rufus and Alexander which family they could stay with, declaring that John and his companions could room with her and her husband.

They talked with Lydia for much of the afternoon, and then John asked if Sophia could record a few thoughts he'd had during the trip. It didn't take long, and by the time they were finished, Bishop Antiomnah had returned. Dinner was served soon thereafter. They were missing Onesimus, who had left for the market when John and Sophia began their transcribing.

After the quite filling meal—Lydia kept guilting them into eating more—Sophia felt sleepy. But Antiomnah seemed full of zeal, and he wanted to talk. John obliged him, and Sophia didn't feel comfortable excusing herself. Onesimus still hadn't returned, though that didn't worry her. It was a safe city.

After a few questions about what was happening in Rome and other areas of the church, which John answered in considerable detail that made Sophia's eyelids feel even heavier, Antiomnah pegged her with a question, preceded by some flattery.

"I hear you are quite the gifted preacher, Sophia. Your mother taught you well."

She urged her mind to come fully awake as she nodded. "Thank you. Yes, she did, among others."

"Like the apostle Paul? He is very close to your family, right?" He made it sound like they were celebrities because of it.

"I learned a lot from him, and I hope I still can. We haven't seen him in a while." Thoughts of the travel-worn apostle who now enjoyed a little time to rest brought her more fully awake.

"He still travels to parts of Spain," added John, "but his body has slowed considerably. I know the Lord is grateful for all his sacrifices, and part of his reward is being with his family again. What a story that is, though he tells me he hasn't written it down yet. I hope he does."

Antiomnah folded his hands, resting them on the low table where they had recently eaten. His gaze returned to Sophia. "What is one of the most powerful lessons he ever taught you?"

She blinked, glancing at John, wishing they could do this in the morning. But a thought came, and she answered. "The Lord's perfect balance of patience and punishment. Everything God does is designed to help us, and that includes when he 'loses his patience.' Many times, my people—the Jews—strayed from the clear path Jehovah had laid before them. He was patient with them, sending prophets, showing other kinds of warnings, giving them every chance possible to turn back to him. But, at some point, it was better for them and their children that the fury of his justice be felt. Unfortunately, too often we stubbornly learn only through tragedy. And yet even in our punishments, he is patient."

She wasn't sure if Antiomnah was Jewish, but he and Lydia nodded solemnly. "The Assyrian invasion," he said, "the Babylonian captivity, the many periods of subjugation by the Philistines,

Syrians, Romans and others … yes, you are right, and I'm not sure I've heard it explained so succinctly."

"It doesn't just apply to the Jews," said Onesimus, causing Sophia to nearly jump off her rump. She hadn't heard him slip in. "The people who occupied the promised land before Joshua led the Israelites across the River Jordan had become so wicked and perverted that they had used up their chances, especially the six 'anathema' peoples, though I can't remember them all."

"I do," offered Sophia. "The Hittites, the Amorites, the Canaanites, the Perizzites, the Hivites, and the Jebusites."

Onesimus cocked an eyebrow. "That's very good. My memory is a sieve compared to yours." She blushed as he continued.

"The Lord commanded the Israelites to utterly destroy those six peoples—man, woman, child, and animal. For any other city that chose to resist peaceful integration as a tributary, every male was to be killed. The only exception to the six 'anathema' nations became the Gibeonites, of the Hivite nation, who proactively dissolved their political and cultural existence and submitted fully to Israelite leadership. Had the Israelite leaders faithfully adhered to the Lord's commands regarding the rest, a multitude of future problems could have been avoided. God knew exactly what needed to be done, for the maximum welfare of all his children, Jew and non-Jew alike, but his chosen people proved too weak and shortsighted to fulfill his commands."

That somber truth rang around the room like a giant bell, causing heads to bow.

"And then the Christ came," said Sophia in a low voice, feeling almost in a trance, "and his own people rejected him, led on by their selfish and ignorant rulers. Even then, he gave them more chances, and some few accepted him in Judea through the ministrations of his apostles and disciples, but the vast majority began to rail against his teachings, his re-introduction of the higher law, even his role as the long-prophesied great atoning sacrifice. Eventually, they were brutally destroyed by Titus and his legions in Jerusalem. Now, Israel is no more. The Romans call Jerusalem Aelia Capitolina, and Judea has become Palestina."

Silence blanketed the room, stretching nearly a full minute. John appeared to be praying, his eyes closed, but then he raised his head and spoke. "Now you see, wise Antiomnah, why I brought her, or rather, why the Lord called her to assist me. Onesimus, too. We have much work to do here, and I trust you and your fellow saints in Leptis Magna can help us arrange some audiences."

Antiomnah bowed low from his sitting position. "Yes, Apostle, we can, and we will. Together, or separately?"

"Separately," said John. "Just assign some of your flock to accompany us at each location."

"Very well. It shall be done."

John dismissed them all, then—except for Onesimus, who scrounged himself something to eat. Sophia gratefully retired to her bed.

Morning came far too early, but she got herself moving. Antiomnah and Lydia's house had some indoor plumbing, which was wonderful, and she soon felt clean and refreshed. She skipped breakfast, though, complaining of an unsettled stomach. That might not have been the best ploy, because Lydia expressed anguished guilt that her cooking had adversely affected her. Sophia assured her it happened to her from time to time. That seemed to allay Lydia's concerns.

Their morning was largely free, since Antiomnah needed time to set up some forums for them to teach in later that day.

John, Onesimus, and she studied and prayed together, seeking the Spirit to help them prepare their approach. At midday, they all refused food, though they took water. By the time Antiomnah returned with the good news that some arrangements had been made, Sophia felt nervous, but ready. A man and his wife would accompany her. Rufus and Alexander would go with Onesimus, while John asked Antiomnah and Lydia to be his companions.

As the eleventh hour of the day came, announced by several bells in the city, Sophia found herself on a small hilltop, surrounded by large homes and a lesser temple, bathed in the sun that wasn't long from setting. The grass of the hill wasn't like what she was used to in Rome—it was drier, thinner, and yellowish. Several curved rows of stone benches formed a half-circle around a central point. Clearly, the area had been designed as a place to present and debate ideas.

As she stood at the center and watched people enter the area and sit on the benches, she noted several curious and skeptical expressions. When it seemed like no more would be coming, she did a quick count: forty-five, all men. The only other woman was the sister who had brought her there with her husband.

"Salvation," Sophia began, her hesitancy softened by her two companions, who sat just in front of her, smiling encouragingly, "is impossible for mere mortals to comprehend. Even lesser gods, if such there are, can scarce grasp it, which is why they gallivant around the world with such importunate spontaneity." She had meant to sound erudite, having rehearsed that line.

"But all things denote there is an all-wise Creator. We did not design ourselves, nor can we sustain ourselves without much assistance. The moon and the stars, moving in their regular courses, also proclaim the wisdom of their Creator, who is God. One God, above all. All-knowing and all-powerful.

"But who are we? Why are we self-aware? How can we reason as we do? Is it because, unlike the animals, or the birds, or the insects, we contain a spark of our Creator within us? Indeed, it must be, for we are his children. And as his offspring, we have our agency, so that we may learn from our experiences.

"However, he does not leave us entirely alone. If he did, we would soon become extinct. History has shown us that stark reality over and over again, and it is only by the goodness and grace of God that we still continue as a human race, sojourning on this difficult but ultimately rewarding planet."

She paused there, gathering her next thoughts. She expected a question or two as well, but it seemed the men didn't yet deign to grace her with one. Or, they hadn't yet decided how they would try to embarrass her.

"By his Spirit, and even by his holy angels, who wield a portion of his power, God grants us a share of his wisdom—not to force us, but to guide us. He also provides us a way to be redeemed of the many sins we have committed, and which we continue to commit day by day despite our best efforts. That great, supernal gift is the atonement of sins performed by the Son of God himself, Jesus Christ, the only person to have lived a perfect life. Through him, we can be forgiven of our sins, so that when we all stand before God to be judged at the end of this life—the inevitable end—we may be clean and therefore rejoice in his presence. Otherwise, we will not be able to abide his glory, and we might wish that the mountains would fall upon us to hide us and our filthiness from his presence."

"You are too young to have seen this Jesus," said one man, eyes pinning her like a hawk's.

"I am," she admitted, "but my father met him. His name was Barabbas. It was he who was set free by Pontius Pilate so that Jesus would be crucified—as God and Jesus knew needed to happen."

The man's eyes widened a little, and whispers arose from the group as they consulted with each other. They would know the name Pontius Pilate, who had later been banished and apparently gone insane. Her father's name was also widely recognized. It clearly surprised them. That was good.

"I am here in your city with John, one of Jesus's original apostles. He traveled with Jesus. He saw him perform many miracles. John, too, has performed miracles, including healings."

"Where is he?" asked another man.

"Teaching elsewhere." She couldn't tell whether he was implying she wasn't worth listening to, especially if one of the famed original apostles was in the city. Of course, 'famed' meant something different to most people than it did to her. To them, Jesus was an interesting legend, orbited by multitudes of stories and parables that could be poked and prodded for intellectual stimulation. But it was their spirits she hoped to touch, not just their minds, or even their hearts. Then they could widen their natural connection to God, their Father, and it would mean everything to them.

"You are intelligent," added the man. "That can be seen, but you are a woman. You have no authority."

She said a silent prayer before answering that insult. "My commission to teach comes from God, through his apostles. If I speak truth, the Spirit will testify of it to all who will open their eyes and ears." She realized she had just cast her own insult, so she looked away from the man and continued quickly. "There are hundreds of witnesses of Jesus Christ's resurrection. This is well documented. And the promise to all of us is that we will be resurrected in like manner, to then inherit the kingdom which we merit based on our thoughts, words, and deeds in this life.

"We have many other evidences of the next life. People have been visited by dead ancestors, including parents and siblings.

Others have died, then resuscitated after a short time, relating what they saw. Yet others have been visited by angels of God, while some, we must admit, have been deceived by servants of the devil. All of this is real, and none of us is smart enough to understand it without some divine help. So don't believe *me*; I am indeed just a woman, as you said." She finally let her eyes fall again upon the man who had made the comment, but without any anger in her tone or expression, before adding, "Each of us can commune with God, without need of a mortal intermediary, and if we are humble and sincere, he will answer our questions."

She had definitely surprised them, which was probably both good and bad. Some seemed to be seriously considering her words, while others obviously grew frustrated and restless.

"Has he spoken to you?" asked a third man, clearly skeptical.

"Not directly, as you and I are speaking. Very few have been afforded that opportunity. But I pray to him every day, and I try to do good, and he constantly shows me he is listening, and paying attention, and helping. I have witnessed far too many miracles to deny his genuine concern and power. I would be the greatest of fools if I tried. I have seen an angel, however ... though for a different purpose."

The man squinted, glancing at a few of his companions. "And what was that purpose?"

"He saved my life from certain death at the hands of a sword-wielding man possessed by a demon. He has since spared me at least once more."

"You cannot prove that."

"Of course not," she said, a touch of snap to her voice, "not physically. But God knows it happened, and God knows you, personally."

There. Let them draw their conclusions. She felt the Spirit witnessing, though it appeared most of the men cut themselves off from its utterings. A man in the back stood, the first of the exodus. Would they all end up leaving? Would her first sermon be an abject failure?

"I would like to hear more," he said, causing her eyes to widen in wonder. "I have witnessed miracles, too, and have never been able to determine from whence they specifically originate. I would also not be accused of having a closed mind."

That seemed to sway a few others, but most turned and chuckled, waving him off and making snide comments about his gullibility, or even his concupiscence, which made her blush. At that point some of the men did leave, followed by others over the next minute or so. In the end, about a quarter of the original group remained, and they congregated closer to her. The Christian couple accompanying her emerged from their rigor mortis, sliding over to allow them to bunch together.

She searched for something else to say, but nothing came, so she took questions. The answers flowed, the Spirit strengthened, and by the time the dinner hour arrived, with the sun hidden below the horizon, she felt spent, mind and body.

After dinner, back at the house, John asked her how it had gone. Onesimus hadn't returned from his teaching, though again, she wasn't concerned.

"It was all men, and a few actually listened." She smiled, reinforcing the joke, and John laughed.

"Well done! We men have minds like mules, by and large, though once you get us on the right course, we generally don't stop." He winked.

"Unless an angel stands in your path," she quipped, reminding him of Balaam's experience.

He laughed harder. "As long as nobody beats me with a staff." He was in a good mood.

"Your preaching went well, I take it?" she asked.

He shook his head, still smiling. "No. It went horribly, actually, but I did my best, and they are my brothers and sisters. They have their precious agency. Tomorrow will bring more opportunity."

"Well, my group wondered why they didn't get to listen to you instead of me, because I'm a woman."

John gave several long nods. "And I'm sure you set them straight on that point."

She looked away shyly. "I tried."

"So, will you continue the conversation with those men tomorrow?"

She returned her gaze to him, feeling the excitement of her answer. "Yes. And some said they would bring kindred and friends. Would you … come with me? Your additional witness will help."

He crinkled his brow, considering it. Then he nodded. "Yes, I will. I'll ask Onesimus to come, too. This appears to be a good core group to start with."

"What about *me*?"

The voice came from the front doorway, and it … it couldn't be.

"Simon?" She leapt to her feet as she turned. And there he was. Her brother, in the flesh.

Onesimus followed right behind him. "Look who I found today." He grinned as Sophia rushed to give Simon a hug. She couldn't help the sobs escaping. She had been thinking about him more than she admitted to herself.

"Where are Mother and Father?" she asked as she held him tight.

He was crying, too. "They left for Rome not long ago. We received a note from Philip about your mission here, and so I came."

She released him, pushing him away slightly to view his face. "You just left your business?"

"It'll keep."

"You wanted to see me so badly?" She raised an eyebrow, giving him a half smile.

"Of course," he replied, shrugging. "You're … Sophia."

"That is my name, yes." One of the dreaded giggles escaped, and she led him back to the group, who had all stood. She introduced him to everyone, then begged them all to sit again. Instead, John and Onesimus excused themselves, as did Antiomnah and Lydia, leaving her and Simon alone. That was perfect. They must have sensed it.

"So, how are you, Simon?"

He rolled his shoulders. "I'm okay."

She studied his eyes, searching for the right words. She knew he was hurting, profoundly. "I'm so sorry about Porcia and the girls. It's not fair."

He stared sadly at the table. "Well, Porcia and her parents think it's fair. And I can't really do anything about it."

"What happened to her?"

He took a couple of deep breaths before responding. "Her parents had a disagreement with the bishop of Rome, something about not granting them a contract for some work. I guess they let that fester, then began criticizing other leaders and members. They shared all of this with Porcia, by the way, without my knowledge. Eventually, they left the church altogether, and convinced her to do the same."

"But why did they want to split up your family?"

He raised his eyes, and she caught both deep pain and a lingering anger. "Because they don't consider me part of their family. Porcia and the girls are, but not me."

"That's cruel, and wrong." She felt her own ire rising.

"It's what happened to Paul." He looked down again.

"That's true. I don't know how he endured that. And for so many years. He finally got them back, though. All of them."

Simon didn't respond. Nary a muscle twitched.

"Is there anything I can do?"

He met her eyes again, wearing a wan smile. "Just being here with you for a bit helps. I'm glad I found you so quickly … thanks to Onesimus."

"What have your prayers been like?" she asked.

His smile went crooked. "I haven't been praying much. I'm too numb, and I doubt the Lord wants to hear me complain, anyway."

Part of her wanted to instantly correct him, forcefully, but she let the pause lengthen.

"I'm happy you're here," she finally said, her voice soft and serious. "And if *I* want to hear from you, how much more does your Father in Heaven? He knows far more than I do. He knows you're hurting, and he loves you perfectly. He can help. He already has plans to help. He helped Paul."

He grimaced. "And it took decades. I'm not as strong as Paul."

She gave a slight nod. "Paul was strong because he submitted himself to the Lord's will and the Lord made him strong. He pleaded for that strength with much faith, too, and it was granted. I … I'm sorry, I can't understand how hard this is for you, or how hard it was for him. I just *know* the Lord will help you. I do. And I pray for you like crazy, by the way." It was true. She did.

He started to sob again, softly, covering his eyes with a hand, his lips a twisted mess. "I know. Mother and Father have been, too. It's just … so hard."

She scooted closer so she could put an arm around his shoulders. He leaned in, and she held him like that for a few minutes, rocking slowly side-to-side, picturing the faces of her former sister-in-law and her two nieces. She had never met Porcia's parents.

"Will you pray now … with me?" she asked.

He didn't respond for several seconds, but then nodded, and they shifted into kneeling positions, holding each other's hands. Simon had always known how to say powerful prayers. This one started out weak and timid, but he gained strength as the minutes passed. Peace eventually settled over them.

———

Several days passed. Her teaching group fluctuated, but it grew more than it shrank. She generally taught in the same place, and Simon went with her everywhere. She asked him to tell the story about when he had run away from home to the prisoner caves on Melita after persecution from some of the Jewish children on the island, and how their father had miraculously found and rescued him. He related how he had come to know Morech and Antonius, who later became the apostle Paul's unlikely traveling companions. He also described the mysterious and supernatural mooring stone, which kept her audience enthralled. Together, they depicted their father's interactions with Emperor Nero, along with Peter and Paul. Paul's rescue and Peter's death elicited strong reactions. Both men were well known.

The day before Simon had to leave, two city officials appeared at the small hill, wearing determined looks and seeming none too happy. Instead of worrying about it, Sophia greeted them like long-lost friends. Others made them feel welcome, too, and before they could lodge any sort of complaint, or threaten her arrest, they had become part of the group, listening intently and even asking sincere questions.

Simon teased her about it before he left the next morning, wondering out loud which one's son she would marry. She slapped him playfully ... and repeatedly. It was difficult to see him go, but his countenance had improved considerably. She felt like she had done some good for him. She and the Lord.

John and Onesimus accompanied her again the day after that, along with Rufus and Alexander, Antiomnah and Lydia, and John asked if any there wished to be baptized. About two dozen men and women stood, and John immediately led them down the hill, through the city, and along the shoreline to a secluded spot, the rest of the group tagging along, including children. A few others joined the group along the way, their total number swelling to well over a hundred.

It was a most spectacular day, and she prayed many more like it would follow.

CHAPTER 10

*He that hath the Son hath life; and he that
hath not the Son of God hath not life.*

1 John 5:12

John hadn't intended for them to spend an entire year in Leptis Magna, but the work proceeded apace, miracles of conversion and healing abounding. That next spring, however, he bought them passage to Caesarea in Mauretania. Before departing, they helped Antiomnah and Lydia make sure all the new members were organized and supported, their names recorded and sent to the new regional headquarters in Carthage. Then they took to their ship.

Rufus and Alexander had already moved on to Cyrenaica with a land caravan. Sophia had thought that might be the best route for John's group, too, in the opposite direction, but John suddenly felt an urgency. She couldn't complain too much. Once they approached Carthage, they stayed relatively close to the coast. The scenery was varied and interesting, much greener than the areas around Leptis Magna, with what looked like real mountains looming near. Carthage itself was magnificent, and she added it to her list of places she would like to either visit or revisit someday.

When they entered the bay protecting Caesarea, Sophia noticed several warships exiting.

"Where do you think they're going?" she asked Onesimus as they leaned against the railing.

He watched them for a few moments. "Not a clue. Maybe they're just training. Or they delivered or picked up someone important. Or they're on patrol. The Great Sea is generally peaceful, but I've heard of pirate activity this far west."

"Pirates?"

"Yes. Piracy ebbs and flows. Vespasian deals harshly with pirates, and he takes enforcement seriously, so it isn't a big problem, unless … well, like I said, we're pretty far west, and this southern edge of the Great Sea is less populated, with more places for pirates to hide."

"How do you hide a large ship?"

He chuckled. "I don't know. I guess you'll have to become a pirate to find out."

She pretended to take him seriously. "Hmmm … I'll have to give that some thought."

"Maybe John will join you," he suggested. "But I'll pass." He maintained his smile as he studied the city growing larger before them. Broad plains extended beyond, with some hills just to the west. It didn't look as grand as Leptis Magna, but the Romans had definitely put their stamp on it. The area produced a fair amount of grain and other commodities, and rich mines dotted the mountains to the south, so the empire kept it well protected. The large, high-walled fort near the water made that clear.

"I miss Leptis Magna," she said, the feeling bubbling up to become verbalized thought.

"Huh," he said, looking at her, "I thought you might. We did well there. The weather was warm, the food good, and we baptized many souls."

"I don't feel as good about this place."

He stood straight, scanning the city and countryside. "Oh, I don't know. I think we'll find a few more Jews here. Perhaps that's where John wants to start. It could be interesting."

She felt a sudden pain in her stomach, reflexively placing a hand on it as a groan escaped.

Onesimus turned instantly, eyes filled with concern. "What's wrong?"

She wasn't sure. She had felt fine just seconds ago. "I don't know, but the pain was sharp. It's still there, just … duller."

"Right side, left side, or middle?"

"Middle."

He breathed a short sigh of relief. "Probably not serious. Food poisoning maybe?"

"I have an iron stomach," she said, but then clenched as the pain intensified again. "My mother … always … said so." She was wheezing at the end, doubled up near the rail. Onesimus took to a knee, hand on her arm.

"You should lie down. We're still a few minutes out, and we don't need to get off the ship immediately. John and I will speak with the captain."

She nodded. That sounded like a good idea. Then she felt a powerful urge to vomit, and she thrust her head over the rail. In seconds, she was emptying her stomach, loudly and embarrassingly. She hoped that would make her feel better, but while her stomach hurt less for the moment, she felt drained and even a little dizzy. She wiped her mouth, then let Onesimus escort her below to the small bed where she had slept. It wasn't a proper cabin, but sheets hung from wooden pegs gave at least a veneer of privacy.

She didn't intend it, but sleep stole upon her almost immediately. When she awakened, it was to scramble up to the deck and puke over the side again. Her insides had become a mass of knots, her body weakened further. She started as Onesimus appeared beside her.

"Feeling any better?"

She shook her head groggily.

"You only slept for about an hour."

She finally noticed that the sun was still up, but she didn't take the time to fix its exact position. She stood for a few moments, then started walking back to the stairs. "I'll be all right. Just a bug. Shouldn't last more than a day."

Unfortunately, it did. She tried to drink some water the next morning, but it came right back up. Same at midday and evening. In her haze, she noticed John had been gone, though Onesimus still attended her.

"Where's John?"

"He'll be back soon," Onesimus assured her.

"He may need to heal me," she mumbled, though she wasn't sure her vocal chords had actually generated any sound.

By the next morning, she was barely conscious of what was happening. John did return, and he brought others. They carried her off the ship, then walked for what seemed like eternity before entering a darkened room which was blessedly cool. She struggled to focus on the apostle as they laid her on a soft bed.

"Can you heal me?" she asked through chapped lips.

"The Lord can," he replied, "if it is his will. I would have already offered if I felt he wanted me to, but he stays my hand for the moment."

"Why?" Her mind had trouble processing all the words, but the general gist came through. It induced a strong protest inside which she could barely express.

"Rest, child. Many of the saints here, me included, have been fasting for you."

As the knots in her belly tightened again, she took small comfort from that. She tried to reach out to Heavenly Father, but found the connection difficult to make. Before long, she had slipped back into an uneasy sleep.

She awoke some time later, pinpricks of light through the blanketed window telling her it was still daytime. She realized at least two days had passed. Her body had become dehydrated. She would need liquid soon. A picture of a palm tree popped into her mind, and she turned her head to see if anyone else was in the room. Onesimus jumped up from a stool, stepping over and kneeling at her side.

"Yes, Sophia?"

She realized she had tried to ask a question, though she couldn't remember what words she had used. She took a pair of labored breaths, trying to clear her head. She tried to produce some moisture in her mouth, but with almost no success.

"Coconut," she was finally able to whisper.

He cocked his head, staring at her in perplexity for a moment, but then his eyes widened and he nodded.

"Coconut milk. If you'd like to try that, I'll get you some."

She attempted to move her chin up and down. She didn't feel it respond, but Onesimus bounded to his feet and left the room. Her eyes closed, and she drifted off again. When she awoke, it was dark. Someone had lit a small candle in the room. As her eyes fluttered open, she spotted John and Onesimus, the latter wringing his hands in some distress. He was immediately on his knees next to the bed. John reached down for a cup on the floor and handed it to him.

"Here," said Onesimus. "The coconut milk you asked for. We … um, we blessed it. John feels you were inspired to ask for it."

She couldn't remember any of that. Her stomach didn't hurt, though, and she was able to nod.

Onesimus reached a hand behind her, cradling her neck as he lifted her head a foot or more. He brought the cup up, coaxing it between her lips, then tipping it. The cool liquid touched, and she sucked a little in, forcing it down her throat with a difficult swallow. The next sip was easier, but then her throat wanted to rest for a few seconds. Onesimus kept the cup in place, thankfully, and she took a few more small swallows before closing her lips tight. He took the signal and laid her gently back down.

John stood at his shoulder, peering down at her with concern shimmering in his eyes. He closed them briefly, then nodded. "You will be well, Sophia. Rest now. We will bring more in the morning."

"I'll stay again," said Onesimus.

"Very well," said John, "but you will sleep this time. Maris will bring you a pillow and blanket."

Maris? She hadn't heard that name before. Her mind couldn't dwell on it, though, as it slipped beneath the waves again.

She had kept the coconut milk down, she realized, as her eyes came open in the morning. She smelled fresh air wafting in from the window, too, energized by an audibly strong breeze. She enjoyed that for a few moments, then forced herself to sit up, surprised she had the energy to do so. As she swung her legs over the side of the bed, she clocked Onesimus in the chin. He had been getting himself to a sitting position, and the timing was perfect. She nearly laughed, even as she winced.

"I'm sorry," she whispered.

He acted like it hadn't even happened. He knelt again at her bedside. "You are feeling better?" he asked, voice somewhat tremulous.

She nodded. "Yes, quite a bit."

"I'll talk to Maris, get you more coconut milk."

"Thank you," she said as he rose and rushed out of the room. His running footfalls took him to another part of this strange house, and then she heard some whispers. A minute later, he reappeared with another cup, flanked by John.

He started to bring it to her lips, but she lifted a hand and grasped it herself. It took him a second to let go, but then he stood, face still creased with worry.

She drank, and not daintily. She was so thirsty! She thrust the empty cup at him. "More, please. And some food."

"Not too much," cautioned John. "You appear to be quite a bit better, but we should be cautious and let you regain your full strength."

"How long since we docked?" she asked.

"Four days now."

She shook her head in disbelief. "So this last sleep was … more than a day?"

He gave a small smile as he nodded. "Yes, and apparently your body needed it. You had us worried, though, especially Onesimus. He hasn't left your side."

She stared at her faithful companion and protector, who seemed a bit embarrassed. "I know, and I'm grateful. But he'll learn." She smiled, letting it broaden until he finally got the joke. His whole body seemed to relax a bit then, and he ran a hand through his hair.

"She's definitely back," he said to John. "No more peace for us."

Within a day she felt normal again. Maybe a little weak still, but normal. In the afternoon, John said he needed to visit a tailor, and Sophia jumped at the chance to accompany him. Onesimus, of course, came, too.

It was the first time she had really seen the city. It was busy, and there were so many children running around she could hardly focus. They were a good distraction, though. After a while, she realized they couldn't have been taking a direct path to wherever this tailor might be.

She mentioned it to John. "Wherever we're going, we're taking the long way."

"Yes, we are," was all he offered in response.

She quirked an eyebrow at Onesimus, on her other side, and he shrugged.

"Why?" she asked John, her tone merely curious, not plaintive.

He glanced at her. "I'm looking for someone."

"Oh. Who is that?"

"I don't know."

She was no longer surprised at such answers. And she couldn't complain. It felt good to be walking. The longer, the better, a notion she never thought she'd entertain.

They finally made it to the tailor, where John picked up a new tunic and cloak. She was glad. She had been avoiding telling him that what he currently wore was so threadbare not even mice could live in it. The new wardrobe had some color, too, which Onesimus remarked on.

"I thought you were colorblind."

"I've been healed," deadpanned John, raising the garment to inspect it. "Plus, now I won't be such an embarrassment to Sophia." He turned to her and winked, and they all chuckled.

"It *will* be a relief to see you dressed properly," she said, then added in a more serious tone, "and thank you for healing me."

His look was one of surprise. "I did no such thing. The Lord helped you through that ordeal."

She felt herself blushing a little. "It wasn't much of an 'ordeal.' Many people have suffered far worse."

"As did the Savior," said John as he led them out of the small shop. "I used to wonder why he felt he had to suffer so many different things, and even die an agonizing death. The excruciating propitiation for our sins should have been more than enough suffering, and it didn't require him to actually die, though the resurrection, of course, did. And even in that case, he could have shed his mortal body on his own, without any 'help' from the Romans, and then taken it back up again. Some of us thought that's what he might do."

Sophia had never thought about it in quite that way, though she had wondered what it was like for the apostles and disciples to be with him, knowing he was the Messiah and hearing him talk about his own death at the hands of evil people.

"So … why did he?" She thought she knew the answer, at least in part. Others, including her parents, had expounded on the far-reaching effects of Christ's willingness to suffer.

John kept his eyes scanning the street. He was clearly still looking for this mysterious person the Lord had prompted him to find. "Because he wanted to know us better, to understand all the experiences of mortality, the good and the bad. He endured not only physical and emotional suffering, of course, but other tests that aren't necessarily mortal in nature, like betrayal and humiliation."

"The humiliation must have been demanding," she remarked. "He was the Son of God, more powerful than all the Roman legions combined, and his own people treated him like a diseased dog … or a leper."

"Some of his own people, yes. But he had schooled and prepared himself. And he never, ever, not even for a sliver of a moment, lost sight of his greatest goal, motivated by his never-ending love for us."

"But he asked if the cup might be removed. He told you that."

"Yes, but he was only asking if there might be another way to achieve the goal, at the point when his suffering for our sins—which we cannot begin to comprehend yet—was at its most agonizing. He never wavered in his willingness to do what needed to be done, and he trusted his Father completely. Given everything, that in itself is truly remarkable, and it never ceases to amaze me."

She nodded thoughtfully, feeling a powerful warmth in her chest, accompanied by an enlightening of her mind. "And he revealed that none of those trials had diminished him when he spoke to the two thieves hanging from their own crosses, and to his disciples who were there. In fact, they had enhanced him further."

John stopped, almost causing Sophia to stumble. She turned toward him, noting the tears in his eyes as he gazed into the far distance.

"I still remember that scene as if it were yesterday. I took charge of his mother at his request. I tried to console Mary over the next two days, but she did more to comfort me than I her. And then the hallowed morning of the resurrection came, and I was blessed to be one of the first to see him in his body again, alive. I thought I had believed before, but I had been a mere child. His return was glorious beyond all description."

"I wish I could have seen that," she said.

"Well," he replied, his demeanor lightening again, "everything is present with God, so someday he can show it to you, as if you were there. And perhaps you were, in spirit."

That was something to think about, and she did, for several minutes as they walked. Their route again became circuitous, but beyond stopping and speaking to a few people and getting to know the area better, they didn't find anything that seemed remarkable to John.

He was quieter than usual that evening at dinner in the home of the Christian couple hosting them, but he didn't mention any concerns. Instead, they made plans for their preaching in the city. John had already spent some time with the local bishop and a few of the elders, and they would have plenty of help. Given her renewed health, Sophia was excited to get started.

The first two weeks were a little slow, but then things began to pick up. They taught together and separately, in conjunction with many of the local members. They preached in homes, in synagogues, in plazas, and on street corners. They even ventured down to the dock areas to engage with the many sailors, though that environment was a little rougher than Sophia preferred. She kept reminding herself that those people were children of God, too. He cared about them, and they had once known him. They could come to know him again.

Baptisms came even more gradually, but each one was a joy. The members worked hard to make sure the new converts were welcomed and nurtured in the way of Christ. They also organized efforts to help the poorer residents of the city, and to improve some of the public works. Not only did that put them in good stead with their neighbors and city officials, it opened new avenues to the preaching of the gospel. That aligned with Jesus's approach, which both relieved suffering and challenged traditional beliefs.

They became so busy that Sophia mostly forgot about John's mission to find this particular person that would apparently join their group. When she did remember, she prayed it would be another woman. Not that she didn't enjoy John and Onesimus's company, of course, and her Christian sisters in the city were wonderful, but it would be nice to have a close female companion in the work … and on their travels.

As they journeyed to a synagogue one morning, they approached a building being constructed—brand new from the ground up. It appeared to be either a very large house or a minor administrative building, which made her wonder why anyone would want a house that looked like Roman offices. She wouldn't.

As they began to pass by, she heard a loud crash, followed by several men shouting, then more chaotic clattering. Dust billowed from one section of the structure, near the back. More shouting erupted, followed by additional disturbing rumblings.

She, John, and Onesimus stopped and observed, though they shuffled to the other side of the street. The dust clouds grew, and while the shouting subsided, several men began coughing. Sleeves over mouths, they emerged from the minor storm, heads low as they squinted. They spread out, eight of them in all, joining her and her companions in staring at the building from across the road. Half seemed relieved, the other half deeply frustrated.

One of them turned to two of the others, his voice the lash of a whip.

"What did I tell you about securing that column? At least three times I said it needed to be done. And now look"—he gestured at the spreading haze—"we've put ourselves back at least a week. Why didn't you listen? Were the words I used too big for you?"

The two men hardened their faces, looking away.

"Answer me!" the man persisted. "Tell me why! If you can't, you're no longer on this crew."

They glared at him, then huffed and walked away. One turned back to say, "You work us too hard. We're not your slaves."

The mention of slaves caught Sophia's attention. She glanced at Onesimus, but he showed no reaction. It was a common turn of phrase.

"Excuse me, young man," said John, tapping the man's shoulder. He appeared to be the leader of the work crew.

The man turned, the consternation on his face still pronounced. "Yes, what is it? You weren't hurt, were you?" Worry joined his expression.

"What is your name?"

The man looked confused for a moment, then glanced at Onesimus and Sophia, pausing longer on her. She tried not to roll her eyes.

"Daniel."

John nodded. "Daniel. Well, we were sent to find you. I am John. This is Onesimus and Sophia."

Sophia blinked, barely arresting her jaw from dropping. *This* was the person they were looking for? A man who worked his men so hard they nearly killed themselves? Then berated them in public? That wasn't uncommon, but it still seemed … surprising. She studied the man for a moment. Dark, wavy hair, brown eyes, strong shoulders that weren't overly broad, a nose less prominent than most Romans, almost as tall as Onesimus. And covered in dust. His hair was probably darker than it appeared.

The man shook his head vigorously, throwing particles of dirt and rock in every direction. "I don't understand. Who sent you? And why? There's no inspection scheduled until next week, and I'm going to have to delay that one." He grimaced, turning to stare at the building again. It didn't look too bad to Sophia's untrained eye … at least not from the front.

"What if I said God asked me to find you? More specifically, Jehovah."

Daniel whipped back around, eyes narrowing. "You're Jewish?"

John smiled. "In a way, yes. We are Jewish Christians."

Sophia expected some sort of exotic eruption, especially from a man with a temper. Most men had tempers, of course, which was one reason she was happily unmarried. Instead, Daniel's gaze became thoughtful.

"So … God showed me to you?"

"Not beforehand, no, and we didn't know exactly where to look. We've been wandering a fair bit. But when I saw you just now, I knew." John's tone of confidence and authority clearly made an impact. But then two of the other workers approached.

"Boss, we need to start cleaning this up."

Daniel glanced at them and nodded, waving a hand. "Yes, go. I'll join you in a minute."

The men gave him a quizzical look, which they also shared with Sophia, Onesimus, and John, but they gathered their comrades and trudged back toward the structure.

"What does that mean?" asked Daniel. He seemed eerily calm and intense. He reminded her a little of Fyodr, and she shivered. "Are the Christians here looking for a builder?"

John's eyes brightened. "Why yes, we are. Jesus of Nazareth was himself a builder, expert in the working of wood and stone, like his earthly father. But he is also a master builder of souls, like Elohim, his Heavenly Father. He calls you, too, to be a builder of souls. Your other skills will prove useful, but they rank secondary to that."

Daniel shook his head again. "I'm confused. You just said you need a builder, but that my skills are secondary to what God is looking for. Do you want my help or not? My crew and I will be working on this building for at least another month, and I have a job scheduled after that which will take about three."

John gave a soft chuckle. "Don't worry about that right now. I can see you have much to do today. We would like to visit you later, though. Where do you live?"

Daniel seemed unsure whether he should tell them or not, but he did, and it was up on the western hills, close to the sea. He said his sister and her family lived there, too. Their parents had passed away of a swift contagion that attacked the lungs some months back. He said a farewell, and their group continued toward the synagogue. John started humming, seeming quite pleased.

"He's probably a member of the synagogue we're visiting," noted Sophia. "I wonder if he attends much."

John paused his humming after a moment. "I doubt it, though he appears to be a good man."

Sophia's eyebrows shot up, and she cast Onesimus an expression of disbelief before lodging her disagreement with John. "He seemed rude, arrogant, and intemperate to me. Why would you say he's a good man?"

John smiled as he looked at her. "He was involved in a tense situation, and he calmed quickly compared to what I have seen with a great many other men."

"We distracted him," she argued. "We were strangers, and maybe he thought we were important, so he needed to behave."

He gave a thoughtful nod. "Perhaps. But I still felt good about him, and the Lord most certainly has chosen him for something. So, we will see. Hopefully we can learn more this evening at his home."

She grumbled a bit at that, but then decided to put it out of her mind. They had a task to perform that morning, and she needed to focus.

Their visit with one of the rabbis did not go well, especially when John told him about Daniel.

"That man is a sinner!" declared the old man.

"How so?" asked John. "Which commandments delivered by the Lord to Moses does he break?"

The rabbi huffed. "Well, none of *those* that I know of, except the Sabbath, I'm sure. He likes to take long hikes, I hear."

John wrinkled his forehead. "The core law is to keep the Sabbath holy and not to do our common work on that day unless it cannot be reasonably avoided. The additional statues that have arisen over the centuries are ostensibly designed to build fences to help us keep the law, but many of them are far too burdensome, and they often prevent us from doing *good* on the Sabbath, which is a critical part of keeping it holy."

"Yes, I know you Christians take a different, twisted view," said the rabbi pointedly, "but you have lost your way following this itinerant, unsound preacher."

John was respectful but bold in his response. "Jesus healed on the Sabbath." He raised a finger. "And not by Beelzebub, but by the Spirit of God, as all those healed attested. He took care of the spiritual—and sometimes the physical—needs of his followers on the Sabbath. And he always, *always* kept the commandments of God while praising the Father for the opportunity. Far from being unsound, he was the only *true* sound coming from the milieu of mostly proud, self-serving, religious dictatorship, whose maniacal focus on the outer vessel blinded them to the corruption festering on the inside."

Well, it was a little more than just bold, but if respect meant telling the truth, even if it was hard to accept, then he was certainly respectful. The rabbi didn't see it that way, of course, so at that point they were asked to leave. Sophia was all right with that. This rabbi was one of the most annoying men she had ever met, and while she hoped he could eventually see the light of Christ through the fog of tradition and social expectation, she wasn't sorry she didn't have to listen to him any further that day.

In the evening, they climbed the hill to Daniel's home. Sophia had asked if she might be excused from that visit, but John encouraged her—in his insistent, apostle sort of way—to come. She didn't complain too loudly, and perhaps meeting the man's sister would prove fruitful.

Ginath was the woman's name, and she had married a local non-Jewish man named Xanthus. The name was Greek, but his heritage was difficult to discern. Their two young children were already asleep when they arrived, and it was quite late—Sophia should have begged John to at least put this visit off a day.

Daniel didn't seem surprised they had shown up, and Sophia could tell he'd already said something to his sister. They were welcomed inside and given soft cushions on which to sit in the front room. Ginath brought them something to drink, and after a few pleasantries, Daniel made the first serious comment.

"I apologize for my rudeness today. I unleashed my temper on two of my workers, and I shouldn't have, especially with others watching."

Sophia raised an eyebrow, trying to discern his sincerity. Why would he feel the need to apologize to them, whether it was heartfelt or not?

"You need not apologize to us," replied John. "You are under significant stress to complete that job, and the damage sounded serious."

Daniel frowned slightly. "Not as serious as I first thought. It did put us behind, of course. The part that frustrated me most was that we had taken over the project from another builder, and we had successfully repaired some unexpected flaws in the foundation. We were well on our way to completing the structure on time despite the repairs, which would have earned us a bonus." He shook his head. "I try to be firm but fair with my crew, and I push us pretty hard. We have done well. I fear I've become too ambitious, though."

"Oh, stop it, Daniel," said Ginath. "You are not too ambitious. You're too picky sometimes"—her eyes flicked to Sophia, who detected … pity?—"but you strive for excellence in your work, and your crew. Their families benefit from that. So do your customers."

Between Daniel's unexpected soul-baring and his sister's flash of compassion, Sophia began to feel uncomfortable. She sipped her drink as she mulled things over, then nearly dropped the cup at John's next words … which shouldn't have surprised her, but did.

"God has a work for you to do Daniel, with us."

The room became quiet. Daniel stared long and hard at John, then at Onesimus, then at Ginath and Xanthus. He avoided Sophia's gaze.

"I suspected it."

"You did?" Sophia couldn't help blurting that out. This didn't make sense. Or maybe she just didn't *want* it to make sense.

He finally looked at her. "After you left, I couldn't get you three out of my head. I knew there was something important about you, and about what you are doing. At times it felt like God was tapping me on the forehead, trying to help me wake up."

"Wake up from what?" she asked, eyes narrowed.

He shrugged. "I don't know, but I'm pretty sure John can help me figure that out." His eyes moved to the apostle, but Sophia drew them back to her.

"You realize we are Christians, right?" She cringed a little at her tone, which made it sound like she was disparaging her own people. That was silly, of course, and she disliked being silly. Heat rose along her neck.

He seemed slightly confused. "Of course. You said as much." He looked to John, as if seeking escape. "What is it God wants me to do?"

John studied him carefully for several moments, letting his eyes wander to Ginath and Xanthus as well. "I cannot say, exactly, but the first steps are clear. We need to open the scriptures with you, and teach you of Messiah."

CHAPTER 11

*Draw nigh to God, and he will draw nigh
to you. Cleanse your hands, ye sinners;
and purify your hearts, ye double minded.*

James 4:8

Sophia assumed that John would ask Daniel to leave his business immediately, but he didn't. Instead, he encouraged Daniel to finish the projects he had already committed to, while they taught him in the evenings. Sophia successfully avoided some of those meetings, finding others to attend. Onesimus, strangely, usually preferred to accompany John, which began to get a little irritating.

Less than a month later, Daniel felt ready to be baptized—another surprise. Sophia refused to be rude and skip it, especially since she had been present for all the other baptisms in the area so far. Ginath and Xanthus hadn't yet agreed to take that step, but they attended the event. No parting of the heavens occurred, but Daniel, John, and Onesimus seemed ebullient. She was happy for their little men's club.

John hadn't said when he planned to move on from Caesarea Mauretania, but it had to be soon, since Daniel wasn't scheduling any new jobs. The apostle also hadn't outlined how he intended their work to be organized once there were four of them. She assumed that she and Onesimus would teach together, while Daniel would be paired with John. That made the most sense, especially since Daniel was new to the Christian faith.

One morning, a few weeks later, John shattered those expectations at breakfast.

"Sophia, we have an appointment to teach a small group up on the west side this evening. Onesimus and I need to travel inland to one of the villages, so I'd like you and Daniel to take that assignment."

He said it so matter-of-factly she wasn't sure she'd heard correctly.

"I'm sorry, did you say me and Daniel?" The food in her mouth had just become tasteless.

"Yes. He is progressing quite well. He'll follow your lead, since you're far more knowledgeable and experienced."

Was he trying to flatter her? No, that really wasn't like John. She *was* more knowledgeable and experienced. And she was *not* an immature, frightened featherhead.

A neutral tone and expression was the best she could do. "Very well. Where will we meet?"

"He knows where it is," said John. "You can meet at his home first, and he'll guide you there."

"You look like you've swallowed a whole basket of bad fish," remarked Onesimus, a smile playing along his lips.

"Very funny. Maybe I'll like working with Daniel better than with you."

He clutched at his heart. "Ouch." He couldn't hold back the full smile, though.

She caught a slight grin from John, though he remained serious. "You will teach well together. He knows a lot of people here, and he has a good personality. I haven't met anyone who doesn't like or at least respect him—well, besides that cantankerous rabbi."

She wanted to say, "Have you met *me*?" but she refrained. She just refocused on their repast, which still lacked flavor. Onesimus chuckled, but she refused to glare at him. She was calmness personified.

―――――――

Or maybe she wasn't. She stood nervously before Daniel's door that evening, staring at the carved lintel. A multicolored cloth braid hung from a nail on one side, reaching halfway down the doorway. She'd barely said a dozen words to Daniel since his baptism. He probably thought she hated him. Of course she didn't, but she worried about working with him. And what about proprieties?

She finally knocked, then waited, hoping Ginath would open the door. But Daniel's face greeted her as it cracked open. His eyes widened as he pulled the door aside.

"Sophia?"

She swallowed, in consternation as much as uncertainty. "John didn't tell you?"

He shook his head. "No. I thought he or Onesimus would come."

"Hmmm ... well, are you ready to go?"

"Oh, um, yes, I am. Let me just grab ... I have some notes. You can come in if you like."

"That's all right. I'll wait here."

She sounded almost imperious, most certainly rude, and she winced as he retreated into the house. He was back quickly, though, holding up a hand to point past her shoulder.

"It's this way. Just a couple of minutes."

She stayed slightly behind him as they began walking, forcing herself to ward off the uncomfortable silence.

"How is your final job going?"

He seemed shocked she had asked him a question. "What? Oh, very well. We'll be done soon, ahead of schedule. I let John know."

She nodded. John hadn't mentioned anything. Not that he needed to, though it might have been helpful.

"How do you feel about teaching?"

He rolled his shoulders, avoiding her gaze. "I've been talking to people, but that's mainly one-on-one, and very informal. I've never done something like this." He sounded deeply uncertain, and a lot humbler than she expected. He was an ambitious, successful builder. He led crews of men on difficult jobs. He definitely didn't lack for confidence in his vocation.

"It's not much different," she tried to reassure him. "And because we're on the Lord's errand, he grants us more help than you might expect. I've been amazed sometimes."

He twisted to look at her, almost running into a small barrel next to a house crowding the road. "John says you're really good at this. I doubt I will be."

She was starting to feel guilty about some of her previous attitudes—more correctly, judgments—about him. "You'll do fine, I promise."

He slowed his pace slightly. "Thank you, but I'll let you do most of the talking."

She stopped, and he stumbled. "You'll *let* me?"

"What?"

"You'll let me take the lead?"

"What do you mean? Of course. Why wouldn't I?" He seemed confused, and she couldn't decide whether to be upset or amused. Then she scolded herself. Why was she being so prickly? She couldn't let her preference for not teaching with this man affect her own feelings; she especially couldn't let it disturb her teaching.

Sons and daughters of God were counting on her. Yes, that helped her regain some focus.

"Never mind," she said. "Thank you for being willing to teach tonight."

He seemed uncertain how to respond, but finally nodded. "Whatever the Lord would have me do."

They resumed walking, but less than a minute later he suddenly stopped, and it was her turn to stumble, and in a most awkward fashion. She recovered, smoothing her robe, the finest one she owned, grateful she hadn't actually tumbled into the dirt.

"We're here," he announced, gesturing toward an impressive home of two stories with large windows in the front. The door and window frames were painted a bright white, clearly discernible even at night in the scant light of a shy moon and infrequent torches.

She gathered herself, then nodded, and he knocked on the door, which was quickly answered. Within a few short minutes, they had been swept inside, introduced to about twenty people, given a brief tour of the house, which it turned out Daniel had built, and then shown to a prominent place in a large, well-lit back room, mugs of cool, refreshing water in their hands.

Sophia tried to maintain a dignified air throughout, but several of the guests had been drinking wine, and it was clear some inhibitions had been loosened. Daniel didn't seem bothered by it, though he did cast a couple of questioning glances her way. He received most of the initial attention, of course. They knew him, and she was a stranger. Plus, he had built the house! She tried to let that part annoy her a little, but somehow she failed.

As the small crowd quieted, some with glassy eyes mostly aimed toward Daniel, she decided she could use that.

"God is the master builder." Amid a few confused expressions, all attention shifted to her. "Not just of this earth and our lives, but of our families, our communities, and even nations, great and small. Like Daniel, God knows where to find the best materials and how to fit them together, following a carefully laid-out plan and utilizing a well-prepared foundation on solid ground, so that the house can withstand the trembling of the earth, the fury of the winds, and the opening of the skies, keeping all within it safe and secure."

She paused, trying to gauge reactions. She hadn't said much yet, just shared a basic concept. She gestured toward Daniel.

"Daniel, what happens if you build a sound foundation on unstable ground?"

She expected him to appear nervous given she was calling on him so early, but he seemed comfortable, at least with this particular topic.

"It will crack, eventually, and then fail, bringing down the entire structure."

"Thank you. Yes, it will fail. Jesus of Nazareth related a parable about a sower, spreading seeds on different types of ground. The seeds that fell by the wayside were immediately eaten up by the birds. Those that fell on stony ground sprouted but developed only shallow roots, so that when the sun beat upon those tender plants, they were scorched and died. Other seeds fell among thorns, which choked them so that they could bear no fruit. The remainder sprang up in good ground and flourished, bearing much fruit.

"The seeds are the words of God, such as what Daniel and I will share with you tonight. You have a choice to make regarding what kind of ground your hearts and minds will be. If you have no desire to hear God's word, which can cut sharply, the seeds will take no root in you. If you accept the word initially, but falter when the going becomes difficult, your shallow roots will perish. If you nourish the word at first, but the cares and concerns of the world take priority, you will develop nothing of lasting value from it. But if you receive the word with gladness, and diligently care for it and nourish it, it will expand your soul and bring you blessings you can scarcely imagine, both in this life and in the inevitable life to come."

A glance at Daniel showed him enthralled by her words, but he quickly regained his composure. She directed another question at him.

"Which material in the building of a house is the most important?"

He pondered a few moments, looking slightly confused, but then a light came to his eyes. "No material is more important than another. Without any one of them, the house cannot be completed and fulfill its purpose."

Sophia nodded, then smiled at the group. "So it is true with the kingdom of God. All are important, and none can say they have no need of the other."

A woman spoke up, sitting at the front. "What is this kingdom you speak of?"

It was a good question. Even some Jews didn't fully grasp it.

"It is greater than any of the kingdoms of earth, which are presided over by flawed mortal men and women. And it will last beyond this life of sorrow and trouble. It is our source of hope for eternal life, our comfort in tribulation, our peace when the storms rage around us, threatening to sweep us under the waves and drag us down to utter darkness. And it is made possible for us here by one man, born of a mortal woman but begotten by God himself, perfect in all his days, faithful in his mission to offer redemption to our souls; that man is Jesus of Nazareth, the resurrected Christ, the Savior of the world."

"But he was a Jew," objected one man in obvious confusion. "The Jewish religion is only for Jews."

Sophia gave him a compassionate grimace. "The Jews misunderstood their own religion, and their role in God's kingdom. They were not the entire house, just a portion of it. They falsely elevated themselves above all other peoples, and Jesus called them out for it, especially their leaders, many of whom he described as whited sepulchers, hiding death and decay within. Jesus didn't come to tear down the Jews, though; instead, he came to remind them of their sacred commitment to be a light to their neighbors, and to restore unto them his higher laws, which he offers to all who are willing to abide them. That they ultimately rejected him reflected their own blindness and pride. And now, the Jewish nation is no more, as Jesus himself prophesied forty years before the blood-soaked siege of Jerusalem."

The atmosphere turned appropriately somber; even those who were slightly inebriated kept the reverence.

"You are Jewish, like Daniel?" asked the woman.

Sophia nodded. "I am, by blood. And my faith is in the one who was long prophesied by my people as the lamb of the world who would become the great and last sacrifice. He offered himself up not just for the Jewish people, but for all people. We are, after all, related to each other through our very first parents, Adam and Eve, who lived here long before the tribes of Israel existed. We are, alike, sons and daughters of the same God, possessing equal potential."

The woman scrunched her brow, deep in thought, while another asked, "We have heard of this resurrected being. It is claimed that many saw him. But none of us have. How can we believe?"

"That is a good question," answered Sophia. "I myself have not seen him in the flesh, and even my parents did not see him after his resurrection, though my father met him before he was crucified. But John, the apostle I travel with, has witnessed his resurrected person, and has spoken with him. I know John, and I trust him. But, more important than that, I have asked God directly for his Spirit to guide me in the truth—not just in this thing, but in many others as well. His Spirit is real. His concern for you is genuine. He will answer your sincere prayers and reward your righteous intent."

She paused, and Daniel spoke. "I can testify that what Sophia has said is true. I had never been taught that I could commune directly with God. In fact, it seemed preposterous, and not just from a Jewish perspective. How many of you would dare claim to have spoken with Jupiter, or Venus or Mars, even through a veil?"

A few mutters and head shakes answered his question.

"One of the most important things I have learned from Sophia and her Christian companions is that I can approach God with confidence that he will hear and answer my prayers, even when I am in dire need of his forgiveness, and even if I am the poorest of persons. Because he loves me as his child."

Sophia blinked, feeling her jaw loosen and try to drop. That was … perfect. He glanced at her, then lowered his eyes to his hands.

The rest of the evening went very well, and even though a few pointed questions arose, the general mood of the group remained positive. She suspected a few would join the Lord's Church, though she felt certain she wouldn't be there to see it. Clear as a bell the message came: they would be leaving soon.

The walk back to Daniel's house was quiet. It was late, and besides some noise from the distant docks, the city rested. Daniel didn't try to engage her in any conversation.

When they arrived at his doorway, Sophia thanked him, adding, "Your testimony is strong, and it helped those people tonight."

"I hope so," he said simply, his expression … perfectly neutral. "You are a great teacher. Thank you. Good night."

Before she could come up with anything else to say, he had slipped inside and shut the door, leaving her tongue to click against the roof of her mouth.

Puzzled, she returned home, only to find that John had just left, even that late. Onesimus informed her that the apostle was finalizing some details for their voyage, which would commence in three days' time. That seemed fast. Then it occurred to her that Onesimus hadn't mentioned where exactly they would travel next.

"Where is the ship bound?"

Onesimus gave her a perplexed look, as if he were still coming to grips with the answer himself. "Joppa."

Her frank expression of surprise made him shrug. "Joppa? We're going to Judea?"

Onesimus nodded. "He plans to visit Jerusalem, then journey to Pella and Galilee. A few saints have returned to Jerusalem. Quite a few families, in fact. It must be difficult, especially since the temple was completely destroyed."

She plopped down on a floor cushion, pondering a minute before looking back up at him as he perched on a chair. "I hope they don't think they're going to rebuild it. That won't happen for a very long time."

"That's what John said. Maybe he means to persuade them from pursuit of that fantasy."

"Perhaps." She tapped a finger on her lips, then gathered her hands in her lap. "I taught with Daniel tonight, and it went extremely well, thank you for asking."

He chuckled apologetically. "Sorry. I'm glad it went well. He seems sincere, and smart. Maybe not as smart as you, but—"

"*Maybe* not as smart?" she asked, cocking an eyebrow. Then she blushed. "Oh my, that sounded arrogant. That's awful."

"It's okay," he reassured her. "I'll remind you of your snoring to keep you humble. And the way you gasp when you see a baby spider." He started laughing as she threw a cushion at him, but then he stopped, his mien becoming somber.

"Seeing Jerusalem will humble all of us."

Her breath caught in her throat, a wave of sadness washing through her. Her grandparents had died there, among nearly a million others. A million! The thought was overwhelming. Onesimus was right. They would be reminded that they truly were the dust of the earth.

The ship's captain must have known they were Jews, and he must not have liked Jews much. While willing to take their coin, he was also more than happy to remind them frequently that they were sailing toward Palestina, and he talked often of the time he had visited Aelia Capitolina. He never mentioned 'Judea' or 'Jerusalem,' implying that such names never existed. He never talked of the Jews, either, referring only to the 'Roman citizens' who lived there. That was probably for the better—she didn't need to hear his specific opinions on her blood relatives.

She realized she did still consider them her people. At least in a few important ways. She was descended from Miriam, Moses's sister, and while Miriam had exhibited her share of weaknesses, she was a great woman. Her people had labored diligently over the centuries to meticulously record the words of the prophets, along with the laws and the statues given by the Lord. Jesus himself had oft quoted those scriptures, which were still valid and contained many valuable prophecies not yet fulfilled. Her people had committed great sins against their generous lawgiver in the past, and they were fast becoming a hiss and a byword across the empire, but they had done great things, too. Many had shown remarkable faith, and a significant number had accepted their long-awaited Messiah and now strived to follow his higher laws and ordinances.

The captain's attitude didn't seem to bother John at all, though Onesimus became rankled by it from time to time. He never made a comment directly to the captain, but he said things within hearing of some of the crew, usually related to unfairly judging people you don't know. It was pretty tame, though.

For her own part, as long as nobody was accusing her of being a snoring witch, Sophia was happy to enjoy the journey—well, as much as she could with the brooding Daniel lurking about. They had returned to saying almost nothing to each other. She understood it was difficult for him to leave his home and his sister and her family, but only John seemed able to coax more than a few words out of him at a time. She began to wonder if he would abandon them once they got to Joppa and then make his way back to Caesarea Mauretania. Men and women could both be unsteady in that way … but especially men. She recalled Paul's falling out with Mark after the younger man had deserted him and Barnabas at Perga. They had reconciled later, but Mark's actions still seemed immature to her.

John caught her at the railing one afternoon, staring at a mass of dark clouds chasing them.

"You and Daniel don't seem to be on speaking terms." He made it sound like a sibling spat.

She raised innocent eyebrows. "What do you mean? We speak to each other."

He chuckled, staring north toward Sicilia as he rested his forearms on the rails. "You are courteous, yes. But the Lord's gospel requires more than mere courtesy."

"We've proven we can teach well together," she objected.

He contemplated that for a few seconds, then turned his head toward her. "Did Jesus teach well?"

"Of course. I mean … well, I'm not *him.*"

"Neither am I. Does he ask us to merely 'teach well,' or does he ask us to do our very best?"

Of course she knew the answer to that, but she mumbled it. "Our very best."

"Yes, and he even helps us try … if we are sincere. You don't seem to even want to try with Daniel."

She gave a defensive shrug. "Well, he clearly doesn't want to talk to me."

"He's intimidated by you."

"I can't help that."

"Can't you? You're incredibly smart. I'm sure you could devise a way to help him feel more … at ease around you."

She knew he was right, though she didn't like it. She stared at the clouds again, then finally gave a deep sigh. "All right. I'll figure something out. I know he's new, so I'll try to teach him, as best I can."

John's smile seemed to scare the clouds back a bit. "That is good. Thank you, Sophia." Then he left her to master her roiling thoughts.

She found an opportunity after the storm clouds had overtaken them, rocking the ship and lashing it with a heavy spray. John and Onesimus, for some unfathomable reason, thought they could be of help to the sailors topside, which left her with Daniel belowdecks—in part because John made sure she was never in an isolated position among a ship full of sailors. She didn't like needing that protection, but it was the way of the world. Raphael had also protected her, she reminded herself. Female angels, too, most assuredly.

"So, what clan from the tribe of Judah are you from?" she began. It seemed an innocuous enough question.

He sat across from her in their modest living quarters, below the end of one of the hammocks. He looked up from a small carving he had been working on. "Benjamin, actually." He returned to his work, seeming to exaggerate his concentration.

"Benjamin," she mused. "The wolf. I am Perezite."

He nodded and gave a slight grunt. "The royal line."

"I suppose, but that doesn't matter."

He was silent for a few moments, tiny wood chips fluttering to the floor. Then he asked, "Why doesn't it matter? David came through that line. As did Jesus."

She shrugged. "Prophecies were made and fulfilled. The genealogy forms just a small part of the proof to our people of Jesus's Messiahship. The Lord doesn't judge us on our bloodlines. Only by our talents, and what we do with them."

He didn't respond at all to that, just kept carving, which was slightly maddening. But she had her commission from John. An apostle, for heaven's sake. "I ... haven't treated you well."

He gave her the briefest of glances. "You've treated me fine. You have no need to apologize."

That hadn't gone where she wanted. "To be able to teach together more effectively, we need to be able to talk to each other."

"Isn't that what we're doing?"

Okay, now he was just being difficult. Typical, obstinate man. She felt the heat rising up her neck to form steam in her ears. "No, not really. Do you not want to talk to me? Have I offended you in some way? Am I ... objectionable?" There. Two could play that game.

It had the desired effect, inviting a delicious rose color to his cheeks. He stopped carving, staring at the amorphous chunk of wood. She couldn't tell what form he wanted it to take yet.

"Of course you're not objectionable," he said, his voice low. "You're amazing." He started carving again, but much more slowly. As a new wave crashed into the ship, she suddenly realized how foolish it was for him to be carving wood during a storm. And useless. Sure, he seemed skilled, but beyond the obvious safety issue, how could anyone hope to create something recognizable under such conditions?

"You can put the knife away and look at me," she said, injecting some authority into her tone.

His eyebrows came together for a moment, but then he stopped, placing his carving knife in a small sheath. With what seemed like great reluctance, he lifted his head and met her gaze. The muscles in his jaw twitched, almost in a pattern.

"I want to tell you about my family," she began again, her voice softer. "Some of it is difficult to comprehend, even for me, but it is all true. After I'm done, I want to hear about yours."

He gave a slight nod, and she launched into her father's early history first, then her mother's, and how they met; the death of her mother's brother Alon and the rage-filled journey of revenge her father embarked upon, ending in long, torturous months in a Roman prison until he was miraculously granted his freedom. At that point Daniel made his first comment.

"Because Christ had to die, you are here." He looked down at his block of wood, rolling it over in his hands.

"Well, I guess it's a little more complicated than that, but yes, I might still be Chanah's daughter, but I certainly wouldn't be Barabbas's."

A chill rippled through her, its provenance many-layered. She paused, then continued with her parents' story, taking Daniel through their life in Jerusalem, then Melita—including Paul's miraculous visit, then Rome and beyond. He seemed astonished at what she could tell him about Emperor Nero, Senator Aviola, and the politics of Rome. His eyes widened as she described her brother Matthew's experiences in Africa, her sister Marian's journey to Britannia, and her own trip to Armenia. It was then he asked his second question.

"The ark of Noah, it lies near Kainepolis?"

She gave a small shrug. "The records indicate that, but the exact location is unknown, as it's buried under snow and ice, high in the mountains."

He nodded, humming as he stared again at the wood. "I would like to find it."

She gave him a blank stare, which he didn't notice. "Well, I'm sure someone will, someday. Certainly, when Christ returns, he'll show us anything we want to see. Nothing will be hidden."

He nodded, looking up at her. "Yes, I believe that."

"Good. Well, let me tell you a little about our trip to Sarmatia. There was a man there who convinced himself I was a witch …"

———

Daniel wasn't bad to talk to—quite pleasant, actually. She never caught him yelling at any of the sailors, either. Not that she truly expected that, but it was good to be wary.

They arrived at Joppa on a blustery day, and John immediately had them on the road to Jerusalem. That left Sophia a little disappointed, because she wanted to meet the Christian woman her parents had discovered there, named Augusta, with her somewhat unique flag on the front of her house. She might not still be alive, of course.

The caravan they joined moved slowly, so it was early on the third day that Jerusalem came into view. They separated themselves, letting the caravan move on. John gazed for long minutes at the once proud city of the Jews, now a humbler, meaner sub-regional capital of the Roman empire, taking its orders from Damascus of Syria, to the north.

"You've seen it since the siege?" asked Onesimus.

John nodded slowly. "Yes, I have. Several times. I remember the temple, and how often Jesus taught there; how much we all taught there. And healed." He raised an arm and pointed. "See the Beautiful Gate? Peter and I healed a lame man there as we ascended to the temple at the hour of prayer. I still remember Peter's words to him: 'Silver and gold have I none; but such as I have I give you. In the name of Jesus Christ of Nazareth, rise up and walk.' The look on that man's face, the transformation of his entire countenance, is impossible to describe." He smiled wanly. "The Council put us on trial for that. And *this* is where that proud and foolish behavior led." His arm dropped, and a deep reverence enveloped them.

Finally, Onesimus asked the obvious question. "With whom will we stay?" John had been vague about that detail during the journey.

John took a deep breath. "Some of Nathanael's family have returned, despite his objections. I fear they are quite poor, but they will take us in, and the Lord will bless them. We will only stay a few nights. I am anxious to move on to Galilee."

"Your home," whispered Sophia.

"Yes. Tiberius, the Romans call the lake now—and even the region. It is still a blessed land to me, and always will be."

True to his word, they stayed in Jerusalem just three nights. They met with most of the members who had returned, and instead of trying to convince them to leave, John sought only to strengthen their faith in the Lord and his sure promises. He did warn them of future persecutions, but he noted that saints everywhere would experience those, including he himself. In that regard, he hinted at a lot more than he said, and Sophia determined she would find the right time to question him about it. He wasn't necessarily prophesying his own torture and death, but he sure left that impression. Sort of. It was confusing.

The roads to Galilee were heavily patrolled. That was to be expected. Small pockets of Jewish zealots still existed, even after the fall of Masada several years earlier, and while they were largely impotent—at least on any significant scale—they caused some havoc from time to time. Of course, for anyone caught in one of their small stings, the scale of their activity ceased to matter.

They stopped only briefly in Pella, just a short jog to the east of the River Jordan, and near to Galilee. John said he didn't want the saints in Pella attaching too much significance to his visit, since the apostles wanted to continue to make clear that the church's headquarters was in Rome, not Pella. Still, he strengthened the saints there, and he gave Sophia and the others plenty of opportunity to do so as well.

On toward Galilee they then progressed. As they descended the hill into Tiberias, John paused at the side of the road and gazed northward toward Capernaum, visible in the distance. Sophia realized she had never actually seen the Galilee, just a few artists' interpretations of it, along with a host of verbal descriptions.

Her lips parted of their own accord. "It's beautiful."

John let his eyes sweep the horizon. "Yes, it is. A sacred place, no matter who might try to defile it. This is where the Lord chose to begin his earthly ministry. This place. Not Jerusalem. Not Damascus. Not Joppa or Sidon or Tyre. Not Athens or Rome or any of the other great cities in the world. Tiny Capernaum, nestled in a picturesque valley filled with simple folk, like fishermen."

"You mentioned that the families of Peter and his widow Jemira still live here," she said.

"Yes. Some of mine as well. I wonder how I will be received."

That comment jolted her brain. It was Daniel who followed up, though. "How could they possibly reject you?"

John turned to clap him on the shoulder. "Not all have chosen to follow Christ. In fact, some who did have since fallen away. They see me as heretical now, obsessive of Jesus to the point of lunacy. It's a shame they have closed their minds, but they were free to do so. All I can do is love them and follow the Lord's directions."

He began walking again, and Sophia shared a look with Daniel, who shrugged.

"Is Jemira here?" asked Sophia, catching up.

John shook his head without looking at her. "From what I gathered in Pella, she is not. She lives here, but travels often to see their children. And she tries to lift the saints in the broader area. I know she's anxious to be with her husband again. Hopefully, her time will come soon."

Sophia understood, though it always seemed odd to see someone's death as a positive thing. Especially someone still healthy, and with loving family and friends around them.

They passed through Tiberius, John purchasing a few victuals for them at the market. Since it was getting late, they stopped at Magdala, where John called upon an old friend of the family who gave them a place to sleep.

John had them on the road early the next morning, and Sophia noted an additional spring in his step. His countenance seemed brighter, too, and his head turned often toward the lake, especially when a shout came from a fishing boat out on the water. There were plenty of those.

Keeping John's strong pace, they arrived at Capernaum in little more than an hour, the day still young. And to their great surprise and delight, Jemira had returned. She spotted John as they passed through the market, calling out as she hurried toward them, a basket clutched in one arm.

John didn't notice her at first, but then expressed joyous amazement as he rushed to greet her. Sophia and the others followed more sedately.

After they embraced, John turned and gestured toward the three. "These are my traveling companions. The young woman is—"

"Sophia?" Jemira's free hand came to her mouth. Sophia nodded shyly. "You were … what, eleven … when I last saw you?"

Sophia bobbed her head again, but with a smile. It seemed like yesterday … but also a very long time ago. She didn't enjoy being reminded she was once a silly young girl, but with Jemira it didn't matter.

"How are you, Jemira?" she asked as she stepped forward.

Jemira handed the basket to John and answered her query with a fierce embrace. Sophia wondered if it was made more intense by the fact that her father had been the only one invited by Nero to witness the execution of Jemira's husband in Rome. The hug lasted several seconds, and then Jemira pulled away.

"I'm doing wonderful, Sophia. You look amazing. All grown up." Her eyes wandered behind her, fixing on Daniel. "And is this …?"

Sophia quickly answered. "This is Daniel, one of our traveling companions. We recently met him in Caesarea Mauretania, and he was baptized. And the other is Onesimus, whom you may have heard of."

Jemira still kept hold of Sophia's arms as she beamed at Onesimus. "Yes, I have. It is wonderful to finally meet you, Onesimus." She laughed. "You should have dragged Paul here with you; it has been too long."

She clearly held no resentment that Paul had been spared while her husband was killed. That was both gratifying and incredible.

Onesimus bowed. "It is nearly impossible to entice him to leave Spain now. He says he knows he will die there."

Sophia would have expected that comment to introduce a somber mood, but it didn't. Jemira just laughed again. "Well, I know he continues to do amazing work, and when we all meet together in the next life, we'll have a thousand stories to tell."

That was true, and a profound peace swept through Sophia, bringing tears to her eyes as she caught the briefest glimpse of eternity. Her mother had described such heavenly flashes of insight before. This was the most powerful one she had experienced herself. Even the awe-inspiring presence of Raphael seemed to pale in comparison.

Jemira clapped her hands. "But let's enjoy the present, shall we? I have just a few more purchases to make, and then you can come to my home. You can stay as long as you like, by the way. I don't know what your plans are." She glanced at John as if that were a question.

He chuckled. "I'm home. I'm not sure I'll ever want to leave. But, alas, that time will come." He took a deep breath, exuding nostalgia. "In the meantime, there is work to do here, and I am positive the Lord's own presence will smile upon us."

Jemira nodded, her own eyes glistening. "He loved this place, didn't he?" She turned, taking John's arm and urging him forward, leaving Sophia, Daniel, and Onesimus to follow. They stopped at various vendors, Jemira inquiring often of everyone what they might like to eat in the coming days. She also wanted to make sure she had enough blankets, since the weather was getting cooler. John offered to pay, several times, but Jemira assured him she was fine.

When they arrived at her home, John stood in the front room and gazed around in wonder. "I had heard you moved back into your original home here. This brings back so many wonderful memories."

Jemira set down some of her purchases on a small table, then followed John's gaze. "Some challenging memories, too, but yes, mostly wonderful." Her smile broadened as she swept her arms wide. "Some of the members here helped me expand it, too. I love having visitors stay with me, so I have three guest rooms, which is perfect for this group. You and Sophia can each have your own rooms."

Onesimus jerked a thumb toward Daniel. "Leaving me stuck with him?"

Daniel seemed unsure whether to look abashed or rib him back. Onesimus didn't give him the opportunity, though.

"At least we won't have to listen to Sophia's snoring."

Sophia cast him an icy glare, while Jemira raised an admonishing finger … softened by a mischievous smile. "Be careful. She knows where you sleep. We both do." She turned and gave Sophia a wink.

Onesimus bowed to her again, voice tinged with sarcasm. "As the lady of the house says." Daniel kept his peace … probably wishing they would all just ignore him. At that point, John announced he wanted to explore the city by himself, and he left. Daniel clearly wanted to follow him, but Jemira didn't let him flail in the wind.

She insisted they all help her get the house ready for their stay, and start preparing some of the food.

As the day progressed, Sophia became more and more aware of the peaceful spirit pervading Jemira's home. Perhaps, she thought, her husband and other angels watched over it. She well deserved that. But her attitude certainly played a part. Nobody could match Chanah, of course, at least in Sophia's mind, but Jemira was a truly remarkable woman.

John returned for dinner, which became a veritable feast. He and Jemira shared stories until well past midnight, at which point Sophia could barely keep her eyes open any longer. She finally excused herself, crawling gratefully into a warm, comfortable bed.

CHAPTER 12

*Remember therefore how thou hast received and heard, and hold fast,
and repent. If therefore thou shalt not watch, I will come on thee as
a thief, and thou shalt not know what hour I will come upon thee.*

Revelation 3:3

They spent the entire winter in Galilee, mostly staying with Jemira, but ranging as far as Caesarea Philippi to the north, Beth Shean to the south, and Cana to the west. Nazareth was another interesting visit. Jesus had first announced his divine sonship in the town where he grew up, and most of the people had wanted to throw him over the cliff. She saw that precipice and tried to imagine the experience.

Teaching with Daniel became more comfortable. He was bright, so he learned quickly, and his manner inspired people to trust him. She wanted to be bothered by that sometimes, even though the same was often said about her. But he was always courteous to her, and he began to open up more—not just about his past, but about his own thoughts and feelings on things. He truly seemed to be a decent man.

By the time John was ready to leave again, Sophia was, too. Jemira had begun dropping not-so-subtle hints about her and Daniel, and she couldn't be rude to Jemira and ask her to stop.

So, happy to be traveling again, she said her good-byes to Peter's precious saint of a wife and set her face toward Tyre, where John intended to catch a boat for Alexandria.

She salivated at the thought of seeing that great city. And the libraries! The original great library had been burned more than a century ago, but others had sprung up in its stead, each striving toward some portion of that once magnificent reputation.

———

Unfortunately, a rain squall hid most of the city from view as they sailed into the harbor. She caught glimpses of the famous lighthouse, but not much more, and when they arrived at the house of the local bishop she was a soggy mess.

"Bartolo, brother, it is wonderful to see you again," said John in greeting.

The rotund bishop exclaimed, "Apostle! It really is you. How long has it been?" Before John could answer, he shouted over his shoulder. "Martha, the apostle John and some companions are here!"

Evening had already come on, but it was difficult to distinguish from what had already been a dark afternoon. Bartolo backed up into his house, motioning them inside. He answered his own question after closing the door.

"It's been at least seven years, apostle, though I must say you haven't aged a day."

John chuckled. "You're very kind to say that. I suppose I've been eating better. And I still walk a lot."

Bartolo glanced down at his own belly. "I could definitely use that exercise."

John clapped him on the arm. "Well, perhaps we'll send you on a mission."

The bishop's face took on a sickly green color, which he tried to cover with a quip. "You would have to reach the utmost bottom of the barrel." He gave an accentuated laugh.

John maintained a broad grin. "We have no idea what the bottom of the barrel really looks like, and we often get it backwards. Only the Lord knows. But don't worry. That's not why I'm here. Philip sent me to visit various areas to preach and to strengthen the saints. And, as you can see, I have some help, which has been most welcome." He turned to Sophia, nodding for her to make the introductions.

She cleared her throat. "My name is Sophia, and I'm from Rome. This is Onesimus, from Colossae, and Daniel, from Caesarea Mauretania. We have just arrived from Capernaum, in Galilee."

Bartolo squinted at her carefully. "I believe I met your parents once. Barabbas and Chanah?"

She nodded. "That is them. They live in Verona now, in Italy."

He nodded, rubbing his chin. "And you have a brother in B'Ashra with Cornelius."

"Yes, Matthew. He married a B'Ashran. Someday I want to visit them."

"I would love to see that place as well," said Bartolo, nodding heartily. "Such amazing things have happened there."

John laughed. "Amazing things are happening everywhere, brother. Here, too! Our Father loves all his children, and he rewards every honest expression of faith he finds."

Just then, Martha entered the room, eyes alight. She gently scolded her husband for not offering to take their wet cloaks from them and hang them on ready pegs along one wall. He jumped to the task, and then she led them back to their kitchen, with a table and chairs. Cups of something steaming welcomed them, causing an incongruous shiver in Sophia's upper body.

After they were all seated, Martha asked after Jemira. "Last I heard, she was doing well. Is that still true?"

John took a sip from his cup and set it back down. "It is indeed. She is a pillar of strength to the community of saints—not just in Galilee, but everywhere. We stayed the winter with her, and she never once mentioned wanting to go and be with Peter. She still feels that, I am certain, but she stays focused on the joy the Lord offers us every day."

"Yes, that is Jemira," said Martha. "Are the authorities treating her well?"

"As for the Romans, yes. The Jewish authorities, fragmented as they are and afraid of the Romans, leave her alone."

"That's ironic," noted Onesimus.

Indeed it was. Romans killed her husband, but now made sure she was unmolested. Movement in Sophia's peripheral vision interrupted that thought. She turned, and a small face disappeared behind a wall. It was a boy, who by his height was probably eight or nine. She focused on John again, ignoring the face's next appearance. John used his hands liberally in telling a story about a winepress in Galilee that had broken, and how he had helped repair it.

The boy emerged a little more, and then Sophia snapped her head toward him, catching him with her gaze. "Oh, hello!" she said, stopping the conversation. The boy jumped, made a squeak, and retreated behind the wall again.

"Oh!" said Martha. "Poly, come out. It's okay. They would like to meet you." The boy peeked out shyly again.

John turned his head, expressing curiosity. "Who is this?"

Martha rose, stepping toward the boy and extending a hand. He hesitated, then emerged and took it, letting her lead him to the table. She placed an arm around his shoulder.

"This is Polycarp. He was somehow separated from his parents, who may have been part of a caravan setting out toward the south. We're trying to find them, but it might take some time."

"How old are you, Poly?" asked John, shifting his chair to fully face the boy.

Polycarp looked up at Martha uncertainly, and she nodded.

"Nine." Sophia could barely hear his voice. His eyes darted around the group, then aimed downward. She detected a slight trembling.

"Nine," echoed John. "It has been a very long time since I was nine. My father Zebedee was already teaching me how to fish. It was hard work, but we still had time to play, too. Where are you from?"

The boy didn't seem to want to answer, so Martha supplied, "He's from a town along the coast, far to the west. We've sent a message, but haven't heard anything back yet. He doesn't have any family or friends here, as far as we've been able to determine. He doesn't talk much. I mean, he *can* talk, he just … doesn't." She gazed down at him with compassion, and Sophia felt a lump forming in her throat. She began to fear his parents hadn't lost him … they'd left him. But why?

She noticed Daniel studying the boy with an intensity that surprised her. "Poly, I'm Daniel," he said. "I'm from far to the west, too. I don't have parents anymore." He sighed. "It feels lonely sometimes."

Poly raised his head and stared at him, bold brown eyes vulnerable. Sophia's heart swelled, and while Poly's lips didn't move, he spoke volumes with that brief gaze. So much pain. So much need.

"He can come with Daniel and me when we teach," she offered, without knowing exactly why. Daniel turned to her and nodded, giving her the warmest smile she'd ever seen from him, causing her heart to move in a different way, which she quickly shunted aside.

"That would be wonderful," said Bartolo. "I'm very busy, and there are limited opportunities for him to accompany me while I work in the law. He hasn't wanted to, anyway." He glanced uncertainly at Martha, who gave Poly a squeeze.

"Poly, would you like to go with Sophia and Daniel sometimes?"

"Like tomorrow," said Sophia, smiling brightly at him.

Poly paused only a moment before nodding, hope flickering across his face.

"Wonderful," said Daniel. "You'll like Sophia, I promise." He winked at Poly, who flashed the briefest of smiles. It was the most adorable thing she had ever seen.

———

Sophia wanted to visit one of the libraries, so that's where they started the next morning. Such forums were also great for striking up philosophical conversations, similar to Paul's sermon on Mars Hill in Athens. Many of the wealthier Romans fancied themselves philosophers superior to even Aristotle and Plato, especially given Rome's greater reach and influence. The Caput Mundi could never fall, they believed; instead, its influence would continue to expand, ushering the world toward greater heights of knowledge, prosperity, and peace.

That was utter hogwash, of course. Her own people had believed the same about themselves, especially during the heady days of David and Solomon. God's kingdom couldn't possibly be destroyed, they proclaimed, asserting it was the Israelites' right and responsibility to rule over the 'lesser peoples' of the world.

But human nature hadn't changed since the very beginning, and never would. God wouldn't violate the precious agency of his children, either, which meant Rome *would* fall, at some point. Many of the apostles and sister leaders of the church had already prophesied it, though not publicly. Her own parents had testified of it as well. The only part that frustrated Sophia was trying to figure out when. Part of her knew it was impossible to pinpoint; the other part kept stubbornly trying.

She chose what many called the Royal Library, in deference to Ptolemy I, who had commissioned the first library in Alexandria almost four hundred years ago. It wasn't as impressive as she expected, but their visit wasn't about her, anyway. Or even about Polycarp, though she hoped it would benefit him.

As they perused some of the shelves, which Sophia wanted to do before they engaged anyone in conversation, an old woman popped out of an alcove holding a scroll. She jumped back, more startled than they were, clutching the scroll to her chest.

"Oh my, excuse me, I nearly ran right into you."

Sophia had her own hand over her heart, and she smiled. "It's quite all right. I'm afraid we were distracted, taking all of this great library in."

The woman glanced around, then cocked an eyebrow. "This doesn't deserve to be called a great library. Not yet." She glanced at Daniel and Polycarp. "But it's nice to see families enjoying it together."

Sophia's eyes widened as she gestured uncertainly. "We're not properly … I mean, we … that is, we just …"

"Thank you," said Daniel, giving a slight bow to the woman. "We are messengers, too, of Jesus Christ, who taught all people to search out worthy knowledge and share it."

The woman scrunched her brow, studying Daniel. "Jesus Christ, you say? The one who was martyred in Palestina?"

He nodded. "The very same. He died so we all might live, even eternally, with God himself. No other man could have done what he did, and I know that with every fiber of my being. I am a Jew, though not from Judea, and I didn't believe at first, but I do now."

"Live with God?" She seemed truly baffled.

"Yes. It is possible, because we are—"

She waved an arm before his face. "I'm sorry, I don't have time for trifles, young man. Be about your business with your family."

"But …" Daniel's voice trailed off as she pivoted and scurried down the hall. His shoulders slumped as he looked at Sophia.

"I'm sorry. I tried. You probably could have done better."

Sophia scrutinized his face for a moment. "How so? You gave a great introduction to what could have been a fruitful conversation. She just wasn't interested."

"Too old and set in her ways, maybe?" he ventured.

She shrugged. "Who are we to say? Maybe." She remembered Polycarp, standing between them. He hadn't made a peep the entire time, not even a loud breath. "What do you think, Poly? Which way should we go now? We need to find someone to teach about Jesus."

He looked up at her with anxiety. The slight trembling began again. But at least he dared speak—that was progress. "I'm sorry. I … don't know much about Jesus." He hung his head in shame, and suddenly Sophia felt awful … doubly so when she realized who they should be teaching!

She glanced at Daniel, and he nodded. Then she put an arm around Poly. "How about we teach *you*, Poly? You're as important as anyone else here … even in the entire city. And you're old enough to learn this."

He stopped shaking but kept his head down and didn't reply. Daniel put his arm around him, too, then pulled them all forward.

"Come on. Let's find a place to sit, maybe in one of the smaller courtyards that's less crowded. We'll tell you all about our friend— and your friend—Jesus of Nazareth."

Shockingly, Polycarp immediately perked up. Sophia could have kissed Daniel. Not that she would, of course, but he was definitely having a positive impact on this boy, who she knew was special. All of God's children were special, of course, but this one would go on to do great things on earth. She was sure of it.

———

Sophia and Daniel spent the next week focused primarily on Polycarp, while John and Onesimus traveled around the city, meeting with the saints and some of the local Jewish leaders. When Bartolo was available, he accompanied John and Onesimus. He wasn't a Jew himself, but due to his capacity as a lawyer, he had many contacts among the large and influential Jewish community.

Sophia and Daniel finally took Polycarp to the temple in Alexandria, a magnificent stone structure redolent of the temple of Solomon, though not as large or fancifully adorned. It seemed so … clean; that was the word that kept entering her mind. The temple in Jerusalem had been built as the house of the Lord, but so often that holy habitation had been sullied and abused, by Jew and non-Jew alike. God did not dwell in unclean places, whether a structure or a person—Paul had reminded them of that many times.

A man and woman just beyond the exterior doors warmly welcomed them, then asked various questions to make sure they were indeed Christians and worthy to enter the Lord's house. Polycarp seemed a little confused by it all … as did Daniel, quite frankly, which made Sophia smile. Daniel was uncertain of some of his answers, explaining that his introduction to the New Covenant was still recent. The couple smiled at his responses, then allowed them to worship in the main room with several others.

Another man wandered from group to group in the room, instructing the worshippers in hushed, reverent tones. When he got to Sophia's group, he thanked them for coming, then opened a small scroll and began reciting some passages Sophia had read before, regarding the very beginnings of the earth; Adam and Eve and the covenants they made with God; also the angels who visited them and the sacrifices they were asked to offer. The man didn't actually refer much to the scroll—he seemed to have it pretty well memorized, which was impressive. He also made mention that Emperor Vespasian himself had visited the temple, agreeing to limit his presence to the foyer in respect of the wishes of the Christians in maintaining a sacred space for their committed adherents. That still seemed amazing to Sophia. How long would it last? What would be the next emperor's response to that restriction? Such powerful people were notoriously prickly, and emperors had been known to tear down offending structures, whether made of stone or flesh.

They left after about an hour, making their way to a different library, where Sophia found some old Jewish texts. They even discovered an account of Jesus's ministry in Galilee, written by a Greek historian who was not a believer. Her perspective was fascinating, her style of writing captivating. Sophia could have stayed the rest of the day in the library, but she was aware how hungry nine-year-old boys could get, and the midday meal time was upon them.

They returned to the bishop's home, where Martha gave them bread, dates, and some cheese. They were about to depart again, to visit the lighthouse, when Bartolo stumbled through the door, thinning hair disheveled, his brow slick with sweat. His eyes were stricken with alarm as he looked at his wife.

"They've taken John and Onesimus!" he said in a rush of breath.

Martha's hands went to her chest. "Who?"

Bartolo leaned on a chairback and took a few frantic gulps of air. "Jewish guards. Sent by Zadok, who is visiting from Damascus. We were speaking with one of the rabbis in his office."

Martha's eyes widened. "Zadok? The one who has been pursuing Apollos?"

Bartolo nodded. "The very same. I don't know why he went after John, but … well, he hates *all* Christians, and he must be frustrated that Apollos still eludes him." He looked down, head drooping, breathing starting to slow a little.

"Where did they take them?" asked Sophia.

Bartolo looked up at her. "The Jewish leaders here manage their own prison, several miles to the south, near the river. The Romans provide scant oversight, as long as the Jews respect their superior authority. They may try to transport him to Damascus. Or they might declare him a heretic and execute him here."

"They can execute him?" asked Sophia, the words barely making it past her throat.

"They must have Roman permission," said Martha in a voice calmer than her husband's.

Bartolo lifted one hand off the chair to raise a finger. "But the Romans don't know John is here. He hasn't been in the city long, and hasn't checked in with any of the authorities, as far as I know. I think Zadok means to take advantage of that. If he can keep it a secret, he can—"

"But he can't keep it a secret," argued Martha. "You witnessed his arrest … his kidnapping. You know too many people who trust you, *including* Roman officials."

Bartolo nodded. "They tried to take me, too. I don't know how I escaped. It was a miracle, really. I mean, look at me." He focused on his paunch, then looked back up. "I couldn't outrun a sloth."

Martha blanched, but quickly recovered. "Well, go, make sure more people know what happened. Lodge a complaint with the Roman authorities, too."

"I'll go with you," offered Daniel, taking a step toward the bish-op, then hesitating and turning to Martha. "Wait, they won't come here, will they?" He glanced at Sophia and Polycarp in concern.

Martha shook her head. "Not likely. Not with Bartolo having escaped. We'll be safe here." She didn't seem fully certain, though.

"She's right," said Sophia. "Don't worry about us. We need to be concerned about John and Onesimus." Fears for them swirled within her breast, chaotic and dark. Involuntarily, she hugged Polycarp close. Daniel stared at her a moment, then nodded. Bartolo straightened, moved around the table to hug and kiss his wife, then led the way back out the front door.

When they were gone, Sophia turned to Martha. "You are right. They won't dare come here. And they'll be worried about the Romans. Which means they won't keep John and Onesimus in that prison long." A thought struck her like lightning. "They might not even wait until the morning to spirit them out of Egypt. They could claim they escaped … or that they didn't arrest them at all. They might even declare that John and Onesimus are on the run for some crime the Jewish leaders accused them of. They can make something up for that." As her mind raced, her feet itched to move. "I have to catch up with Daniel and the bishop." She looked at Polycarp. "You'll be okay?" The boy nodded, as did Martha, eyes wider than before.

"Go, then," Martha whispered. "They'll be heading north first. And the Lord be with you."

Sophia dashed outside, turning north toward the center of the city. Her sandals slapped hard against the dirt, and she kept her hems raised to reduce the chance of tripping. She scanned ahead, trying to spot the pair, doubting they would be moving very fast; Bartolo had already seemed exhausted.

Gratefully, she found them quickly, just as they turned onto another street.

"Daniel!" she called out, then twice more before they halted and turned toward her.

She slid to a stop in front of them, uncertain at first how to start. She looked at Bartolo.

"Where is this prison, exactly?"

Bartolo blinked, his expression uncertain. "Well, it's quite a distance south. Why?"

"Because the Jewish leaders might transport them out of Alexandria before the Romans can respond, and then we'll have a devil of a time finding them before the Jewish leaders decide to do something truly awful."

Bartolo's jaw went slack as his face filled with concern. He looked at Daniel, then back at Sophia. His lips tightened in frustration.

"But what can we do?"

"I don't know, exactly," said Sophia. "But something. Daniel and I will go visit the prison. Just tell us how to get there."

Bartolo gave her a wide-eyed stare, as if she had grown another head. But he didn't object. Nor did Daniel, thankfully.

"All right. But I will do what I can to help the Roman officials understand the urgency. I may use your father's name as well, Sophia. I know he has met with Vespasian and has his favor. That will impress them."

"Thank you, Bishop Bartolo."

After brief instructions, and a prayer offered in a narrow alley, led by Bartolo, Sophia and Daniel made haste toward the prison, knowing the walk would take them the rest of the day and into the night hours, even at a fast pace. She wished they had horses. Hitching rides on wagons might save their legs some soreness, but not much time in those busy streets, and of time they had precious little. She knew that to the depths of her soul.

About halfway there, Sophia suggested they alternate walking and jogging, and Daniel agreed. Sophia didn't run much, but she *could* run, and need drove her beyond what she thought herself capable. Which was a good thing, because the Jewish prison lay a bit farther than what she had interpreted from Bartolo. They didn't get close until the third hour of the evening had already passed. She prayed fervently they weren't too late. Darkness had fallen nearly two hours ago, and the Jewish leaders would take advantage of the night for cover. In a similar way, and also illegally, they had done so with Jesus, too.

They passed the entrance to the building, a two-story stone affair with narrow slits for windows along the sides. The façade appeared normal, with broader windows featuring shutters, and the front was where the guards and the steward would reside. When they reached the end of the block, she stopped and turned to Daniel.

"What do you think?"

He raised both eyebrows. His breathing wasn't as heavy as hers, but he had longer legs, which didn't seem fair. "I don't know. This was your idea."

"True. But … have you had any thoughts?"

His eyebrows climbed higher as he shook his head. "No. I've never broken someone out of prison before."

She concentrated, trying as she had the entire afternoon and evening to come up with something. "My dad did, with Cornelius. They freed Paul, in Rome. But they had to go through the sewers, and they had some direct guidance from the Lord."

"Well, we definitely need God's help."

She took a deep breath, squaring her shoulders, and then she remembered something.

"Shortly after Christ left, Peter and John were thrown into prison by the high priest in Jerusalem. An angel let them out that same night."

"So … if an angel can let John and Onesimus out, why are *we* here?"

She frowned. "I don't know. Unless …" She looked around, then whispered, "Raphael? Raphael, are you here?"

She waited, but the streets were quiet. Besides a dog barking somewhere nearby and the muted wail of a baby in the distance, she detected very little noise. Certainly nothing to indicate Raphael's presence. She tried again, hoping against hope he could hear her and would respond. But nothing came.

"You've told me about Raphael," said Daniel after a few more seconds, keeping his voice low. "Does he usually come when you ask him?"

She shook her head, temporarily defeated. "No. He comes when he's needed, though, and surely he's needed now. And we have enough faith, don't we?"

Daniel looked away, down the street. It was hard to make out his expression. "Perhaps I am the problem. I don't have enough faith."

For a brief moment, her mind latched onto that idea. But then the feeling came—and strongly—that it was ridiculous, and also a product of her pride.

"No," she said, "that isn't it." She looked back down the street toward the prison, squinting at it as if she could burn a hole through the front windows. What could they do? The Lord had brought them here, she was certain of that. Slowly, an idea began to form, and while it seemed utterly mad at first, she didn't push back on it. Finally, she looked at Daniel, tone firm.

"We're going into that prison, and we're going to bring them out."

Daniel blinked. "What do you mean? How do we get in? Do you know of a way through … the sewers?"

"There aren't any sewers here. This isn't a heavily populated area, and the water table is too high. No, we're walking through the front door."

"Through the what?" His look of perplexity was priceless.

She took a calming breath, feeling the Spirit confirming her thoughts. "*We* are the angels the Lord sent tonight. We're going in, and we're bringing them out."

He shook his head. "Just like that?"

"Yes, just like that."

He whipped his head toward the prison. "But how do you know it will work? How *can* it work?"

"Take my hand," she said softly.

His head came back around to her, eyes wide, then narrow. He looked down after a second, then grabbed her hand. She felt warmth and strength at his touch, even though doubt still filled his eyes.

"Do you trust me?" she asked.

He didn't respond at first. She wasn't sure she could blame him.

"Do you trust the Lord?"

He glanced at the prison again, then locked onto her eyes. "I trust you both. So … we're just walking in."

She let out a long breath. "Yes. And it's no use waiting. We're hungry, thirsty, and tired … but that's probably the best time for the Lord to guide us."

He took his own deep breath, then gave the hint of a smile, squeezing her hand. "All right, then, here we go. Crossing the Red Sea."

It wasn't quite as dramatic as that … or was it, in the circumstance? She started walking, strangely grateful for his hand, his presence. She felt calm at first, but as they drew closer, her heart began to beat faster. By the time they reached the door, it thudded in her chest like a row of drums, frantic and without consistent rhythm. She lifted her hand as if to knock, then dropped it to the latch. Amazingly, the door was unlocked, and it swung open easily for her.

Inside, two lamps burned, one on a long table, another on a plinth by a wall. Three men occupied the front room, which spread across the entire front of the building. One lounged in a chair, eyes nearly closed. Another sat at the table, reading some documents. A third posed before one of the windows, looking out into the night. It was a painting, perfectly serene.

Not one of them looked at her and Daniel, and she gently closed the door. She was about to speak, but her tongue stuck to the roof of her mouth. Daniel still held her hand, and she squeezed, looking up to see his eyes nervously dancing among the men, two of them obviously armed.

A door on the rear wall led farther into the building. It looked thicker, banded in iron and bearing a stout lock. Taking another calming breath, she stepped toward that door, Daniel accompanying her in slow motion. The men continued to ignore them, and none said anything, not even to each other.

She tried the door, and her eyes widened as she was able to pull it open. Shouldn't it have been locked? A glance a Daniel showed him gaping, but he stayed with her as they passed through. A long, narrow hallway presented itself, with doors on either side. Each door featured a small window with crossed iron bars. She lifted herself up on her toes to peer through the first door on her side, while Daniel looked through the opposite one. Their hands remained clasped, even though a part of her thought it seemed silly.

They moved on to the next set, and then the next, until finally Daniel squeezed and pulled. She moved to stand next to him.

When she looked through, her heart flickered with relief. John and Onesimus were there, dozing, apparently unhurt. Thank the Lord!

Again, she almost knocked, but instead grabbed the door latch firmly and pushed. Miraculously, but unsurprisingly now, it opened, and she stared up at Daniel in dumbfounded amazement, his expression mirroring hers. At that point, he let go of her hand while she stepped across the small cell to rouse the false prisoners.

John reacted calmly, but Onesimus jerked as if he'd seen a ghost. After his gaze passed between them a couple of times, he grunted, getting to his feet to stand next to John, whose smile seemed to bathe the room in a warm glow.

"You are the angels," he said to Sophia, who looked up at Daniel before nodding.

"We ... didn't know how this was going to work."

"Well," said John with a low chuckle, "we're only halfway through the process. I suggest we get moving."

Sophia nodded wholehearted agreement, then led everyone out of the cell and back down the hall. The heavy door opened just as easily as it had the first time, and the men in the front room seemed not to have changed position at all. How strange. She preceded her charges through the front door, and when she closed it, she heard the lock click securely into place. Just to be sure, she tried to open it again, but it wouldn't budge. Mouth agape, she stared at John, who shrugged before turning to walk up the street, for all the world like it was daytime and he was making a trip to the market.

They all followed him, catching up as he reached the first cross street.

"That was ... incredible," Sophia said.

John stopped and turned. "Yes, your faith was indeed amazing."

"No, I mean—"

"Your faith, and Daniel's—and mine and Onesimus's, I suppose—made that possible. There quite literally isn't anything God cannot do. He just demonstrated that again tonight, and we'd best not forget it."

How could she ever forget? Such a notion seemed impossible. But she was mortal, and mortals tended to forget quickly, unless they focused on reminding themselves. She vowed to keep reminding herself of what had just happened—not only the actual events, but the feelings and heavenly communications which accompanied them. She would have to write them down, too. Her mother and Marian would love to read the account. Maybe Marian could even include something like it in one of her stories. She smiled as she thought of that, then broadened the smile as she realized she and Daniel were once again holding hands. She couldn't recall which of them had initiated it.

John said he wasn't worried about still being so close to the jail, so they found lodging for the night. By the time morning came, the marvelous events had already faded to an alarming degree in Sophia's mind. She was still delighted and amazed that John was free, of course, but the details were somehow growing fuzzy.

Sore legs, plus feet that had begun to blister, were a sharp reminder. She didn't have the callouses for running so much. And then there was Daniel. Suddenly, she couldn't get him out of her head. What was worse—or better, she had a hard time deciding—was that she couldn't get herself to be upset about it. Or about him. Or even about John's and Onesimus's occasional knowing glances at them as they ate breakfast.

John found a small wagon to take her and Daniel back to the vicinity of Bartolo and Martha's, claiming that the Lord needed him and Onesimus to visit other people along the way. He only asked that they reassure the pair that he would be back in their home within two days.

Since the Romans had made recent improvements to the road the wagon traveled, the ride was smooth. Daniel didn't say much at first; in fact, he seemed uncertain what to say. So she broke the silence.

"Thank you again, Daniel."

He stared at the street falling away slowly behind them, the clop of the mule's hooves echoing in slow staccato. "I didn't do anything. It was you."

She swallowed. She knew that wasn't true, but how could she get him to see that? "You came with me. I needed someone there … all the way through." She gave him an earnest look, and he finally turned his head to meet her gaze. "I couldn't have done it on my own," she continued, "and, well … it wasn't Raphael's job to help me. It was yours."

His eyes still looked almost stricken. "I faltered. I couldn't understand what was happening, and I was scared. You helped *me* follow through."

Without realizing it immediately, she brought a hand up to his face, then remembered all the times she'd seen her mother do the same with her father. Her heart … expanded. She couldn't come close to describing the feeling. Warmth spread throughout her body, chasing fear into the deep corners.

"We helped each other, and the Lord helped us."

He blinked; not once, nor twice, but three times, before he answered. "I trust you both."

She nearly spilled out of the back of the wagon as her bones melted. Tears blurred her vision. Her hand remained on his face, his beautiful skin. She couldn't believe the words she said next— bold, like her mother's had been long ago.

"I want to marry you, Daniel."

By the time they reached the bishop's home, she realized just how completely the dam had broken, and she had no regrets. In fact, she wondered why she had wanted so adamantly never to marry. Whatever the reasons, it had turned out well, because she had waited until meeting Daniel—yet another example of the Lord's perfectly orchestrated plans.

John and Onesimus arrived two days later, as promised, and true to form, John didn't act surprised when Sophia and Daniel made their announcement. In fact, he seemed to have expected it, and rather than encouraging them to wait through a long betrothal period, as was the Jewish custom, he advised them to move forward quickly.

She felt the truth of his counsel, and since it also wasn't practical to invite her parents to travel there, they made a small whirlwind of minor arrangements to be married in the temple in Alexandria, with John officiating in the ordinance. John the apostle, marrying them!

Daniel seemed surprised at how fast things were moving, too, but he never even hinted at a complaint. Polycarp, for his part, was ecstatic, and Sophia marveled at how quickly he emerged from his shell. He could talk a mile a minute when he wanted to, and he often did. Still no word had come from his village, and none of Bartolo's contacts across the city and among Roman officials had heard anything about his parents or other family members returning to look for him.

So it was, then, that Sophia married Daniel in the house of the Lord, under the happy gazes of John and Onesimus. She thought she could almost see Raphael smiling as well.

CHAPTER 13

I can do all things through Christ which strengtheneth me.

Philippians 4:13

Vespasian died in June. It was the seventy-ninth year since Christ's birth, though the Romans used different numbering. Many people mourned; Vespasian was quite popular, well respected for his wisdom as a ruler.

As they sat at the table in Bartolo and Martha's home, John addressed the subject.

"Very early in his reign, Vespasian asked Philip if he would die peacefully, in tacit admission that Philip is a prophet." He looked at Sophia. "Your father, as you know, was with him that day. Now, in fulfillment of that prophecy, the Lord has taken his son Vespasian home. I cannot say what judgments and opportunities await him in the next life. He treated the Lord's people relatively well. We have thrived and expanded. Much good has been done; many roots planted deep. While the church will be persecuted in the future, and even fall away from the fulness of the truth, the seeds of the gospel will remain. Reformations—even restorations—will be needed at some future day, but the faithfulness of this generation has laid a permanent foundation on which truth and righteousness may thrive when the people are willing."

Sophia would have expected such a prophecy to sound somber, but that wasn't the impression she received from either his tone or his expression. In fact, he seemed hopeful. Perhaps, she thought, he was mirroring Christ's own personality, which was hard for her to reconcile sometimes. How could the Lord view all the gross wickedness of the world and be optimistic? She knew the answer taught by his followers and confirmed by the Spirit, and she believed it at some level, but she found it difficult to grasp fully in her heart. And now that she was married—oh my, she was *married*—and might have children of her own to nurture in this world, new fears arose.

"Will Titus or Domitian succeed him?" she asked. "Or will we have another war of succession?"

"According to Philip," John answered, "it will be Titus, and he feels strongly that Titus will be better than most people expect." That brightened her outlook a little, until he added, "But, according to the Spirit, Titus will not rule long." Now his voice was somber. Right when she was starting to feel calmer!

"And then we may see more war," observed Onesimus, lowering his head.

"Perhaps," replied John. "Or Domitian may ascend to the throne without opposition. That man should rightly be feared. I have seen his face in my dreams, and we will not be good friends, nor will he be an ally of the Lord's Church."

"Will he … kill you?" asked Sophia, voice trembling slightly. She knew he had just prophesied.

"No, though he will try." Suddenly, John's countenance metamorphosed into pure joy and positivity. It almost knocked her off her chair.

"I have much yet to do, and I rejoice that I get to do it. And with friends like you!" He raised his cup high. "May the Lord continue to bless us, and may our faith in him be an unwavering beacon in the storms of life!"

She couldn't help but absorb some of his sudden positivity, and her worries faded into the background. Here she was, with the apostle, and with her new husband, with the promises of the Lord to guide them. It would all be set right in the end. It would.

———

Two weeks later, as they continued their ministry in Alexandria, they received the news that Titus was indeed the new emperor. A month after that, John announced they would soon be leaving for Rome.

Word had recently arrived from Polycarp's village that his family had never returned, and nobody could say where they had gone. Sophia feared something awful had happened to them. Daniel shared his thoughts on the subject: Poly's parents had indeed abandoned him. That's when an idea that had been forming in her mind for a while sprouted fully. Daniel agreed, and they found a time to speak privately with Poly about it.

"Poly," she began, hands resting on his shoulders as they stood in a small room in the Royal Library, "what would you think about joining our family?"

Poly's eyes widened in surprise and some confusion as his gaze darted between them several times. "What … do you mean?"

"Well"—Sophia glanced at Daniel, who put an arm around her shoulders—"you could be our … son." The idea had seemed so logical and delightful in her head, but now she was staring into the eyes of a nine-year-old boy who had apparently been rejected by his parents. She had assumed he would love the proposal, but perhaps she hadn't allowed herself to think it all the way through. How could Poly trust them? Fear spiked in her chest, triggering tears.

Poly suddenly hugged her, hard, burying his head in her bosom. She instinctively wrapped her arms around him and kissed the top of his head, tears falling into his hair. Daniel put an arm around Poly, too, enclosing both of them in his embrace. Her crying turned to sobs, and Poly squeezed harder, which nearly made her heart burst from her chest. How did she love this boy so much? And how had she been so blessed? She caught another glimpse into heaven, and concerns about who was emperor of Rome dwindled into nothingness.

It was mid-August before they departed. John had resolved a few issues in the city, which included calling a new bishop to take over from Bartolo, who had served faithfully for nearly ten years. That was a fascinating process to watch, and it was clear that the Lord directed John to the right man and his wife, for surely they served together.

The Great Sea glittered like a priceless jewel as they left the harbor, and Sophia caught the full magnificence of the lighthouse. The captain promised a swift journey, though they were fully laden with grain bound for Italy and the boat sat low in the water. She had grown used to such blustery, empty boasts. This one just made her smile.

As expected, they progressed slowly, though the captain often remarked in their hearing how they were "making good time." He was a funny man, and if she had met him on the street, she would never have guessed he was a sailor. He looked more like a statue, well proportioned and dressed for leisure. He was also fairly young. He might be a scion of a wealthy family who had been allowed to captain a highly valuable grain ship for a while, but she didn't ask about it.

She still felt astounded every time she noticed Daniel and Poly on the ship with her. And she devised at least a hundred different ways to break all of the joyful, surprising news to her mother. She imagined the look on her face, over and over again, especially if she were to play a bit of a trick on her. Yes, that's the direction she leaned.

After passing between Sicilia and the tip of the boot, they hugged the western coast of Italy, staying within sight of the land. The south was dryer than the north, but still beautiful, even in August. Poly enjoyed watching the landscape pass by, and he never seemed to get seasick. Sophia loved observing him, and cherished talking with him and Daniel more than anything in the world. Not even John, the famous, beloved apostle, could hold a candle to them.

Their final full day of sailing dawned clear and beautiful, and before long they were passing near the city of Neapolis, near mighty Mount Vesuvius. Oddly, smoke wafted from the top of the mountain, but then she remembered that it sometimes did that. She'd never witnessed it, though.

John suddenly appeared at her side, eyes intent on the mount. She hadn't even heard him approach.

She blinked. "Is something wrong, Apostle?"

He took a slow, deep breath, not looking at her. "The Lord's will be done." The words came out almost as a whisper, and then Sophia felt the earth beneath the sea heave, in a way so profound she imagined her own body linked directly to it. Vesuvius belched a massive plume of smoke, and she gripped the railing hard while placing a protective arm around Poly. Daniel was down below, but he would likely come up to find out what was happening.

The captain shouted orders to steer the ship away from the coast. John, Sophia, and Poly—shortly joined by Daniel and Onesimus—migrated toward the stern, trying to stay out of the way of the bustling sailors tying and untying ropes, yelling to communicate, and casting about both curses and prayers.

The earth continued to rumble, and with increased frequency. Then, the entire top of the mountain seemed to explode, rushing outward and upward in eerie silence. The sound didn't hit them until a few seconds later, after John advised them to cover their ears. Sophia had never experienced anything so loud and powerful. It seemed like the earth was cracking apart. She glanced in concern at John, who returned her gaze just as a massive wave of wind pummeled them from behind. It was indeed fortunate—and wise—that the captain had turned the ship.

After the gale had passed, John said, "This is not the end of the world. When that day comes, it will be like ten thousand of these. But this is a somber day. Many of God's children will be returning home, most of them unprepared." She followed his gaze back toward the coast, eyes widening as she noted the height of the massive plume. She had read about volcanic eruptions, but witnessing one went well beyond what she had imagined. Her eyes snapped to the cities near the base of the volcano: Neapolis itself, Pompeii, Oplontis, Stabiae, Herculaneum. How many thousands of people? Which way would the lava flow? Where would the torrential amounts of ash and rock fall?

The captain shouted, gesturing toward them.

"Get down below! We're attacking the tidal wave!"

At first she was confused, but then she remembered something she had learned from one of her tutors. Volcanic eruptions also involved earthquakes—and tidal waves. She prayed it wasn't an over-large one. But what did the captain mean by 'attacking'? Oh, yes, they were sailing straight into it, to reduce its influence on them. She prayed again, and kept praying. Down below, John led them in joint prayers—not just for them and the sailors, but for the people near the volcano. Many, doubtless, had already died, and many more would. Countless others would suffer intensely.

The ship survived a series of tidal waves, though it was damaged badly enough that the captain chose to put in at Formia, about fifty miles northwest of the destruction. Given what she had witnessed, Sophia's feet hit the solid ground with some uncertainty, though no volcanic mounts loomed over Formia. At least no known ones. John led them to one of the homes converted for weekly Christian worship services in the city, where an elderly couple still resided. They would shelter there for the night, after which he was certain others would come from the south and fill it up.

"Many people need help around Neapolis," said John as they sat on benches and partook of a light meal. "Our journey to Rome must wait. Tonight, we must organize the saints and any others who will join us to assist the suffering. I hope to procure many wagons of supplies we can take with us. Poly, you can stay here and rest, with either your mother or father."

Sophia was glad he had said that, but regardless, there was no way both of them would leave Poly, even for part of a night, not after what had happened to him before. She looked at Daniel. "You go. I'll stay with Poly."

He nodded, then kissed them both on the forehead. My, how she loved that man. He was so gentle, so smart, and so determined to do good. And he had never even hinted at complaining that they had instantly become parents of a traumatized nine-year-old boy.

After the men had left, she lay down with Poly on some blankets the old couple brought in. She tousled his hair as they stared at the ceiling, wondering how the night could be so peaceful for her and so tragic for so many people just a short distance away. She'd often reveled in how amazing the earth was, thinking that mankind was the problem. But the earth had fallen as well. It wasn't perfect. In fact, it was long departed from the Garden of Eden it used to be. It didn't provide all the necessities of life without a great deal of coaxing. Some babies were born with deformities, or died during childbirth, sometimes taking their mothers with them. Its natural forces could and did kill. The eruption replayed itself in her mind. She felt again the burst of sound and the shockwaves. She took some solace in the fact that most who had perished died instantly, but thousands more still suffered.

"That was scary," said Poly.

He had been so silent she thought he had already fallen asleep. "Yes, it was. Which makes me glad to know that this life isn't the end, and God is in control."

"Did God cause the volcano to erupt?"

Such an innocent question, yet so profound. "God knew the volcano would erupt. He created this earth, and he designed it to challenge us. We need that challenge, because we're his children."

"So … it's a good thing?" His obvious confusion pulled at her heart strings.

"Well, what we define as good isn't always good, just like what we define as bad isn't always bad. The best example is Jesus Christ's crucifixion. It was a horrible, cruel, awful way to die, and yet, in God's great wisdom, that death, followed by the resurrection, was the most wonderful thing that has ever happened, or ever will.

"The apostle Paul was shipwrecked once, coincidentally on the island where my family lived. I was your age. A horrible storm hit their ship, and everyone on board thought they would die. Except for Paul. He told them everyone would survive, and they did. My father and brothers helped pull people out of the water. My mother, sister, and I brought food and blankets. And then Paul was bitten by a poisonous viper, which didn't seem fair. Only it didn't hurt him. That miracle showed many people who he really was, and who he represented. That led to the growth of the Church of Christ on the island, and a great increase of faith and hope.

"Sometimes, we need to be reminded that we need both God and each other, and that this life is a preparation for something far more important. It's hard for us to fully understand, but our Father in Heaven loves us very much, and he is so patient with us. He loves you, Poly. He knows you personally. I know we've told you that before, but at times like this, it's a little easier to understand and remember. That's a good thing, even though what is happening seems so awful."

She wasn't sure she had explained it well enough, even to herself, but he nodded. "I know God loves me," he said, snuggling next to her, "because he sent you and Daniel. You're my real parents."

Her jaw clenched as her throat tightened. She fought off a sob, but couldn't hold the tears in abeyance. She squeezed her son tightly. Her son. She was his real mother? Yes, she was. Eternally. They had formalized it in the temple before leaving Alexandria. That was one of the greatest mysteries of God, which she didn't fully comprehend yet: relationships beyond the grave, not just for enjoyment, but for *purpose.*

"Thank you, Poly. We love you. God sent you to us, too, which shows how much he loves all of us. And tomorrow, we get to share that love with others who need help."

"I'm glad we get to help," he said. He turned on his side, still snuggled close with an arm under his head, and soon he was asleep. Sophia, despite her best efforts, wasn't far behind.

Twenty wagons. Sophia stared at them in shock, noting they had already been filled, teams in the harnesses ready to go.

At least fifty people clustered around the wagons, shouldering bulging packs.

She looked at John. The men had just returned, with the sun not even showing half its circumference above the hills to the east. "How?"

He shrugged, his eyes clearly tired. "People want to help. There are good people everywhere. They felt the eruption here in Formia, and the plume was visible. They know what happened. News is racing up and down the coast, and inland. More help will come. So, now we depart. He turned and spoke to several men, and seconds later the creaking of harnesses heralded the departure of the relief train. John walked alongside one of the wagons. Onesimus was farther back, while Daniel joined her and Poly.

"Why are you walking?" she asked John. "Surely you can ride with one of the drivers."

John shifted his own pack slightly. "I suppose I could, but these legs are still good. I can rest later. We'll stop at midday and when it gets dark. And I won't slow this procession—not even a little." He turned and winked, and she was amazed at the new vitality in his eyes. She also felt guilty. She and Poly had slept soundly, while the men hadn't gotten *any* sleep. Well, her time would come. They would likely arrive late the following day, and then the work wouldn't stop, not for a long while.

———

Word came that afternoon that more relief caravans were on the road from various places, including from Rome herself. Two men on horseback, racing ahead, stopped when they saw John, and he recognized them from the church in Rome. They said Philip had sent them to start organizing things closer to the devastation, while he and thousands of saints prepared to follow.

"Excuse me," said Daniel. "Did you say thousands?"

The man nodded as his horse pranced. "Yes, with as many supplies as we can gather quickly. Hopefully two hundred wagons. Many laden mules as well. We've been preparing for something like this, especially after the Great Fire."

John nodded at him, peering up into the bright sky. "Well, Godspeed, then, brothers. We'll be there soon."

———

John urged the caravan to greater speed and an early start the next morning, so that by mid-afternoon they got their first look at the utter calamity. Herculaneum was gone, buried in a great slide of earth from the slopes of the mountain, which still belched smoke and had lost several hundred feet in height. The ash was still falling, mainly toward the east, so it was hard to tell what had happened to the other cities.

The great flow of stunned humanity moving in the other direction gave them bits of information. Pompeii, they reported, had been completely buried under lava and ash. Oplontis and Stabiae as well. Neapolis had escaped the brunt of the desolation, as had Misenum across the bay. Many people had been so badly burned they had no hope of recovery; some survivors had even taken to putting them out of their excruciating misery.

The relief party drew from their supplies to help the weary, traumatized travelers as the caravan pressed on into the hazy ashfall. When it became too thick, John called a halt, ordering that they set up a camp and start organizing the supplies for distribution. He also sent out scouting parties to gather more refugees, cautioning them to keep their faces covered as best they could and carry extra strips of cloth so that those they found could do the same.

He called several of the elders, teachers, and sisters from Formia to him, including Daniel, Onesimus, and Sophia.

"Brothers and sisters, the Lord has given us tools to use in such dire circumstances. Many we encounter will require healing, and they will be desperate for it. Most will not know of Jesus nor have any faith in him, but we must lend them our strength as best we can and call on the Lord's guidance. I can promise you that many *will* be healed, to show forth the power and mercy of our loving Heavenly Father.

"Some will not, of course, but in every case we will minister in the Lord's name as his representatives and do our best. This is our calling and purpose. Let us give it our all."

Heads bowed as the apostle prayed, his heaven-directed words among the most powerful Sophia had ever heard or read. And then they went to work.

———

Sophia kept Poly by her side, staying close to the camp while Daniel and Onesimus ranged farther. They stopped for sleep in brief, rotating shifts, but the work never abated. More people emerged from the ashen fog every minute, throughout the night and well into the next day, until the skies began to clear a little. At that point, several wagons were sent ahead to see if a path to Neapolis could be found. Aid would come by sea, too, but they didn't know when.

Sophia participated in nearly a score of healings, but she was surprised and saddened at how many people refused to even let them try. On the one hand, she could understand the deepness of their traditions, and even superstitions; but on the other, it made little sense, especially given the extremities of their situation. God generally wouldn't heal anyone unless they wanted him to, and it wasn't because he was cruel or offended. In fact, each time, she sensed the deep pain he felt for his children's suffering, in a way she hadn't experienced before.

Poly proved to be a valiant companion. He never complained about what she asked him to do, which included changing bandages that had become so filled with blood, pus, and tissue that they did more harm than good. He also helped cook and distribute meals, pack up mules being led to other destinations, and fetch water from covered wells a good distance away so they could keep bodies and equipment clean.

Fear of disease began to grow, but over the next several days more caravans arrived, carrying a large supply of bandages, plus alcohols and salves meant to slow infections. Additional fresh water, too, as nearby rivers and streams became polluted not just with ash, but with dead and decaying flesh. Not only humans had died, of course. Scores of thousands of animals had also perished, and soon the flies became so thick they resembled an ashfall themselves.

Philip arrived, along with Luke, and John gave them a full report on what he had seen so far. With the additional supplies and equipment he had brought with him, Philip asked that their camp move off the road a bit farther and expand considerably. He explained that the church was setting up similar camps at strategic locations, and that they would remain at least through the fall. Even after that, saints would rotate down to help survivors and returning refugees dig out from the ash and rebuild. He revealed that Titus was sending two legions to help as well, which would be a massive boost—both in manpower and morale. The new emperor had already expressed his surprise and respect for how quickly the saints were able to mobilize.

As they counseled together late one evening, Sophia finally mentioned that she had married Daniel. Her husband had returned that afternoon from delivering supplies, and sat next to her near the large cooking fire at the center of camp.

Philip's eyes sparkled in the flames. "That is wonderful. I didn't foresee it, but your mother recently told me that when you fell, you would fall hard and fast."

Sophia blushed a little. "Is that right?" asked Daniel, teasing.

She gave him a gentle nudge. "She told me that, too, and I laughed at her." She looked into his eyes, and they both smiled broadly.

"Well, it's the mothers who know," said Philip, his own grin nearly splitting his face in two. "John told me a little about Polycarp, too. Is he …?"

"Yes, he's our son now. And he's been an amazing help here." She turned to her other side and put her arm around him. He smiled up at her shyly.

Philip rested a benevolent gaze on him. "Much fruit. Your name was well given, young man." Poly sidled closer to Sophia, and she laughed, looking down at him.

"That is very true. If my womb never bears fruit, we will always have Poly, and that is enough."

Poly kept his eyes down, and for his sake, Sophia changed the subject. "What is Titus like? John said he would be better than most people expected."

Philip gave John a curious look, then nodded. "Our relationship so far is better than I expected, too. Many see him as a cruel man, especially after how he dealt with Jerusalem, and I agree he has that in him. But he seems determined to govern like his father, with a lighter, wiser hand. It's Domitian I worry about, and he seems to be hungrily waiting in the wings."

"Agreed," said John. "But this talk of emperors bores me. They are all tyrants, more alike than they are different. And unless we come unto Christ, we, too, are too much alike, mired in selfishness and the cares of the world. With the Lord's light, our individual personalities shine in brilliant diversity, for we glimpse a potential far beyond mere mortal influence. That is what I see in the face of each person we're trying to help here; that is what I'm trying to help *them* see."

Philip gave a solemn nod. "Well said, brother. Our mission isn't just humanitarian. It's spiritual and eternal. This volcanic eruption took many lives. But perhaps it will save many more, for it has energized us to give up ourselves and do good."

Sophia caught Poly staring in open amazement at the prophet, and she realized another piece of the puzzle had fallen into place for him. Her precious son. God was indeed good.

CHAPTER 14

For the great day of his wrath is come; and who shall be able to stand?

Revelation 6:17

After three more strenuous weeks, they departed for Rome, Philip preceding them by a few days. The legions had arrived, and their centurions directed the work now. The saints had done much good, earning the sometimes grudging respect of bedraggled refugee and grizzled warrior alike. Just as importantly, the name of Jesus Christ had been heard by countless people, many for the first time.

Since the guest house on the temple grounds overflowed with refugees awaiting the opportunity to return south, they were given rooms in Senator Aviola's mansion on the Quirinal. The senator and his wife were still away in Asia, but Venesta, the chief cook, was a familiar face. Apparently, Manius had wanted to take her with them, but Venesta didn't want to leave her family, and Manius acceded. Sophia and her little family were the beneficiaries—Venesta had to be one of the best chefs in Rome. The views from the top of the hill were magnificent as well, though she missed having the temple just steps away.

Daniel expressed both amazement and unease. He had worked for many powerful people, he explained, and didn't trust most of them. He had never met Senator Aviola, of course, but he also made a valid point about good people becoming corrupted. Christ himself had often warned about that, as had Peter, Paul, Joanna—who had been married to Chuza, Herod's chief steward—and many others.

She, Daniel, and Polycarp had just returned from a walk on a beautiful fall afternoon when an insistent knock came at the main doors to the mansion. One of the stewards answered it as Sophia and Daniel watched from just beyond the foyer. The steward backed up a step in surprise, giving an awkward bow. Sophia glanced at Daniel, eyebrows raised.

The steward retreated further, still bent forward, and in swept two legionnaires, followed by Emperor Titus and his brother, Domitian. She only knew it was Domitian by the decorations he wore. Portraits of Titus were plentiful, so she knew what he looked like.

"Your Eminence," said the steward, straightening slowly, "to what does the house of Manius Acilius Aviola owe this great honor?"

Titus let his eyes wander the foyer, pausing briefly on Sophia and Daniel, before answering. "I heard you had some new guests, one of them a daughter of Barabbas. My father held him in high regard. I came to welcome them to Rome."

The steward had no idea she and Daniel were watching, so he jumped when she stepped forward and spoke. "I am she. Sophia. And my husband, Daniel. We have a nine-year-old boy, too, named Polycarp."

Titus's penetrating gaze quickly became unsettling, and she lowered her eyes as Daniel moved up next to her.

"You are indeed a princess," said Titus softly. "You need not lower your eyes from me." Feeling even more apprehensive, she met his gaze again, glancing at his brother's face, too, which seemed darker and more calculating. They were both powerful, dangerous men, but John's opinion of Domitian appeared apt. She didn't want to be anywhere near Rome if and when he ascended to the throne.

"I was not aware you had been married so long," Titus continued, removing his riding gloves. "Your father didn't mention it."

"We were only recently married, in Alexandria. We adopted Polycarp, who was abandoned by his parents."

"Ah, that was kind of you. Polycarp. From the Greek. Much fruit. I don't think I've heard that name before." She suddenly realized he was speaking Latin, and she right along with him. She hadn't used Latin in quite a while, but it still seemed perfectly natural. Daniel probably couldn't understand much, though she hadn't actually asked him how much Latin he knew. It hadn't come up.

"He is a bright boy. God was kind to place him in our path."

Titus nodded, slapping his gloves once in his hand before placing both hands behind his back. The steward seemed about to invite him and Domitian further inside and offer refreshments, as was appropriate, but Titus cut him off. "Well said. You were married in your temple in Alexandria?"

She nodded, lowering her eyes again for a moment. "Yes."

"My father talked about his visit, shortly before he passed. Did you know that Philip, your … prophet? … predicted that he would die peacefully, of natural causes?"

She nodded again, well aware of that fact, which had become quite famous among members of the church.

"I wonder if he might have a prediction for me."

She tilted her head slightly. "You haven't asked him?"

His lips drew briefly into a tight line. "I have. But he has demurred, telling me he needs to consult with your god."

"And that worries you."

He quirked an eyebrow, not quite menacing, then surprised her by admitting, "Yes, a little." He twisted his head to indicate Domitian. "My brother is not complaining, though."

Her eyes popped a little as they darted to Domitian and back. She couldn't tell if he was joking or not, and Domitian's expression gave nothing away. City of a thousand knives. How grateful she was not to have been born into one of the powerful families of Rome!

"Would you … like to come into the sitting room?" she asked, noting the steward growing more anxious.

"Yes," he replied. "The guards will remain here by the door. Lead on."

Daniel turned with her, and they began walking toward the entrance to the large sitting room. That told her he at least understood some Latin. When they were all seated—Titus sitting straight and formal, Domitian lounging comfortably—Titus restarted the conversation.

"Senator Aviola is doing a fine job as governor in Asia Minor. He has a firm grasp on Roman justice, and I can trust him not to betray his duties … or me."

"He is a good man," Sophia agreed.

"His Christian faith is part of that."

"It is."

"He does tend to show more lenience with escaped slaves, however. I have received a few complaints about it."

His tone didn't quite frame it as a challenge, but Sophia still took the opportunity. "I have traveled much recently with a man named Onesimus, a former slave. He is also staying in Rome, along with the apostle John. We teach in our church that all people are children of the same God, who loves them equally. As his children, we all have the same eternal potential, no matter the circumstances we inherit in this life. Also as his children, he gives us the freedom to choose how we treat each other, while cautioning us that we will be judged, in the end, for that behavior. Slavery is a gross sin in God's sight. Prosperity is not an excuse. Neither is revenge, nor even supposed compassion. There are far better ways to make progress."

Her neck felt warm, but it wasn't anger. She had just spoken frankly about the evil of slavery to the emperor himself. Why had she done that? Before her worry could peak, though, a calmness spread from her heart, filling her with peace. Somehow, she had done the right thing. She wondered what Daniel thought, but didn't dare break her focus on Titus. Instead, she stared intently at the emperor, ignoring Domitian.

Titus narrowed his eyes, studying her for several uncomfortable seconds.

"You would have made a fine empress," he said. His voice was soft again, evoking the same fright as before. "Regardless, there isn't much I could do about slavery across the empire. It is too firmly entrenched, and I have no desire to start a massive civil war. Perhaps, if you Christians can convince enough people of a 'better way,' something can be done. Eventually."

He suddenly relaxed, taking on much the same posture as his brother, letting the soft furniture embrace him. He even smiled. "Now, I wish to make an invitation."

Oh, no. Her father had warned her about 'invitations' from emperors. Especially when they were smiling.

"The Flavian Amphitheater—or as some like to call it, the Colosseum, owing to that hideous statue of Nero next to it—will open in the spring. Many slaves labor now toward its completion, but"—he raised a finger—"we treat them well. I would like you, and Philip, and John … and even this former slave you mentioned … to be my guests on the day of the first games. And your husband, of course."

He gave Daniel a glance that made her shiver, but the calmness reasserted itself. It felt as if an angel stood beside her, and she almost turned her head to verify.

"I thank you for the invitation," she said with all the grace she could muster. "Philip has already convinced us to stay in Rome for a while, so I don't see why Daniel and I couldn't be there. I cannot speak for the others."

"But you will pass along the invitation, and then notify me?"

"Yes, most certainly." He sat straight again, paused as if to add something more, then suddenly stood. He looked at his brother, who seemed loathe to give up his comfortable position on the fine couch. "Come, brother, we have other business to attend to." He gave a slight bow to Sophia, who had jumped to her feet as well, followed closely by Daniel. The steward, entering the room with a tray full of drinks and fruit, nearly dropped it.

"I will say one other thing," Titus continued, staring at Sophia. "I wanted to execute your brother-in-law, Corun, when he deserted us at the siege of Jerusalem. But I couldn't. It was not possible, no matter how much I wanted to. That vexed me; you have no idea how much. But, I have accepted the fact that your god is powerful, and he will smite me if I attempt to harm your family. Perhaps Philip, too, I do not know. It seems somewhat capricious, but who am I to understand the mind of a god? I look forward to seeing you at the games. In the meantime, if you need anything, send word, and it will be done."

Sophia felt like her bones were becoming jelly. She started to sway a little, but Daniel's strong arm held her steady. Not only did she feel the unmistakable presence of the Spirit, but she was shocked to her core. Far from being threatened, she now had the emperor's personally promised protection? It was not possible. And yet it had happened. She didn't let most of the air out of her lungs until Titus and Domitian had departed and the front doors were once again shut. Then she felt slightly nauseous, and found their room so she could lie down.

When Sophia told John of Titus's invitation, he groaned, acting like his stomach suddenly hurt. When she asked him why he seemed so distressed, he declined to explain. Two weeks later, he invited Onesimus, Daniel, and Sophia to a meeting with Philip at the temple to discuss what they should do. They left Polycarp in the care of Venesta, to his palate's delight.

Philip had chosen a room on the top floor, with windows looking east, away from the city. The leaves were fast changing, and the view was spectacular.

After the prayer, Philip began. "Many of our members express open excitement about the amphitheater, and, to be fair, some of its events will be … worthwhile entertainment."

"But many will not be," said John, frowning at the oak table before them, "including the games he has invited us to attend as his honored and notable guests. Blood will be spilled, and the people will cheer it on. Evil drives such emotions."

Philip nodded. "Most of the people aren't evil, but they *are* deceived by leaders who seek to distract them from both the difficulties of their own lives and the corruption that pervades the ruling class, which often endangers and impoverishes them."

"Many slaves are used, too," noted Onesimus solemnly.

"Or people who are given no other viable choice," said John, "which amounts to the same thing. A few of those who go to train at Capua seek fame and fortune from the games, but most are purely prisoners, desperate to earn their freedom."

"How can they earn their freedom if they die?" asked Sophia.

"Not all die," said Philip, "and in fact, some of the people's favorites are afforded extra protection, their battles designed to improve their odds of victory. This is all about entertaining the people and keeping them happy, though most of the elites—including the emperor and the senators—do indeed enjoy watching men, women, and God's creatures perish in a gory spectacle."

John nearly growled. "That's often what it is."

Philip gave a heavy sigh. "Well, I do not see how we can decline the emperor's invitation without inviting severe persecution for the church—primarily from his brother Domitian—so, how should we approach it? Not only must we worry about the saints, but all the people of Rome."

"They are all God's children," Daniel whispered, staring intently at his clasped hands. Sophia reached over and set her hand atop them.

"One thought I've had," offered John, seeming suddenly much calmer, "is to prepare a special proclamation—not just for the saints, and not specifically about the games. We could distribute it right after those first games, and it should focus more on positives, not negatives."

"Positives about the games?" asked Onesimus, brow furrowed.

John shook his head. "No. About life. About families and their eternal nature and purpose. About finding joy together that uplifts the soul instead of just firing the emotions and driving one into a stupor. Satan seeks to sift all our souls as chaff, and we cannot let him achieve his aims so easily."

"We must be cautious in the wording," said Philip, "and yet bold in promoting correct principles."

"Like Jesus taught, 'Wise as serpents, yet harmless as doves,'" said Sophia, hoping she wasn't repeating the mantra too often.

"Yes," agreed John. "Jesus *was* bold—he did indeed bring a sword—but he knew when to be diplomatic as well, and he laid out the truth in such a way, and in the right circumstances, that those in charge had difficulty denying it."

"Our goal isn't to stop the games," said Onesimus, clearly surprising everyone. "The people would revolt en masse, including against the Christians. "But we must encourage progress, which will take time."

"Indeed," agreed Philip. "Well put, my friend. People can only progress if they choose to progress, and no number of appearances from angels—or even legions of angels wielding swords—can alter that reality. If we want to be joint-heirs with Christ, we must actively follow him of our own free will and accept his grace. The justice of God can neither be denied by us nor in any other way controlled by us."

After a few seconds, Sophia said, "So … families? That seems like a wonderful focus to me. And it will have an impact. I know it will."

John chuckled. "You seem excited about it. Good. You can help us write it."

"Me?"

John raised an eyebrow. "Don't look so surprised. With the amount of valuable writing you've already helped me do, I have no doubt your talents and faith will help us align with the Lord's will in this matter."

"You … give me too much credit."

John looked at Philip, then Onesimus, then Daniel, and finally back at her. "Do I? We all have our parts to play, and the Lord understands those far better than we do. I know his gifts when I see them. I will not be guilty of ignoring them."

She had no rebuttal for that. Daniel grabbed her hand in both of his and gave it a gentle squeeze.

"We should start with a list of the key points to emphasize," said Philip. He reached to a side table behind him and retrieved a wax tablet and stylus, and instead of handing them to someone else, he took the stylus in his own fingers and poised it above the tablet. "I'll begin. Our identity as sons and daughters of God, loved unconditionally by him. Without that knowledge, we are utterly lost."

Everyone nodded solemn agreement with that sentiment. Then John said, "The pattern for families, provided by heaven itself, and demonstrated through all ages of history. Men and women, covenanting with each other and remaining faithful to that covenant, loving their children in ways similar to how God loves us, teaching them and showing them a good example."

"Wonderful," said Philip, scribbling furiously on the tablet.

"Moral agency," added Sophia after giving him a few moments, "and how its righteous exercise empowers us, sustains us, and makes us joyful, even when we toil under the vicissitudes of life."

"Well put," said Philip.

"Forgiveness," offered Onesimus. "Justice and peace cannot be achieved through revenge, inside or outside the family. Grudges are a curse, dragging us down to despair."

"Excellent." All eyes, eventually including Philip's, went to Daniel, as if it were now his turn. He glanced at each of them uncertainly, then cleared his throat.

"Happiness is based primarily on our attitudes, and how we treat other people. We can never feel true joy at the suffering of others; only a counterfeit satisfaction that ultimately leaves us empty."

Philip nodded thoughtfully. "That is a bit more direct with regard to the games, but I like it." He began writing again, and after a few moments, John chimed in.

"The fidelity between man and wife must include obedience to God's law of chastity. Such obedience brings tremendous blessings, far beyond what we can contemplate. Nations that ignore this law always begin to deteriorate, until they collapse. Many Romans already know this to be true, but in their hubris, they believe Rome could never fall, and therefore their multitude of indiscretions does not matter."

"Indeed," remarked Philip. "Many of their own philosophers, and those among the Greeks, said much the same thing. It will be good to remind them of that. No nation that continuously flouts the basic laws of God can long survive, and the nations that exist on earth now will not exist when we get to the next life."

"Everyone dies," noted Onesimus with a somber nod, "and there is nothing we can do to stop that. But we can prepare for a better life to come, and that preparation will benefit us both here and in the hereafter."

"Very good," noted Philip, tongue sticking slightly out of his mouth as he concentrated on capturing everything on the tablet. After a minute, he set the stylus down and looked up. "I think we have enough to start, and we have some time. I'll ask Luke to work on a first draft. Sophia, you can assist him. We can come up with an official title later, but provisionally we'll call it 'A Proclamation from the Church of Christ on the Central Importance of the Family and Moral Strength.' It's a little long, but for now it will do."

Nobody lodged any objections, and Sophia waited for Philip to ask someone to lead them in prayer before they departed. Instead, he pushed aside the tablet and stylus, folded his hands on the table, and announced they would study the scriptures for an hour, and then ask the Lord to reaffirm the ideas they had just recorded.

It turned out to be a wonderful suggestion.

Over the next five months, the document took form, passing through various revisions. Sophia marveled at the process and her privileged part in every step of it. The first draft was sent to the apostles and senior sister leaders not in Rome, and most responded, including Paul, whose letter came in late March and included a greeting from her parents, who had decided to visit him on a whim. She still hadn't been able to make the grand reveal to them about her marriage, and she was starting to worry the news would reach them another way.

Much of the feedback on the document came in the form of minor suggestions, but entire new sections were proposed as well. In every case, Philip and the Senior Council of the Lord's Church debated them and prayed fervently about them. Though the proclamation became quite long after all the initial suggestions were included, she and Luke cut the manuscript down by more than half, refining and focusing it until it shone like a celestial body.

In keeping with the spirit of the message, Sophia made plenty of time for being a mother to Polycarp, a wife to Daniel, and also one of the Lord's ministers in Rome. The Roman saints were marvelous, so energetic and faithful. It reminded her on occasion of how Porcia, Simon's former wife, used to be. She had been so alive in the gospel, and then … she was not. And their girls. Her heart yearned for those girls, and for her brother. She prayed for them often. Perhaps, someday. God had a plan.

At last, the inaugural day of the games in the massive, brand new amphitheater came. She had largely avoided the structure over those several months, but now that they all approached it, accompanied by Luke, who Titus had agreed could also attend, she was awestruck. It was said to have a capacity of more than fifty thousand people. *Fifty thousand.* The arena floor could be transformed into a lake, where sea battles could be simulated. The arches along the second and third elevations all held large statues, expertly made, and at terrific expense, surely. More than two hundred masts at the top supported an enormous velaria to provide some shade, and the venue boasted more than seventy entrances. The scope boggled her mind.

Inside, a constant din of noise buffeted them, even though they had arrived early. One of Titus's aides led them to his private box on the first level, where Sophia felt guilty at being granted such a special place.

Philip, John, and Luke wore nothing fancy, but they still appeared regal to her. Onesimus maintained a calm demeanor, although she imagined that inside he had difficulty contemplating what was about to happen, more than the rest of them. Daniel looked … well, like Daniel, the most amazing man she had ever met, those strong shoulders and wavy dark locks somehow signifying to her that everything was right in the world. Well, at least in her world.

The sun blazed from a nearly cloudless sky, but of course the emperor's box was covered, and several servants waved large palm fronds to keep the guests cool. Titus himself didn't arrive for nearly another hour, past the time the games were set to officially open, but that didn't seem to lessen the energy of the capacity crowd. Everyone knew, of course, that emperors were always on time … whatever that time turned out to be.

A great cheer arose when Titus finally showed himself, flanked by several family members and a pair of powerful senators. Many other senators had boxes nearby, with their own frond-waving servants. Or slaves. Most likely slaves.

Titus greeted Philip and the other Christians coolly, then stepped up onto a small rostrum at the front of the box, raising both arms high. The crowd went silent.

"Good citizens of Rome!" His voice boomed, and Sophia wondered how they had designed the acoustics. "My father's dream comes to life today. This great Flavian Amphitheater is his gift to you, in gratitude for your loyalty and sacrifice. May the games this day please you, and may you remember that Rome is, indeed, the capital of the world!"

Sophia found his use of the word 'life' ironic, since men and beasts would die this day. And Rome as capital of the world was a stretch. The headquarters of the Lord's Church resided in Rome, however, and at least that said something worthwhile.

"The gladiators you will witness today," continued Titus, "are the finest anywhere. Some have trained and fought for many years. You know their names. They bear Rome's glory through their bravery and skill. Honor them with your cheers and your wills. And now, a warmup!"

He clapped his hands high, twice, and within seconds more than a dozen large doors had opened in the floor of the arena. Men emerged in small groups, running to different areas and then stopping to raise shield, sword, and spear. They shouted in unison, martial slogans from Rome's illustrious history of conquest. Then they paired off, sparring in exaggerated fashion, exhibiting a portion of their talent as they warmed up their muscles for the coming combats. Sophia felt the energy of the masses as a living thing, and she shivered at the lustful anticipation it represented. She wondered about the men in the arena, too, and … wait, was that a pair of women sparring? Indeed, it was. Rome didn't use females in their armies, but other nations did, at least in limited fashion, Sarmatia being an obvious example.

Her stomach turned a little as she observed the women shouting and spinning, thrusting and parrying, part of the show. Would Titus allow women to die here? Of course he would, she reasoned, especially if these women were slaves. Under Nero, several Christian women had been slain publicly, and the people of Rome hadn't revolted against that.

She felt Daniel's arm slide around her shoulders, and she realized her breathing had quickened.

"It will be all right," he said into her ear, and even so she could barely distinguish the words above the din. "God is aware of all of them."

That sounded like something she herself might say. She reached for his other hand and squeezed it, turning to look into his eyes and mouthing a "Thank you." She caught a concerned glance from Philip, too, clearly meant for her. At that point her pride kicked in. She didn't need to be coddled through this. She could handle it.

Easier thought than done. The gladiators retreated underground, and then the actual games began: gladiators fighting gladiators, gladiators versus animals, and animals pitted against each other. Few of the contests ended in death, except most of the animal battles, but there was so much blood, so many grievous injuries … and so much full-throated cheering and groaning. Bets were obviously being placed—a different level of perverted pleasure. Titus never shouted, as that was beneath his station, but he smiled often and occasionally clapped, even standing a few times to do so more vigorously.

Sophia and her companions never clapped for any of it, and she began to fear Titus might be offended. Though he sat with his back to them, lower and slightly closer to the action, he surely noticed their lack of enthusiasm for the grand games gifted to the people by him and his father. What could they do, though? They couldn't pretend to enjoy something they clearly loathed. Surely Titus had some idea that they didn't favor such blood sport. Was he setting them up for something horrible? John and Philip had both reiterated that Titus didn't concern them. But his brother did. Where was Domitian, by the way? Shouldn't he be here? A thought struck her, sending a chill down her spine.

Perhaps Domitian was offended at Titus's invitation to the Christian leaders, and his absence was designed to send a message. His disdain would likely grow once he heard about the lackluster reaction of the Christian dignitaries at the games. Once again, she was reminded of how much her father detested the politics of Rome. In that moment, she decided it was silly of her to keep planning an elaborate, sneaky reveal of her new family for her parents.

Immediately upon returning to Manius's home, she wrote them a long letter, overflowing with gratitude. And within a week of receiving her letter in Verona, her parents arrived in Rome to celebrate with her.

CHAPTER 15

*He that loveth not knoweth not God; for God is love. In this
was manifested the love of God toward us, because that God
sent his only begotten Son into the world, that we might live
through him. Herein is love, not that we loved God, but that he
loved us, and sent his Son to be the propitiation for our sins.*

1 John 4:8-10

The inaugural games at the Colosseum lasted more than a
hundred days, but Titus never extended another invitation
to Sophia or any of the others. Nor did he say anything about
that first day, or send them any messages related to it. He became enormously popular with the people, and not just because
of the games. He was handsome and charismatic, and the crisis
in Campania, where Mount Vesuvius had wreaked such massive
destruction, afforded him the opportunity to show his empathy
and goodwill toward his people, which he did in abundance.

To his credit, he never complained about the Proclamation on
Family, Fidelity, and Faith which the saints distributed the length
and breadth of Italy and beyond, nor did he seek to undermine
it. That seemed a major miracle.

Unfortunately, late that year a powerful fever overtook him,
and he passed away. Rumors swirled that Domitian had something
to do with it, but nothing could be proven, and the legions were

still happy to support one of Vespasian's sons. He was quickly installed as emperor.

John left the day after Titus died, not in fear, he said, but out of a wise caution. Onesimus agreed to accompany him to Ephesus, where John hoped he still had a home. It had been a long time. Sophia continued to wonder at how much energy he had. It seemed he hadn't changed at all in the past eight years.

She and Daniel decided to purchase a home near the temple site in Rome. Daniel had been granted some lucrative building contracts—perhaps influenced by Titus, for which Sophia was grateful—and he was hard at work. Polycarp spent time with him, absorbing what he did, while also being tutored at the church's school, where Sophia spent much of her time mentoring students. She also served on various councils of the church, lending her experience of having visited so many areas while learning to exercise faith in myriad ways.

Just before that year ended, Philip took ill as well. Sophia and Daniel visited his apartment in an upper suite of the visitors house, which had recently been expanded. He expressed both great hope and great concern for the saints, but as for himself, he was happy. He even predicted he would die soon, leaving Matthew, Bartholomew, and John as the only surviving original apostles. Ironically, word shortly arrived in Rome that Matthew had died of natural causes while visiting Ethiopia. Within a week, another letter arrived—Bartholomew had passed away peacefully in Armenia while ministering to the saints there.

Philip and the other apostles had prepared for such events, and Philip rejoiced that two apostles had passed in succession without violence. He didn't promise it signified progress, but Sophia hoped it did. Timothy was called to replace Matthew, while a man named Linus, originally from Alexandria but serving as a bishop in Upper Germany, was chosen to replace Bartholomew. Philip suggested to the others that Clement, an elder from Rome proselyting in Gaul, replace him when he passed, and they appeared to favor the recommendation while expressing ardent hope it wouldn't happen soon.

It did, however, and Sophia mourned with the church. Its second leader had passed. Both Peter and Philip had been great men who served the Lord and his people faithfully. She had no idea who the Lord would choose as the next chief apostle, and perhaps some time would pass before he would do so. The quorum, as a group, could collectively fill that role, at least for a while.

The next year-and-a-half passed in a frenzy of activity. Her parents visited twice more, apologizing that they weren't there more often. Simon still needed their help, and she understood. Her heart ached often for her tender-hearted brother, and she had sent as many letters to him as to her mother and other siblings. Polycarp grew several inches. He would pass her in height all too soon. The church continued to thrive, even without a chief apostle, though the feeling grew that the situation would change soon.

Just a few months after John left, she had received a letter from her brother Elhanan in Ephesus, who reported that John hadn't been getting himself into trouble with the local Roman elites, which was good to hear. He and Onesimus still traveled a lot, though just within Asia Minor. They focused on strengthening the saints there, and they performed many miracles. In some cases, the miracles caused people to flock to them, while in others they prompted resentment and outright rejection. That was hard to figure, but it was the way of the world. Fallen humans were capricious, and often incredibly shortsighted and cruel.

Another stark reminder of that had come with a new missive from Elhanan just weeks later, written in a tight script and beginning with the words, "My dearest Sophia, please do not be overly sad." What a terrible way to begin a letter! Or maybe it was the perfect way, at least for this one.

Her heart thrummed with dread as her eyes progressed through his message. John and Onesimus had attracted the ire of the mayor of Iconium. That area was long noted for its occasional waves of anti-Christian sentiment; Paul had been stoned at Lystra by those coming from Iconium and Antioch the Lesser. In this case, the mayor had complained to the local prelate about John trying to cause an uproar and sedition in his city, and before any word could reach Senator Aviola, a mob had descended upon the pair.

Onesimus, tragically and almost unbelievably, had died in the stoning. John, though he survived, had been arrested. Sophia stopped there, unable to read further. Her breathing slowed, then increased dramatically, and she could barely see through her tears. Her dear, brave, faithful friend. Friend to all, actually. How could people let the devil control them so easily? Intense rage flared in her breast, but only for a moment. She knew Onesimus would counsel her not to let anger consume her. Perhaps he was whispering such to her in that very moment. Either way, she would honor him.

She finally controlled her breathing, just as Daniel walked into their bedroom, where she sat on the edge of the bed. It was the Sabbath, so he wasn't working. He and Polycarp had been out delivering some food to a needy family.

"What's wrong?" he immediately asked, sitting next to her.

"Onesimus." She barely got the name out before a sob wracked her entire body. He hugged her tight, then let her cry, which she did for several minutes, the letter still held loosely in one hand.

When she finally recovered, she wiped her eyes and looked up at him. "Anti-Christian zealots stoned him to death in Iconium." She held up the letter and started reading again, this time aloud.

John had been sent immediately to Ephesus, where the proconsul had announced, under authority of an obscure order sent by Domitian more than a year earlier, that John would be thrown into a cauldron of boiling oil.

Sophia's breath caught again. How insane and heartless! Her dream from years ago flashed before her ... the dragon—Domitian—dropping John into the fiery lake. Satan was attacking the apostle through his witting and unwitting minions. But in the dream, he'd come out of the lake just fine. What did that mean? She kept reading.

The order had been executed. John was indeed dropped into the vat. And then ... he climbed out of it. Elhanan wrote that he himself witnessed the event. The apostle emerged as if he'd just enjoyed a pleasant swim, then asked for towels. The proconsul, watching from a platform a few feet away, had a heart attack, collapsed, and died. It was then that Manius finally arrived with a century of soldiers, intent on rescuing John. But the Lord already had. Astounding. Almost beyond belief.

"Daniel in the lions' den," whispered Daniel in awe.

"Shadrach, Meshach, and Abednego in the fiery furnace," added Sophia in the same reverent, awestruck tone.

"Keep reading," he encouraged.

John had immediately returned to Iconium to retrieve Onesimus's body. Manius and his soldiers proved useful, because the mayor wanted to resist. Onesimus was taken to Ephesus, where the saints procured him a tomb. John presided over the memorial services, attended by thousands of people, including many who were not members of the church. John left shortly thereafter for Smyrna.

After that, Elhanan talked about his own family, and how worried Junia and he sometimes became when thinking about the world their children would inherit. But, he noted, as long as they had their faith in the Savior, everything would turn out all right in the end. Elhanan was a good man.

When she finished, Daniel waited a few moments before saying, "I'm so sorry, Sophia. You were right. John, too. Domitian—and his master, Satan—want him dead."

"They want all of us dead," she replied, tasting the bitterness of her words.

"Not all of us," he ventured, daring to correct her in that tender moment, "just the ones he knows he'll have the hardest time turning. Like John. And you."

She swallowed. Not her. She was still far too proud, and Daniel's praise didn't help. But his heart was in the right place. His mind, too. "John, indeed, he can never corrupt. And I don't think he can kill him, either. God will not let him. That is comforting, but—" Another sob caught her by surprise, and she nearly choked. Daniel's supportive arm was there again.

"Onesimus. I know. But he is at peace now. I didn't know him as well as you, but I will miss him, too. Did he have any family? I never felt comfortable asking him more details."

She shook her head as she calmed again. "Not that he had been able to find. Alive, that is."

"Well, he is meeting some of them now, right?"

That seemed to brighten her mood considerably. She had always pictured him as their companion, but still somehow alone. Now he was indeed enjoying many happy reunions with his family and friends. Her very soul broke out in a broad smile, and she cried again, but for a different reason.

By the time summer came again, Sophia felt strongly she needed to leave Rome. She had spoken with Daniel about it before, and he seemed supportive. She didn't want to force it on him, though. Or on Polycarp, who had adjusted well to his new life and was flourishing.

"Are we too comfortable here?" she asked Daniel one evening as they sat on their front porch, enjoying a warm, gentle breeze.

"Has it become too easy, you mean?"

"Yes, partly. People cater to us a lot."

"I know. You've shared this concern before. It makes us proud, and a little lazy, too."

She turned to him and quirked an eyebrow. "It makes me proud, and you lazy."

He laughed. "Fair enough, yes."

Her expression grew serious. "It appears I might not be able to conceive." She knew that didn't have anything to do with her first statement, but she felt it keenly in the moment.

"That's nobody's fault. And it might be because of me."

"You just said it was nobody's fault."

He smiled. "I know. But sometimes a bull can't inseminate a fertile cow. That's not the cow's fault."

Her eyebrow arched again, then quivered. "Did you just compare me to a cow?"

His smile broadened. "No, I did not, and you understood exactly what I said."

Daniel had changed. Matured, as had their relationship. Drat. It challenged her to find new ways to tease him.

"You're an angel," she said, again growing serious.

"I'm no Raphael," he responded.

"True," she agreed. "You're better."

EPILOGUE

But the Comforter, which is the Holy Ghost, whom the Father will send in my name, he shall teach you all things, and bring all things to your remembrance, whatsoever I have said unto you. Peace I leave with you, my peace I give unto you: not as the world giveth, give I unto you. Let not your heart be troubled, neither let it be afraid.

John 14:26-27

Isca Dumnoniurum. What a ridiculously long name. What Roman general had conjured it up? Had he done it after eating something rancid? Or as he was dying of a gut wound?

Despite the long and silly-sounding name, though, the area was beautiful. The coasts of Britannia had surprised Sophia. And they felt … inviting. Yes, this was the right place for them. She, Daniel, and Polycarp had prayed about it, and each felt good with the decision. Poly showed some apprehension, but he was a brave boy, turning into an impressive young man.

After they docked, Sophia led them to the merchant whose name Luke had given her. He should be able to arrange some transportation for them and their considerable baggage, which included a rather large number of documents she couldn't bear leaving behind.

They spent one night in the port town, trying out some of the food, which left a great deal to be desired compared to Italy. Then they began their trip to Nazaretum. Daniel still harbored some worries that they hadn't let Marian know they were coming, but Sophia wanted to surprise her sister more than anything in the world right now. If she had been able to, she would have commissioned a painter to be present to capture the moment. The look on Marian's face. Her husband Corun's reaction.

When the man driving the wagon carrying them and their goods turned onto the short spur road to Nazaretum, Sophia felt the butterflies swarming in her stomach. She was more excited than she thought she would be to see her sister. Daniel could tell, because he laughed. She stuck out her tongue at him, and then at the driver when he looked over at her.

"Reliving your youth, are you?" teased Daniel. She punched him in the ribs. Not hard enough. He was right, of course.

They approached the sign Marian had described before, which arced over the entrance to the city. It appeared to have been moved recently, which made sense. Nazaretum had become a significant presence in the region, and many traders visited now. Marian claimed it had nearly tripled in size just since she and Corun had gotten married eight years ago.

The driver pulled off into an area designed for the offloading of wagons, giving her a nod.

"Thank you," she said sincerely, feeling a little embarrassed at sticking her tongue out at him.

He touched his forehead as he nodded. "My pleasure, ma'am, sir." He glanced at Daniel as well. Polycarp lay curled up in sleep just behind the seats, among some of their goods. They woke him, then began offloading their possessions.

A middle-aged couple came hurrying up, the woman lifting her skirts as they both puffed. Sophia spied a large building several blocks in—had they come from there?

"You're new!" she said, coming to a stop. "Welcome. We're Paerin and Teresa. You"—she tilted her head one way, then the other—"you must be Sophia, Marian's sister."

Sophia's mouth opened in surprise. "You *recognize* me?"

Teresa gave a firm nod. "Of course. I can see the similarities in your cheekbones, your eyes, the shape of your chin. If you weren't sisters, you'd at least be cousins."

Her husband Paerin looked a bit perplexed, and he gave a slight shrug to Daniel. Sophia just hoped Teresa wouldn't spoil the surprise she had planned.

"Well, thank you for the welcome, Teresa. This is my husband Daniel, and our son Polycarp, who we adopted in Alexandria. He's a little nervous, as you can understand."

"Of course," said Teresa, focusing on Poly. "We have many young men about your age in Nazaretum. You'll make some friends fast, I promise." Her smile bubbled from her face, and Poly's eyes brightened. Sophia squeezed her son's elbow.

"See, I told you the people here would be nice." That was still a premature thing to say, but Poly nodded eagerly. Sophia turned her attention back to Teresa.

"Do you know where Marian is?"

"I'm not certain," she replied. "She might be at home. Corun is on a patrol with one of his deputies."

"His … deputies?"

"Yes." Teresa laughed. "Didn't she tell you? Corun is our new sheriff. Well, it was pretty recent. He was doing fine as a farmer, but I know he didn't love it. This position suits him much better, and he is perfect for the role, which requires both the right skills and the right temperament. And courage."

"Do you have many … problems?" asked Daniel.

Paerin answered him. "No, not in the town itself. Minor things, for the most part, though people are people, everywhere you go. But some of our neighbors try to sneak in and steal from us occasionally. Their town officials don't seem too keen on punishing them, either, since, you know, we're Christians. So, we have to be vigilant."

"We're growing in influence, too," added Teresa, "and many of the local gentry aren't too thrilled by that. We try to be good neighbors, but …"

"But some people aren't interested in being neighborly," supplied Sophia. "Yes, we're familiar with that." She looked at Daniel, then tousled Poly's hair.

"Are you … planning to stay?" asked Teresa.

Sophia gave a firm nod. "Yes, we are. Rome … has lost its luster for us. We needed something simpler, more pure."

Teresa nodded as if she knew exactly what she meant. "Well, you'll find that here. And if you're interested in some of the local history, there have been some exciting new developments, including a small stone monument someone just discovered on a hill a few miles from here. It appears Jesus himself inscribed a few words on it, including his name, when he was a teen visiting with his uncle Joseph of Arimathea. Very exciting."

Sophia's eyes widened. That *was* interesting. Mary had written a little about some of her son's journeys prior to his ministry, but not much. Most of those documents resided in the church's library in Rome. She sensed the spirit of this place seeping into her soul, and it felt good. They would be happy here, and they would have much work to do as well.

Marian wasn't home, but Sophia's plan allowed for that. They let themselves in, and while Sophia and Daniel secreted themselves in a back room, Polycarp remained in the front room with just a small pack. She invited him to sleep—or at least pretend to—until Marian came back.

Less than an hour later, the front door opened, and Sophia heard her sister's surprised voice amid the pattering of several pairs of feet. Her children. Sophia could hardly keep herself from jumping out right away so she could lay her eyes upon them.

"Oh, hello. Who might you be?"

She heard some shuffling as Polycarp got to his feet. "I'm David," he said, as instructed. "I … I was hoping I might be able to stay with you? For a while?"

After a slight pause, Marian acted as expected. "Of course you can. Who sent you here? Was her name Teresa?"

"Um … no," said Poly, again as planned. "I don't know her name."

"Oh, well, that's all right. How old are you?"

"Twelve."

"Almost a man. Well, you can be a big help here. Where did you come from?"

"Rome."

Another pause followed, longer this time. "Rome, as in Rome, Italy, capital of the empire?"

Poly's voice grew softer. "Yes."

"How in the world did you get here?"

"An angel."

Several seconds passed. "Extraordinary. An angel, you say? Did the angel have a name?"

Sophia could almost feel him nodding. Here came the reveal. "Yes. Sophia."

Marian gasped. "Are you sure that was her name? I have a sister named Sophia. Oh, no, I wonder if—"

"And here I am," announced Sophia, bouncing into the front room, Daniel following more circumspectly behind her. "Not dead!"

The look on Marian's face exceeded all expectations. Shock, confusion, and even a tinge of panic preceded the narrowing of her eyes as she tried to put on a pretended anger. "You tricked me, and scared me half to death!"

Sophia moved swiftly to embrace her sister. "I'm sorry. I didn't mean for you to think *that*." Tears filled her eyes as she drew back and gazed at Marian's children, who were six, four, and two, naming them one by one. "Joel, Hannah, Henric. I'm your Aunt Sophia. Me and my husband Daniel, and our son Polycarp, have come to live here in Nazaretum."

As Marian squealed in sudden delight at that announcement, Joel's face screwed up in confusion. "Where is Polycarp? And who is David?"

Sophia laughed. "David is Polycarp. We were having a little fun."

Joel gave her a surprised look, which morphed into a timid smile. "Oh, I get it."

"Are you seriously moving here?" asked Marian, hugging her again.

Sophia tilted her head, the moment settling on her. "Yes. I mean, I think so. It feels like this is where the Lord wants our family."

"Oh, that is wonderful!" Marian moved to briefly embrace Daniel, and then Polycarp. "Corun will be excited, too. Do you need to stay here for a while?"

"Well … if that's all right. We brought quite a few things. They're all still sitting near the gate."

"Of course it is. Don't give it another thought. We have plenty of room, and we will absolutely love having you here. Fair warning, though: I'm going to pick your brain constantly for ideas I can use in my stories."

Sophia laughed. It felt wonderful. She and Daniel had both been nervous about finding a temporary place to stay.

"Thank you. I look forward to getting to know everyone here. We already met … um, Paerin and Teresa."

"Oh, they're great people. You'll like them a lot. Probably even more than me."

They shared a brief laugh, and then Sophia said, "They told us about some recent discoveries."

Marian nodded, light sparkling in her eyes. "Yes. I found the latest one. Me and Joel." She turned to give her oldest a fond look, and he beamed. "We'll show you."

"And Corun is the new sheriff? Of the whole town?"

Marian nodded, her pride in her husband obvious.

"How many people live here now? And are they all Christians?"

"Well, we don't exclude anyone, but almost all those who come are Christian, yes. I think we have about five thousand people. And the Spirit has been telling us to expect more. Many more. You, I think, are the vanguard of the next wave."

Somehow, that sounded both ominous and extraordinary. She glanced at Daniel, soaking in the strength of his soul, and at a smiling Polycarp, who had found a seat next to Joel, his cousin. Her heart swelled with gratitude and wonder. Then she turned to her sister with determination.

"Well, we'd better get our things then. It's time to show the Lord what we can *really* do."

END

IN LATE 2020, M.D. HOUSE semi-retired from a successful career in Corporate Finance and Business Leadership that allowed him to experience all facets of designing, producing, marketing and selling products to customers across the world. He enjoyed that career, and still consults part-time, but being able to pursue his passion for creative writing has been a tremendous blessing.

Many years ago, while writing on a very limited basis, he came within a hair's breadth of getting a science fiction novel traditionally published. Since embarking on his new journey with much more time and focus, he's published that book and a sequel, along with five religious historical fiction novels (which were a surprise). He's starting to get some award recognition, along with a favorable review from Kirkus for The Servant of Helaman, a spy thriller and the first book submitted to them.

His docket is filled with new projects, including his first fantasy novel, a movie script for The Servant of Helaman (along with a sequel), and book 3 in the Patriot Star series.

You can learn more about M.D. House, including interviews with people like Eric Metaxas, Tricia Goyer, Carmen LaBerge, Roger Marsh, Chautona Havig, Jaime Vaughn, and Dr. Paul Reeves, at mdhouselive.com.